About the Book

Quarton: The Payback

Arrix's latest attempt in his relentless quest for eternal life has failed. Thanks largely to Mackenzie and Chuck, the Garial Bridge has been destroyed and with it Arrix's army of warriors. But Arrix's defeat has come at a cost and there is no guarantee that he is no longer a threat. Indeed, a new alliance seems to be in the making between Arrix and the equally ruthless, Klavon.

The coding continues to evolve and grow ever more powerful. Unless it can be destroyed or, at the very least, controlled, Earth will never be safe.

With new devastating attacks on targets within President Lessey's control and Fen's life hanging in the balance, it is left largely to Mackenzie and the Southern Alliance to step in to help. But they know they cannot do it alone.

The scene is set for one final encounter between the four Garalians who were on the original bridge. Whoever can control the coding, can control the future.

The quartons and the coding have not quite finished wielding their influence just yet.

Author note: Reincarnation is a complex enough issue to deal with without characters transferring into other bodies too, which is what happened in Quarton: The Coding.

With that in mind, I have produced a guide at the back of the book. It lists the names (or descriptions of people where there is no name) connected to the main four characters – Rana, Pella, Arrix and Klavon – who started this all off in book 1. There is also a list and description of other main characters, like Mackenzie and Chuck, from all three books.

The character list might also serve as a reminder of some of the main events to date and how they link in with each other.

The Quarton Trilogy

Quarton: The Bridge
(Part 1 in the Quarton trilogy)

Quarton: The Coding
(Part 2 in the Quarton trilogy)

Quarton: The Payback
(Part 3 in the Quarton trilogy)

A trilogy dedicated to my own special trilogy

Ang, Abbey and Joe.

Ian Hornett

Quarton: The Payback

Prologue

Fen

Fen and Mark stood helpless as Arrix effortlessly grabbed Chuck round the stomach and carried him out through the portal's door. Mark took Fen's hand and held it. Virtual strangers in this life but, in reality, brother and sister – Rana and Pella from Garial – facing death together. Again.

Arrix was outside now, intent on causing as much misery as he could before he gained control of the MASH. With it, he would be able to finish it – finish them – for good. Of the four, only he would be left and only he would have control of the coding.

Taron, Arrix's warrior, had been given the job of killing Fen and Mark before the MASH would take away their souls. He was taking his time, prolonging the pain. Maybe that was part of the package Arrix offered his warriors for complete devotion: the promise of eternal life plus eternal pleasure from making others suffer. It explained why Arrix and the coding was such a good match, why he was its keeper. 7,000 years of searching for quartons told her that the coding fed on pain and misery. It was hotwired into it, part of its intricate code. She knew that.

But she now knew a lot more about it too because the coding had revealed itself to her. When Taron eventually decided to kill them, she was not going to die. For her daughter, Martha's sake, she was not going to die. For the memory of her dead husband, she was not going to die. For the revenge she would inflict on Arrix, she was not going to die. She would stand proud and face Taron, knowing that whatever Arrix did, this was not the end.

Taron deliberately stepped forward and she readied herself to take her last breath in this life. A loud jarring sound from outside made the huge warrior pause. There was another second when Taron raised his visor to reveal a disfigured Garalian face, pocked with scars. He looked directly at Fen, and then he, Pella and everything around was ripped apart and scattered into billions of atoms.

She felt her own body disintegrate and spread with them, yet all the while she retained an awareness which enabled her to look upon the process with a strange inquisitiveness. Her mind was cocooned, wrapped up in some sort of mesh which was holding enough of her together to maintain her feeling of self as the dark energy that had powered the bridge through the quartons was thrown into reverse. The coding held her tight, fighting to stay and to keep them together on Earth – her, Arrix, Pella, Klavon, the quartons and the bridge – to finish what it had started. She fought with it, knowing that her only way of seeing Martha again was to stay there, to live and to fight Arrix for full control of the coding. Yet it seemed impossible.

Outside the portal was even more chaotic. The quartons, the bridge, the warriors and the hardware they brought were, in an instant, swept away in a tsunami of the physical merged with the spiritual. Fen did not remember it, but something similar, in reverse, had happened after the Garial Bridge was destroyed. She, as Rana, with Pella, Klavon and Arrix had been spat out onto Earth with the quartons, trillions of miles across the galaxy. The force again was all in one direction, this time away from Earth and the portal, and she soon realised she was in a battle she could not win. All she could do was survive and somehow keep her body together. Maybe even try to work with the coding to shape the outcome.

Where she would end up, she had no idea, but at least she would be alive.

So she hoped.

Part 1

One year later

Mackenzie

The door frames were far too low, even for normal-sized people. Mackenzie had to stoop whenever he went from one end of the building to the other. It was causing havoc with his back to the extent that he had seriously considered crawling as soon as he set off anywhere. Nowhere was built for six foot eight giants. Still, this place was ridiculous.

He rubbed his back as he sat down on a chair and faced his good friend, Don Berretti, now a colonel in the Southern Alliance. The chair creaked under his weight – tiny rickety furniture was another bugbear of his – but he was not in his office to spend time complaining.

Don briefly looked up from his console, nodded and then spoke to someone down the line. Mackenzie could not hear the other end of the conversation, but the long pauses between Don's responses suggested that a lot of information was being directed his way. Mackenzie thrust his hands in his pockets, leant back in the chair and looked for something interesting in what was a sparse office. Some of the other officers projected 3D pictures of coastal or mountain scenery, even pictures of their kids, onto their walls. Not Don. He liked to keep everything straight and above board, so there was nothing to keep Mackenzie even remotely entertained as he waited for him to finish. Fortunately, he did not have to wait long.

'How are ya, Mac?' Don was one of only two people who Mackenzie allowed to address him by his shortened name. The other person was – had been – Chuck.

A year, almost to the day, had passed since he had seen his best friend give up his life to prevent an alien invasion. The image of Arrix in his full Garial regalia holding Chuck up above his head, presenting him to the Garalian fleet that thronged around them, haunted him still. Those sorts of memories were hard to get rid of. And the hurt from not having Chuck around had lessened hardly at all. Not that he often let it show.

'Good, Don. I'm good,' he said. 'I won't bother asking how you are – stressed and overworked by the looks of things.'

'You could say that. I'll get straight down to it, Mac. You said to me a year ago after Arrix and his warriors had been defeated, that you could not guarantee that was the end of the matter. Correct?'

'Correct.'

If he and Chuck had used the MASH as it was originally meant to be used by hitting them with an overload of dark energy, Chuck was convinced he could have physically obliterated anything they directed it at – Arrix, warriors, bridges, even planets. That had not been possible in those last crazy moments. Instead, Mackenzie had put it into reverse and extracted the dark energy from the quartons. They had vanished along with everything and everyone else connected to them. The big question was to where?

'And since then you have spent your time at HQ, overseeing a project to develop Chuck's system to monitor fluctuations in dark energy across the globe.'

'Correct again, Don. That's why I moved to Australia. It's what I do. It's my job description, set out by my employer. You are my employer. Is this a performance appraisal of some kind? If it is, then count me out. Mark me down as 'needs to work on his doorframe avoiding skills' and I'll get back to work.'

Conversations between the two friends often went along these lines. They both enjoyed to banter but could switch onto the serious meat of the subject when required. It did not take long for Don to do exactly that.

'Mac, I need to ask you something. Both you and Chuck said that dark energy was the key to the Garialans' form of space travel, for want of a better term.' Mackenzie said nothing. It was not a question. Neither he nor Chuck ever got to the bottom of exactly how Arrix and the Garalians used the quartons to bridge a gap across space, a gap measured in light years rather than kilometres. All they knew was that they had managed it. Given that Mackenzie was convinced the Garalians could well come back, he had urged Don to give him the resources, through the Southern Alliance, to get a team of scientists together to keep a watching brief on changes to dark energy levels. That was in place now at the Alliance's main headquarters in Melbourne. So far, no abnormalities had been detected. Which was good news in terms of an alien threat, if somewhat misleading, as he was about to find out.

'What if,' Don continued, 'they found another way?'

'We've discussed this before, Don. That is entirely possible. The Garalians are an advanced race. I wouldn't be at all surprised if they did develop some other means. Dark energy fluctuations, as I keep explaining to your superiors at every resource committee meeting, are one indication of extraterrestrial activity. It's one, but an important one, because Arrix, Fen and the other two were all linked to it through the quartons. If Arrix is coming back – let's hope he won't, let's hope he's a real goner – but if he is coming back, then the likelihood is that he'll use existing technology in some form which might involve dark energy. But, perhaps he won't.' He shrugged. 'We can only work with what we know.'

'Take a look at these, Mac, and tell me what you think they show.' He flicked a duplicate screen across so that Mackenzie had the same view. A memory of a similar conversation with Fen and Sam, studying the early images of the hole that had appeared over the Severn Bridge, flashed into Mackenzie's mind. It still hurt that neither of them were around. Lives lost that he wished he could have saved. Fen had been instrumental in helping to decipher those images. But he did not need any help with the ones Don was showing him. Sadly, his early experiences in the Southern Alliance had thrown up many situations very similar to these.

'More wrecked communities,' he said. 'Recent, I assume?'

'Very. Earlier today.'

'What happened?'

'We're not sure. That's the problem.'

Mackenzie swiped through twenty or so pictures taken from different angles. They all showed a similar scene: flattened buildings, rubble, glass, rooftops blown off. 'Location,' he said and inserts with names of places and maps popped up in the corner of each image. 'There's a pattern,' he said. 'All fishing communities, small populations – less than five hundred – all of them ... hang on. Now that is strange.' The chair groaned as he sat forward. '... All of them hit at exactly the same time of day, nine-ten European time, and all locations under French-Irish jurisdiction: three in France, three in Ireland and three in the area that used to be under their control, the western corner of England. This is a concerted attack against our favourite president and what's left of her alliance.'

'Agreed, but by who?'

'Are you thinking these are alien attacks, Don? Says here in the provisional ground reports that they have the hallmarks of explosives and guns being used. Humans at work here, surely?'

'Look at the death toll – six in each. All victims killed right on the perimeters of the communities. No other injuries. People were either out on boats or down by the shore involved in fishing related activities. Mac, this was very specific, calculated to show or prove something. It took some kinda organisation.'

'Who is out there capable of doing this? Do we know of any countries or organisations that would hold this kind of grudge against Lessey?'

'Plenty who hold a grudge, but none who would want to go this far. Think about it – these were all done at exactly the same time – exactly, to the second – across nine widespread locations. Synchronised. All had almost identical levels of damage.'

'Quite a feat, but it doesn't scream alien attack to me.'

'Not in itself, maybe. But it does scream sending out a message.'

'To Lessey?'

'No, to us. You said last year's shenanigans were possibly not all over.'

'I said I couldn't guarantee it was all over because I don't know where the quartons Arrix brought over with him on the new bridge would have ended up. The experiment Chuck and I did before we carried it out live, left us with no clue what happened to the things we extracted the dark energy from. Neptune, the sun, another galaxy – they could be anywhere.'

'On this planet?'

'Yes, in theory. Hopefully, Arrix has been terminated with his quartons. But I take your point. If somehow he has survived, we could be looking at the threat coming from within rather than from Garial.'

'I'm not saying it's definitely him, Mac. But look at the data. This is a highly unusual attack, perpetrated by an unknown for no obvious reason. I'm looking at it from a military point of view. We are not at war with anyone. No one is. That's the only good thing to have come out of the Power Wars. Things aren't perfect, but I repeat: there are no countries or groups that I know of that would want to do this, however nasty Lessey is.'

'Isn't she a reformed character?'

'I wouldn't go that far. She's had her wings clipped after having to give up that corner of England and has been less prone to stir things up. I've got a feeling that won't last long after this.'

'So, no obvious motive, yet this was carried out by someone with the capability to do a lot of damage. It's worth looking into.'

'I'm glad you agree. What do you...' Don was interrupted by a shrill ring on his bracelet.

Mackenzie did not need to guess who was trying to get hold of Don as he took the call. The use of the word *feck* every few seconds made that abundantly clear.

It was difficult for Mackenzie as he stepped off the plane onto the same airstrip at the same airfield where he and Chuck had spent several years building the MASH. The place had strong associations with his long-term friend. It had also been where he had met up with Sam and Fen and begun to plot how they all might tackle the threat from Arrix and his warriors. Could he have imagined back then returning without any of them? Probably not.

The area was instantly recognisable, although there had been some changes. The large hangar was still there, as were the two pods to the left of it that Chuck and he had lived in. But it was far busier than he had ever seen it before with a significant amount of aircraft and ground vehicles of various sizes and functions littered around being attended to by maintenance staff. There were two new buildings to the right of the hangar, one of which, with its two stories and uniform windows, looked like accommodation. The other, smaller, low and flat, with the French and Irish flags fluttering above the entrance, was the new focal point for the alliance's aeronautical operations. This part of northern France, just outside Paris, was close enough for the short hop President Lessey would occasionally take to meet with her French colleagues... when she could be winkled out of her base in Dublin.

Apparently, Lessey did not travel much these days – Don had said on the trip over from Australia that word was she had lost some of her confidence after what she referred to as, 'The Energy Anomaly' in official documentation post the Garial attack near the Severn Bridge. The fact that there was a larger military presence in France than in Ireland might have suggested that the balance of power could be shifting away from her. That was as maybe, but, at the moment, at least, she was hanging on to the presidency with typical Lessey determination.

The two men headed straight for the main entrance to a smaller building where they were greeted by a familiar face.

'Ah, Major Shaw,' Don said holding out his hand. 'It's good to see you again.'

Shaw's response was rather stiff and formal. 'Gentlemen, I hope you had a pleasant journey.' He shook Don's hand and nodded a cautious greeting towards Mackenzie. The last time Mackenzie had seen Shaw was at the military site set up to monitor the hole which was the precursor to the Garial Bridge arriving. He and Don had briefly been held prisoner in one of the pop-ups there but had escaped Shaw's clutches, leaving the major and some of his men slightly worse for wear, thanks to Mackenzie. With Lessey shell-shocked and in denial about her alien encounter, Shaw had organised a rapid withdrawal of their troops. Mackenzie guessed that his presence here today was acknowledgement on Lessey's part that he was not as hopeless as she had previously made out her major to be. It seemed, though, he was prone to bear a grudge.

'President Lessey is waiting for you in her office,' said Shaw. 'Vice President Geron is already with her and I shall be joining your meeting.' Mackenzie detected a hint of boastfulness and self-importance in his tone which did not make him any more likeable. He had not much appreciated his attitude towards Fen in particular last time round. Shaw had had a rather closed mind on the origin of the hole which aligned with his president's own sceptical point of view. It would be interesting today to see what sort of view they took towards the causes behind the attacks on their villages and whether either of them had shifted their opinions about what had happened last year. The fact Lessey had called on Don and Mackenzie was a hopeful sign that she was, at the very least, receptive to taking advice.

'Follow me this way,' Shaw said taking them through a security door and into a corridor.

'What is it with military establishments,' Mackenzie said ducking as he walked, 'that specifies you have to be less than six feet six inches to walk comfortably inside? Is this an international agreement or something?'

Shaw, who was significantly shorter than Mackenzie, turned his head. His expression suggested that he had taken his question as a personal dig. Mackenzie tried to form his face into a picture of innocence. With his ginger beard covering most of it, he usually had to rely on his pale blue eyes to do the talking, but in this case, they were too busy looking out for dangerous obstacles, like low lights. The next obstacle arrived pretty swiftly in the form of another door frame as Shaw changed direction and took them into a small waiting area with a few seats and a water dispenser.

'I'll check to see if they're ready for us,' said Shaw. 'Take a seat, if you wish.'

18

'I'm fine, thanks,' said Mackenzie, forcing himself not to comment on the squat nature of the furniture for risk of offending him further. As Shaw followed his knock into the next room and pulled the door to behind him, Mackenzie whispered to Don, 'Did you know our friend was going to be involved?'

'No. Is it going to be a problem?'

'Not for me it isn't. It does largely depend on his and the president's attitude, though.'

'She approached us, remember? She could have spoken to anyone in the Southern Alliance, even the big boss, but she came to us. As I said on the plane, let's see what she wants. She's asked us to come here and she's gone out of her way to meet us, if not halfway then at least partway. She's off her own patch in Ireland. I think that's significant.'

'S'pose so. Seeing Shaw here has made me a little suspicious. We'll see, I guess.'

The door opened and Shaw, with his back propping the door open, ushered them in. 'Do mind your head as you come through, won't you?' he said, his voice sounding just a little harsher. Mackenzie twitched his whiskers, an action that could be interpreted as a smile or a grimace behind the mass of hair.

Lessey and Geron were sitting at either end of a long desk. Geron pushed his chair back in preparation to stand up in welcome as they entered, but Lessey remained seated, her eyes fixed to the far wall. 'Colonel Berretti and Mister Ingles. Thank you for coming all this way,' he said with just a trace of a French accent. Geron was a man in his fifties who looked like he had lived at least thirty more than that. His shoulders were slumped and he winced as he

19

straightened his back. His grey hair was obviously thinning, but what was left on top had been shaped and gelled into a wave that sat precariously towards the back of his head, joining up short sides that must have needed constant attention to keep them so short. His paunch suggested that he had long been enjoying what was left of any fine French wine that had survived the Power Wars and his dark eyes peered out from under wispy eyebrows, a good place to retreat to should the need arise. Working with Lessey and her renowned short temper, Mackenzie imagined, Geron probably needed the safety of that particular haven.

'You know President Lessey, of course,' Geron said.

Lessey's eyes flicked towards them and she gave a little nod upwards in recognition, before turning her attention back towards the wall. To Mackenzie, it seemed like she was embarrassed to see them again after last year when she had been overwhelmed. He had never understood her insistence that the whole event, from the Garial Bridge appearing through the hole to the attack led by Arrix, was a stunt organised by the Southern Alliance to push her own Alliance out of the Western corner of England. It had seemed remarkable in the face of so much evidence to the contrary. Maybe she had had a change of heart, despite the official line she had taken subsequently.

Shaw invited them to take the two seats next to each other at the centre of the table. He walked round to Lessey and stood next to her with his arms hanging loosely by his side. With Geron at one end and Lessey and Shaw at the other end of the table, it did not suggest total unity within the government. Mackenzie looked from one to the other and then, as was often the way, found his mouth speaking before he could stop it:

'So, have you decided on a new national anthem now there's just the two nations left?' He immediately regretted saying it as his friend's elbow found his ribs. Don hurriedly followed it up with a more diplomatic line about being pleased to be there and reiterating his condolences for the loss of life during the recent attacks which made Mackenzie feel even worse about his rashness.

'Thank you, Colonel Berretti,' said Geron. 'That's very kind. Now, can I suggest we get down to business?'

Lessey, extraordinarily in Mackenzie's opinion, still had not said a word. Last time they had been together, not even an alien-neutralising beam had been able to stop her talking. Now, she was strangely mute. Mackenzie did not like it. It suggested she was building up to something.

It turned out that he was right.

Fen

It was so vivid.

Martha could not stop giggling as she made a play of sneaking up behind her dad to snatch up the weeds he had just dug up. She scurried away, delighting in the danger of being caught red-handed, to the opposite side of the garden where she had her own trowel and patch of ground. Fen was right nearby, in charge of supervising – her job was to make sure Sam did not notice. In practice, she was looking out for spiders which had their own habit of scurrying about, an actual danger in this part of the world. Martha dug separate holes for each weed and replanted them. Fen loved the way the tip of Martha's tongue edged out as she concentrated on her work. The final patting down of the soil and then Martha was off again, ready to fool her dad who was all too aware of what was going on. Fen had never felt such contentment. She could not believe her luck. After all she had been through, all the heartache and pain, somehow it did not seem real. It felt all... wrong.

It felt wrong because it was wrong. Despite her efforts to hang onto the reassuring images and sounds, they faded away and she was forced to assess a new reality.

She was, in fact, flat on her back on a hard floor. Her first thought was that she was in her old room, the one she had shared with Lee at the scavenger's base, trying to sleep after a day spent searching through piles of rubbish in some grotty corner of the city. What had woken her this time? A rat scuffling about? A distant clang of an old pipe? The bitter cold seeping through her sleeping bag? None of these things, she realised, as it began to dawn on her what she had just been through.

Everything around her had been ripped apart, each particle in danger of dispersing to far flung corners of the galaxy. But she had kept herself together – physically and mentally (so far, at least) – and she had done it by using the coding. She had allowed herself to become part of the intricate code and immersed herself within it as the dark energy had whisked her away from the portal. It had protected her. Rather, she had let it protect her, a significant difference, because she now had a semblance of control, something that had been hinted at back at the portal.

Although, on reflection, maybe not that much control since she had no idea where she was now, nor was she entirely sure she wanted to find out.

Small steps were required, she decided, until she would open her eyes. The air was good enough, if a little stale, but she was breathing – always a good sign. No headache and her chest felt fine. She tapped her hands lightly over her stomach before gradually stretching her arms out and walking her fingers down her thighs. Then she tensed the muscles in her legs and wriggled her toes. Her back ached as she moved but, apart from that, everything seemed to check out. She was in one piece, definitely in one piece, and definitely in control.

Keep telling yourself that, Fen, she told herself, and you might be able to believe it.

Eventually, she summoned up the courage, took a deep breath and opened her eyes.

Mackenzie

Mackenzie and Don sat while Geron updated them on the latest situation at the sites that had been attacked. The death toll was the same, no injuries and, crucially, no clues as to who had carried the attacks out. Investigation teams had been sent to all three locations and were still conducting enquiries, but indications were that, whoever was responsible, was incredibly well organised, had been razor-sharp with the accuracy of the attacks, and was deadly. No trail had been left, no one had claimed responsibility and no motive had been established. There had been a rumour that a group, opposed to the French policy of economic cooperation with China before the Power Wars, had been re-formed to protest against the Irish and French Alliance. Judging by their previous modus operandi, this type of attack might have appealed to them, but the idea was quashed. Even at the height of their powers, a coordinated attack on this scale would have been beyond them, let alone nowadays with far fewer resources being available. That was the problem. No organisation, other than another country possibly, would have had the wherewithal to do this with such precision and with such a devastating effect. And there was no country in the world that would have any logical reason for doing so.

Geron finished his briefing and then looked expectantly towards Mackenzie and Don. Mackenzie happened to be looking directly back at Geron at that point, having spent the last couple of minutes swivelling his head from side to side from one end of the table to the other, checking Lessey for a hint of a reaction. Throughout, she had maintained her silence and fixed stare.

Don placed the flat of his palms on the table and prepared to stand up to speak. It was at that moment that Lessey decided to finally say something.

'This was delivered to me via Major Shaw, just before you landed,' she said, her voice quiet and subdued. 'I opened it but haven't shown anyone else yet.' From underneath the table, she pulled out a small white envelope which she slid down towards Don. There was a red seal, plastic or wax, which had been broken, presumably when Lessey had opened it. The last time Mackenzie had seen anything as antiquated looking as that had been in a museum pre-war.

'Pick it up, take a look inside,' she said.

Don had to stretch a little to reach it. He placed it between himself and Mackenzie and the two men examined it. The red seal was thin and was probably plastic rather than wax, Mackenzie concluded. The point of the flap had been torn and tucked back inside. Don flipped it over. Handwritten in black was one word: Lessey.

'Go ahead,' said Lessey. 'Open it. Read it out loud. Geron needs to hear it.'

Don turned it back over, lifted up the flap and pulled out a piece of paper with his forefinger and thumb. He unfolded the paper and began reading from it. 'Ex-President Lessey. Your office and institutions are finished. The French-Irish Alliance is no more.'

Don looked up at Lessey. 'That's it? Nothing else?'

'That's all there is in that envelope. There's one here addressed to you too.' With that she produced and slid down another similarly marked envelope with the red seal, broken again.

'You've opened it,' said Mackenzie.

'Of course,' Lessey replied, shrugging.

Don collected the second one, turned it over. It was marked, handwritten again, 'Colonel Berretti'.

'What's it say?' asked Mackenzie impatiently.

Don read it to himself and, without looking at Mackenzie, held it out for him to take. Mackenzie read it out loud. 'Colonel Berretti, your office and institutions are finished. The Southern Alliance will be no more.' He handed it back to Don who placed it on top of the envelope on the table.

Lessey still had not shown any of the fiery behaviour she was so famous for and Mackenzie was beginning to wonder whether Don had, in fact, understated her transformation of character. It was particularly surprising given the reaction he heard over the phone when she contacted Don, and now with the threat stated in the letters.

She looked directly at Mackenzie now. 'There's one for you, too,' she said.

A third envelope was slid down the table, this one with no seal on it. Don picked it up and handed it straight over to Mackenzie who immediately flipped it over. Again there was just the one word – 'Mac' – this time, though, the writing was different.

Mackenzie recognised the barely legible scrawl straight away. 'It's from Chuck,' he said. 'This was given to you, President?'

Shaw interjected. 'All three were found inside this unmarked one, left on my desk.' He held up a larger brown envelope.

'Where's your office?' asked Don.

'Next door and, before you ask, I've had security run through the visuals. Nothing and no one has shown up in them. I had been in my office all morning. I came in to see President Lessey and when I came back it was on my desk. They're going through all the visuals of the entire area again – I'm not hopeful.'

Mackenzie turned the envelope over several times. 'You know what's inside this one too, President, I see,' he said noting the tucked in flap. Lessey said nothing.

'You okay?' said Don quietly.

'Yes, fine,' Mackenzie replied feeling, suddenly, anything but fine. 'Let's see what the little fella's got to say.'

Lessey

Moira Lessey had always considered herself a strong woman, able to handle anything that came her way. In a world where men still dominated in positions of power, she had fought her way to the top through shouting louder than anyone else, and not caring much whether what she shouted caused hurt. Male, female, neither, large, small, Irish or foreign, she started from presuming everyone was incompetent or stupid, unless she decided otherwise. She had not so much earned the respect of those around her, rather imposed it; she always had something to say in any situation, and had a way of saying it that pummelled opponents into submission.

Latterly, since 'The Energy Anomaly', she had been less prone to the tantrums she was famous for. She had not felt at all well after the incident inside Mackenzie's contraption. They – 'they' being the Southern Alliance and their partners – had put on quite a show that day, to their credit. Very convincing with spaceships and alien like creatures descending from the skies. Their technical department had gone overboard with all their virtual reality 3D trickery. At one point, she had wondered whether it was, actually, real. That was what had sent her into shock at the time, she reflected afterwards. It was not the fact there were aliens running around everywhere, more the fact that she had briefly believed that there were aliens running around everywhere. The unshakable confidence in her own abilities – and her own belief system – had taken a knock, from which, she was loathed to admit, she was still recovering. She was going ever so slightly soft, and she hated herself for it. Why, she had even given Major Shaw more responsibility. He was the biggest of all eejits – what on Earth was wrong with her?

So when she had heard about the attacks on her territory, she had assumed that Don Berretti and the Southern Alliance were up to their tricks again. She had given him an earful, yet had not felt the indignation and fury she would have felt prior to last year. That kind of understated reaction was happening more and more these days, even at meetings with Geron and the other sub commanders. She tried to shout and bawl, but it was hard to sound so right in every situation these days. It used to not matter whether she was right or wrong.

Which was why she had asked for a meeting with Don and Mackenzie in France with just Geron there. The Irish members of her cabinet had been more awkward recently, maybe sensing a weakness in their President, so to be away from them would be useful, plus the fact that the base they now had outside Paris was a good place from which to coordinate a response. Don had agreed not to involve his bosses too much at this stage, other than to keep them informed, which suited her down to the ground because she still did not trust the Southern Alliance. But she trusted him; he was willing to take risks and operate outside of the usual rules, much like her.

He had insisted he brought Mackenzie along with him. Because of the big man's connections to what happened last year, she was not totally comfortable with him being there, but her instinct, annoyingly, was telling her that it was right. Hopefully, between them, they could shut the whole mess down without too much fuss.

Then the letters arrived. The manner in which they arrived, as well as the content, knocked her off kilter. She had received many threats before and seen them as just that: threats, nothing more because, normally, they were without substance. It came with the territory of being President – there was always someone trying to knock you off the top. But this threat was different – 'Your institutions are finished.' It was such a bold statement. How would they do that? There were no weapons of mass destruction anywhere in the world. After witnessing the devastation to England, in particular, and the retaliatory response on Beijing, every single nation with nuclear capability from China through to Russia and the States had dismantled their armouries, each nation sending representatives to oversee each other's actions. It was a safer world – different, but definitely safer. No one could wipe out her Alliance. No one would want to. Yet something about this made Lessey believe it, and she believed the threat to Don and the Southern Alliance was as serious. She believed it because of who those two letters were from. On the back they were signed simply: Lee. No person in official circles other than Shaw, possibly – not even Geron – knew about her connection with Lee and how she had tried to use her to gain access to Chuck and the inner workings of what was going on by the Severn Bridge.

It soon became obvious that Mackenzie and Don knew something about Lee too as Mackenzie, his voice quivering with emotion, read out Chuck's letter to him.

Dear Mackenzie,

I am sorry, old friend, if you are reading this letter as it means I have ultimately failed in trying to put right the mistakes from long ago. The one piece of good news is that, if you are reading it, you are alive, at least.

Lee is by my side now as I write. I have agreed to do this as part of the conditions of her helping us to defeat Arrix. If things go well and I live, the letter will never see the light of day. If things go well and I die, the letter will never see the light of day. In both cases there will be no need because it means both parties – myself and Lee – are fully satisfied with the outcome. Since you are reading it now, I would suggest that, unfortunately, trouble lies ahead.

Be strong, Mac. Listen to what Lee has to say. Believe her. I hope what she has got to say is not as bad as I fear.

Once again, I'm sorry.

Your friend, always,

Chuck

Mackenzie coughed. 'There's a micro disc attached to the letter,' he said, his voice wavering. 'You played this yet, President?'

She had not. Lack of time was the official excuse. Unofficially, she did not have the courage. 'No,' she said simply. 'Major Shaw?'

'I'm on it, Madame President. I have located a suitable machine which will allow transference of the data from the micro disc onto our current wave 3.5 digital systems. It will convert any of the old three-point-three and three-point-four audio formats to...'

Lessey snapped, 'Just play it, Shaw, for Chrissakes!' She put her head in her hands in the expectation that when she looked up again she would be listening to what was on the disc. That proved to be correct, although the voice that came out of Shaw's converter surprised her.

Her irrational side had told her that it would be Lee, gloating at her from the other side of the grave. Lessey had gunned down Lee outside the portal and knew she was dead – Shaw had checked that with Don after they had withdrawn – yet she still feared she had, somehow, survived. Her rational side told her that it could be Lee, maybe her voice from the past, recording a message at the same time that Chuck wrote the letter.

What Lessey did not expect to hear was a young girl's voice – the same young girl she had tried to get information from near the portal. What was her name, Ruby, was it? She had never been keen on children and this one had been of little help other than mumbling on about something called quartons without any real explanation.

As the girl began to speak now, something struck her. There was something about her manner that did not fit with the way young children normally talked. It was a child's voice, yet it sounded grownup, confident, full of intent. There was a hint of sarcasm laced heavily with an undertone of malice that Lessey did not like at all.

It definitely was not Lee's voice, yet take away the higher pitch and the youthful nature, it might just as well have been.

Fen

Her first instinct when she looked directly up was that she was outdoors since she could see blue sky with patches of reds and pinks. Something caught in her nose making her half sniff, half sneeze. The slight echo back took her by surprise. She shivered involuntarily, suddenly aware of the dankness seeping up from the floor through her clothes and into her bones. She needed to get up before she froze to death. She started by easing up onto one elbow.

Directly in front, not far away, was a wall. Light from above bounced off it sending out tiny multicoloured rays, flickering and dancing in all directions. The light dimmed and the show faded away, leaving a smoky feel to the room. Was it a room, though? She checked behind and to the sides. The wall she had been looking at seemed quite close, but other walls were not visible. She looked up again. What she thought was blue sky was in fact some sort of dark covering. Between that were the patches of pink, much further away, that could have been sky, maybe a sunset or sunrise. It was hard to get a true perspective from the floor.

Somewhat groggily, she turned over onto her hands and knees and got to her feet. She stood for a few moments to make sure her balance was okay then looked down. As she hoped, she did indeed seem to be all there. Her head ached a little and she felt tired – absolutely exhausted, in fact – but otherwise she was okay, which was incredible given what she had been through. What she had been through... that needed further thought, but she could find an excuse to put that to one side by exploring and establishing where she was.

Intrigued, she approached the wall with a vague recollection that she had seen something like it before. It was further away than it had first appeared, but as she walked towards it, she felt some strength and stability return to her wobbly legs. Another shaft of light broke through and the wall came to life again. Now she was closer, she could see the wall was a large barrier of ice with liquid flowing gently behind it. Every now and then the movement would catch the light and send ripples of colours off in different directions.

She stood mesmerised for a moment until the source above faded once more and with it the wall. Slightly disappointed, she turned round. The haziness had returned to distort her view so, with nothing specific for her eyes to latch onto, she plumped for the practical approach and decided she would walk until things became clearer, or something stopped her going much further. The floor was uneven so she proceeded with caution, aware too that there could be obstructions she might trip over.

At first, it felt like she was walking down a slope but, after a short while, that changed and she began to go up. The slope became steeper as she walked, so much so that she began to feel the strain in her thighs and she started to pant with the effort. At last, it flattened out and she continued walking as straight as she could, a difficult thing to judge with few reference points and no sign of an end to the room or anything obvious to the sides. It occurred to her she might be in one of those shopping malls they used to have in cities.

Ages ago with Lee, she had scavenged in one in London which had been partially flattened by the missile strike. There had been the remnants of a long walkway and smaller areas off of it which used to be retail outlets. (It had been a productive day, she recalled. They had found quite a variety of goods under the rubble – surprising really considering how close it was to their base and the likelihood it had been visited before). Fen could almost imagine she was out scavenging now, scoping out a new place, not knowing what she might find. Except, whatever this place was seemed endless and devoid of anything at all.

Noticing that the smokiness was subsiding, she stopped and looked up again. The roof – or whatever was left of it – had opened up to reveal an all pink sky. It was a deeper pink than any she had seen before, solid with none of the usual patches of whites, oranges or reds. There was no direct sunlight shining through at all, but she could make out three objects in the sky, staggered and spaced apart, slowly coming into full view. Looking up was making her feel dizzy and she decided to sink to the floor before she crashed onto it. Once down, she stretched out her hands behind her back and waited for the dizziness to subside before leaning back and looking up again. The three objects were now clear to see. Instinct had told her that they might give her a reference point. They certainly gave her that.

She felt her stomach lurch as she realised where she was. The objects in the sky, without any doubt whatsoever, were the three moons of Garial. Fen was back on her home planet. In fact, she could be quite specific as to her location because she had been here before, a long, long time ago.

She was sitting on the floor of the huge science complex Arrix had built to research and design the Great Garial Bridge. Fen had worked here for a brief period before she found out about Arrix's true motives and decided, for the future of her planet, she needed to stop him connecting the bridge to Earth.

The complex had been built in the mountains, some hundred miles from where the bridge was constructed. It hugged the outside of one mountain, starting just over halfway up and creeping round the outside to the peak at the top. She remembered that she had walked up and down this open space many times, mainly to admire the incredible artwork on display at one end towards the bottom of the complex. The backdrop to that, she was sure, had been the multicoloured ice wall that she had just been puzzling over – a natural phenomenon exposed early on in the construction and retained.

The large gaps in what had been the roof and the lack of other proper structures nearby, suggested the complex had deteriorated massively. That was hardly surprising, given how long ago she had been here.

She slumped back onto the floor and shut her eyes again as she tried to take in the full implications of what she had just discovered. After over 7,000 years, the combination of the coding, dark energy, and maybe her own will, had contrived to throw her across the galaxy, back to the planet where she, as Rana, had been born.

Fen and Sam had answered the call for help when the hole had opened up near the Severn Bridge in England. They had agonised over being so far away from Martha. That long journey from Australia to England paled into insignificance compared to the trillions of miles she was now away from the person she loved more than anything.

Ruby

'A message for President Lessey, Mackenzie and Major Shaw. Can you guess who this?'

<It is not necessary to start in such a foolish manner, Klavon.>

I do know what I am doing, Arrix. And this is more enjoyable.

<We are not doing this for enjoyment. Get on with it.>

Very well.

'I hope you have read that letter from the little man in the chair. Such a funny old thing – so clever, so brave but, ultimately, so useless. So clever because, when he wrote it, he actually predicted the future. He predicted he was likely to fail. And he has.

'Our organisation has carried out three attacks on three sites. We have hit villages of similar size in three locations belonging to what used to be called the Western-French-Irish Alliance. Death numbers are the same in each, damage almost identical and they were all done at exactly the same time. But you know all this, don't you? You will also know that it shows that we are well organised and dangerous, so when we say your Alliances are finished, we mean it.'

<That is good. Our followers know what we can do. They do not. They need to believe a young girl is capable.>

Perhaps we should be more specific and tell them who we are?

<They have probably guessed, yet it will still disturb them to hear a young girl making threats. Don't question my judgement.

Making decisions and planning is what I do best. Frightening people is what you do best.>

On that last point we are agreed. We would be nowhere if our followers weren't scared of me. I shall finish off the communication.

'You will hear from us again. Do not try to find us. You will not be able to. That is all for now.'

<Better, Klavon! A strong finish to your message and the start to getting who and what we want. In addition, it will set things up nicely for when we take over. A world with countries and alliances not trusting each other will make it easier to dominate.>

So, you admit I was right about Lessey?

<Yes. She is trouble, and in an ideal position to stir things up... with our help.>

Ruby stood up from the kitchen table she had been sitting at and walked out to the closest and smallest of the three barns near the farmhouse. She entered the building where eight people were busy at work checking over weapons. About half of the hundred or so other followers – the workers and foot soldiers – were scattered around the farm doing the more mundane jobs that kept a small army going. They alternated with the other half out now in the French and neighbouring German countryside and towns, foraging and scavenging for the resources that an army needed.

Ruby held out her hand and waited for Jerome to take the recording disc from her. Nine times out of ten, when something was needed, it would be Jerome who would be first by her side. He was the most keen, the most ready, the most violent of all the followers. Everyone complied – that was why they were there – but

Jerome was the one Ruby counted on the most. He had been their first recruit and had other assets which were useful, often acting as her enforcer.

As Jerome went to take the disc, she forced eye contact before she said anything, smirking as Jerome, a bulky man well over six feet with biceps the size of bowling balls, averted his eyes. It did no harm to remind him who was boss. It was the part that Klavon enjoyed the most about his role in this double act which had worked so well since they had been joined by the coding. He definitely liked being the nastier one of the two, and saw it as a challenge to stay that way.

From the moment Ruby had left the Severn Bridge area in England and made her way first east, and then gradually south towards the coast, she had found people were terrified of her. Nine years old was no age, yet she quickly realised the eyes were her greatest asset. They somehow told a story – a story of two dark twisted souls inhabiting a young girl's body that would do anything to get what they wanted. Anyone who doubted that – as Jerome did when they first met in northern France – would soon find themselves on the receiving end of Klavon's natural tendency to violence. In Jerome's case, it was a slash across the stomach from a broken glass bottle. It had been more than enough to convince him there was something different about the girl, and he was quickly on board and more than happy to be with her rather than against her. Ruby's uniqueness, maturity way beyond her body's years and sheer magnetism were enough to draw to her those who felt isolated from the new society being forged from the ashes of the

Power Wars. Very soon, she had the makings of a loyal group and eventually a small army was formed.

Arrix had been here before, of course, with the warriors, and knew instinctively how to handle people like them. He did not promise them eternal life – he could not – but he promised them revenge against the authorities who had ignored them. Klavon's caveman like threats, on occasion, were useful, but what could be more of a motivation than the opportunity to put right perceived wrongs? It drove them on and it was part of what motivated the combined life-forces now called Ruby.

After that pause, Ruby said, 'Take the letter, too, Jerome. You know what to do. Timing of delivery is crucial, just before our friends land from Australia. It will give Lessey time on her own to get nicely worried about our threats. Take Odette with you.'

A young girl came forward. Discounting Ruby, at sixteen Odette was the youngest member there. A technological genius, she had helped to build and refine most of the powerful weapons that had been used in the recent coordinated attacks. She had also helped develop systems that would easily override the security at Lessey's base in Northern France.

'Stay nearby and tell me what happens, both of you,' Ruby said.

With a nod of understanding, Jerome and Odette left and Ruby returned to the farmhouse kitchen.

<What do you find so funny now, Klavon?>

It's this place and this huge kitchen we are in.

<What about it?>

It reminds me of a kitchen I spent a bit of time in. It's old and shabby, just like the one I killed Fen's partner, Sam, in.

39

<Not the last person you killed though?>

No. Some humans can be so annoying. Still, we have a satisfactory selection now after weeding out a few.

<It's a fine balance between using violence for a means to an end and using it for the sake of it.>

I didn't know you had a caring side to you, Arrix.

<I don't, Klavon. You would do well to remember that.>

Mackenzie

'Wasn't that the girl who was in the Garalian transporter?' said Don. 'The one we lost before you destroyed Arrix. My staff looked everywhere for her after it was all over. We never got to the bottom of who she was.'

'It sounded like her.' Mackenzie pushed his chair back and stood up. 'Give me a sec – I need some air.'

He headed for the door, aware that Don was following him out and saying something to the others about it being a shock for Mackenzie to have received the letter from Chuck.

Shock was a good word for how he felt – sadness, despair, confusion could be added to the list – but he would be okay, providing he could focus on the job in hand. Getting out, would provide the opportunity to do precisely that by talking over the situation, in private, with Don.

On the way, he noted the two sets of security doors that whoever had left the envelopes would have needed to get through to access Shaw's office. They had opened automatically for Shaw on the way in, and they opened for him and Don on the way out, presumably at someone else's instigation. How had the messenger not been noticed?

Once outside, he walked over to the only tree immediately outside the building, spotting it was the sole source of shade from the late summer sun's belting heat. He leant against the trunk.

'Mackenzie, are you...' Don began as he joined him.

'I'm okay, Don. It's just a lot to take in.'

'Are you sure?'

'Really, I'm fine. Well, as fine as anyone could be when they get a letter from a dead friend, followed by an eerie message from a little girl who threatens the next apocalypse.'

'I take your point. Ruby... her name was Ruby. It was definitely her voice, wasn't it?'

Mackenzie nodded. 'I reckon. And she's an obvious link because she was there at the end.'

'She spoke with uncanny maturity.'

'That's because it wasn't actually her, Don.'

'Arrix? This body transference business?'

'Possibly, but the way she spoke – she was brash, sarcastic, nasty. I know we only met Ruby for a few minutes, but that wasn't the impression I got from her. It was certainly the impression I got from Lee, though, whenever I met her. And before you say anything, I know Lessey shot Lee... several times... and I know she had an autopsy done, and I know she was cremated. Remember what Fen told us, and remember who we are dealing with here. This could be Lee – in other words, Klavon – in that poor girl's body.'

'But we still can't discount Arrix from being involved.'

'Definitely can't. My God, what have they done to that girl? Dreadful.' It was unthinkable, but there was no time to dwell on it. 'We've got to deal with her as if it is Klavon or Arrix. There's no other way.'

'Agreed.'

'We also need to discuss Lessey's involvement here. As soon as we found out what had gone on in the villages, both of us, I think, realised this looked bad. On the face of it, Lee, with some sort of following she's managed to build, is getting at Lessey. But that's not the whole picture. She and they want more. They want us and specifically, they want me, and what I've got access to.'

'The MASH.'

'Yep.'

'They could've targeted you directly.'

'They could, but this way they have leverage. The threat of obliteration is a powerful tool. They know I – you, us, Lessey, the northern hemisphere – will respond. If they just went for me, they couldn't guarantee I would react. I could go into hiding.'

'You still can.'

'Not likely, is it?'

'But do they really have the threat that they say they have?'

'Do you doubt it bearing in mind who we're dealing with here? Lessey doesn't doubt it, that's for sure. She's worried, Don. Understandably. You saw her reaction – nonexistent. Does that sound like the Lessey we know? She's being played here, like a fiddle, just as we are. She doesn't like it because she's not in control. We need to handle her carefully, as well as dealing with

42

the threat. If we don't, we run the risk of the whole thing blowing up in our faces – quite literally.'

'You're right. Geron seems a reasonable sort. How about we go back in and listen to what they've got to say, suggest we need a bit of time to think about our response and in the meantime try to talk to Geron on his own?'

'Agreed. I'd also like to have another listen to the recording. I'll get Shaw to send it over to our bracelets.'

Mackenzie unfurled Chuck's letter which he had tucked into his pocket and scanned it again. "I hope it's not as bad as I fear," Chuck had written. Mackenzie had to smile ruefully. It could not be a lot worse.

Part 2

Fen

Fen had fallen asleep where she lay. Trying to process the implications of being on the other side of the galaxy had proved the final straw to a body that had been through hell. She would have slept on if she had not been shaken awake.

She tried to focus on the face that owned the hand on her shoulder. She could have cried when she realised who it was. It was the last human face she had seen in the portal before she – they, apparently – were whisked away back to Garial.

'Pella! Is it really you?'

'Yes, the latest version of him, anyway. Can you stand?'

'I think so.'

He helped her to her feet and said, 'I don't feel safe out in the open here. We'll move to one of the rooms over there. Can you walk?'

He offered his arm out for her to hold, but she rejected it. 'I'm okay, thanks. Just show me the way.'

Pella set off with Fen following close behind. He moved quite quickly towards a bend along what she could see now in the improved light used to be a wide path. She risked a quick glance up – Garial's moons were no longer in sight. They had been replaced by a much lighter pink sky. She must have been asleep for a long time – right through her first full night back on Garial.

'Just in here,' Pella said taking her through an open doorway into a room with smooth plastic type walls. Whatever had once filled the room had turned to dust. There was a gaping hole above their heads which led to more floors with similar holes as far as the eye could see. At the far end of the small room was a large jagged gap with a view out onto the mountains. The rays from the morning star were shining directly through one of the ridges and Fen had to hold her hand up to her eyes to stop it dazzling her as she approached it. Keen to drink in the outside Garalian air, she stopped for a moment while Pella continued through a door in the corner into the next room. She had always wondered what had happened to her planet in the millennia she had been away and whether it had recovered from the pollution and rising temperatures that had threatened its future all those years ago. Were her people even around anymore? If they were, had they evolved in any way? Arrix had brought a huge army of warriors with him. Perhaps they were just a small part of what was now populating the whole planet. There was a lot to discover. A lot, maybe, still to fear.

The air tasted fresh and unspoilt, much like the air back home in Australia, and not at all like the air she had to put up with in London which had been contaminated from the fallout after the Power Wars. Even before that, as a child, Fen could remember her mother complaining about the pollution in the air. When it was very bad, she suffered breathing problems and was reliant on her daughter to fetch her medication. That same acrid taste and smell had been common on Garial before she left – a sure sign of a planet in distress.

Pella urged her into the room he had just entered. Originally the door would have been made up of scattered molecules which could be remoulded into clear or coloured barriers, depending on what the occupants of the room wanted. There was no way of shutting the door now, but at least they were away from the main area and out of sight of any prying eyes. This was a much bigger room than the last, complete with four walls and a ceiling. Against one wall were a couple of pieces of furniture which remained intact. One was a chair – built for a Garalian much bigger than her – but, nevertheless, an obvious place for her to at least lean against. She did not have the energy to clamber up on it. Pella stood beside her looking rather awkward and apprehensive.

'Are we safe here?' she asked.

'For now, I think.'

There were a few moments of silence. She had a heap of questions for him, but was unsure where to start. Eventually, she said with a touch of irony, 'Are you pleased to be back home?' It was a stupid comment, she knew, yet it broke the ice and Pella smiled.

'Not exactly. Although, there were hundreds of times in all those crazy lives we lived on Earth that I would have given anything to be back here with you and our parents in our stack.'

'My God, the stack! How do you remember that? That system of rotating the living spaces to be nearer the star, just to get a few more drops of energy. Seems crazy now.'

'It's what started it all, if you remember. Your journey as an eco-warrior, out to save the planet.'

'And your journey as a scientist, happy to abandon it.' She regretted saying it as soon as it came out. 'Sorry,' she added hurriedly.

'That's alright. Rana...'

'Fen. Call me by my Earth name. It's who I am now, who I want to be.'

'Understood. Fen it is. It's what I knew you as when I was Forrest. Strictly, I'm Mark now.'

'You don't look like a Mark.'

'What does a Mark look like?'

'Don't know, but not like you.'

'Okay, let's stick with Pella.'

She was pleased. 'Deal.'

'So, Fen, somehow, we're back on Garial?'

'Yes, and I'm pretty certain this is the science complex we worked in with Arrix.'

'And I'm pretty sure this is my office. I can remember going up and down slopes from there to get here. It was on a bend and had the small anteroom which I shared with some of the other scientists.'

'No!'

'It was on the same floor as the ice wall – do you remember that?'

She nodded. 'That's where I woke up.'

'I woke up here. I've been exploring some of the floors above, looking for food.'

'Any luck?'

'Not yet. We might still find something edible. The packs they kept food in were meant to last forever.'

Fen glanced around the room. She would have come here to see him when he was Pella in her brief time working on the complex, though she could not remember it. No doubt, it would have been full of other things then but, like everywhere else she had seen so far, it was now mainly dust. It was a miracle the chair she was leaning against had survived 7,000 years.

All of a sudden the questions she wanted to ask came out in a flood. She did not expect him to have all the answers; it was more a question of trying to establish some sort of reality, no matter how perverse it might be. He was equally keen to exchange information.

It turned out that Pella's experience since the portal was similar to hers. He remembered Taron, the warrior, being poised to kill them, followed by a highly confusing sequence of events where he was only partly aware of what was happening. He had assumed that, finally, he was going to die – properly die and not come back. It was obvious he did not share the same degree of insight into the coding that she had as he did not speak of seeing it or of it offering protection. Pella said he had no idea what had happened to those outside of the portal, so Fen told him what she thought had happened.

'I'm pretty sure that inside the portal was different. Did you get a feeling of being split apart, molecule by molecule?'

'Sort of.'

'Well, I could see that happening to me. It was strange to say the least. It looks like we've been held together.' Subconsciously, she patted her arms and hips. Pella copied which made her smile. Then she said, seriously again, 'Outside, I was aware that they were blown apart. Scattered.'

'You mean Arrix and all the warriors? What about the bridge?'

'All of them, and it, gone.'

'You're certain? How do you know?'

That was a difficult question to answer. 'I just know. I could kinda feel or see it happening. As we were held together, they were dispersed. What happened to us was more controlled.'

'Controlled by what? The coding?'

She nodded. 'What do you know about the coding?'

'Not much, but I gather it was in the quartons and us too. Well hidden from us engineers. What about you?'

Fen felt a sudden reluctance to share everything she knew or felt about the coding. She did not want to tell him it was her – her power, her determination – that had kept her body together and, most likely, his too; that she controlled the coding, not the other way round. When all four Garalians had been inside the portal together, with her unconscious on the floor and Arrix and Klavon vying for dominance, it had revealed itself to her. She had always sensed its presence through the quartons, but never before had it shown its beauty the way it had then. She wanted it and she knew it was tempting her so it could choose her to be its keeper over Arrix. Yet, in that moment, she knew she could better it.

She shifted her weight from one leg to the other and felt that shooting pain in her leg which made her wince. It was a good excuse to dodge Pella's question.

'You okay?' he asked, concerned.

'It's nothing.' She held his gaze for a moment. 'I'm pleased we're together, Pella.'

'Me too, Fen.' He grinned at her and she could see the Pella of old in his eyes. 'So, what now? It's a relief that we don't have to worry about Arrix here.'

'Agreed. Arrix is not our problem at the moment. Getting back to Earth is our problem.'

'Will he be there?'

'Who knows? If he is, then he'll be our problem.'

'You think we can get back?'

'I'm alive now because of one thing and one thing only. That's the motivation to get back to Martha, my little girl.'

'You've got a daughter?'

'Yes.'

'Me too. Ruby.'

'The girl I kidnapped?' In her haste and desperation to get transport back to the portal, Fen had taken Ruby from her home to a place of danger – he should be furious with her. She looked for signs of annoyance or anger in his face, but there was none, only regret.

'When I say she's my daughter, she's the daughter of the real Mark, the person whose body I occupy. She feels like my daughter. I messed things up for her on Earth. She hated me.'

'I'm sorry. I thought she needed help. That's why I took her, kind of on impulse. I tried to keep her safe.'

'Last time I saw her,' said Pella, 'she was still safe. I left her in one of the Garalian flyers. If she's not okay, it's my fault, not yours. I was the one who forced her away from me, and then I was the one who left her when I should have stayed with her.'

'You did what you thought was right.'

'We both did.'

There was an awkward silence broken, eventually, by Pella. 'I have to get back, Fen. I really do. I couldn't bear it if I never saw her again.' A gulp and the slight tremor in his voice betrayed an attempt to hide his upset. There was a long conversation to be had about how he came to be in Mark's body, but that story would have to wait, as she turned back to their current predicament.

She moved the subject on to it by very deliberately looking around his former office. 'There's not much for us here, is there?'

'Not much.'

It was time to get into solution mode. 'So, Pella, formerly known as Mark, renowned engineer and scientist, how precisely are we going to get back? Ideas?'

'Maybe we can go back the way we came, if it was something to do with being in the portal. It had a large concentration of dark energy – maybe it held us in a sort of tunnel and we can do the same in reverse.'

Pella's positivity gave her some hope. That was until something significant about the journey from Earth to Garial suddenly hit her. In her battle to survive, she had not been aware of Pella at all which was why she was surprised to see him there. The fact that she and he had been in the portal and survived could very well mean something else.

'I'm so stupid,' she said. 'The warrior – Taron, I think he's called – was with us. If we're back on Garial, then he's probably back here too.'

A sudden thunderous crash coming from the room next door suggested that she could well be right.

Mackenzie

Lessey seemed to have recovered some of her usual verve by the time Mackenzie and Don returned to her office. She may not yet have been her old belligerent self however, Mackenzie spotted a renewed spark in her eyes as she welcomed them back with a sarcastic, 'Hope your little chat behind my back was useful.'

Shaw had left to oversee the search of the surrounding area which had started as soon as the letters had arrived, insistent, according to Lessey, that the mysterious messenger would not have been able to get far away. Mackenzie's opinion was the same as Don's: if they had been able to sneak in undetected then they would have been able to sneak out the same way. Neither was counting on the perpetrator being found as a way in to dealing with this latest crisis.

Just before they returned, Don had updated the Southern Alliance Council of the situation. They were taking the threat extremely seriously and making available three European based units to support any action decided on the ground. When they sat down again, Don explained that he had been given authority to liaise with Lessey and coordinate any action they decided between them. Diplomatic as ever, he opened it up to Lessey to ask how the Southern Alliance could best support her.

'Well, you can start by making sure you don't treat this as an alien hunt.'

'You know our views on that, President Lessey. The last encounter was an alien encounter. If you read my report...'

'I did read your report, Colonel. Can I speak off the record?'

'If you mean can you speak without me telling my superiors, then I would have to say no... officially. Unofficially...'

'Good. Don and Mackenzie, you are being duped.'

'Duped? How and by who?'

'By your superiors. You have to realise that everything that happened last year, and is happening now, is a charade – a game being played by your bosses. I have given this a lot of thought. At first I assumed you were part of the cover-up, but now I realise that they are fooling you as much as they are trying to fool me.' Mackenzie tried to interject but Lessey held up a hand. 'Hear me out. There's a conspiracy going on here that's much bigger than you, me and both our organisations even. It is sophisticated and it's dangerous.'

Mackenzie sat back and puffed out his cheeks. His hope that Lessey was somehow changed by events last year was disappearing fast. Her quieter personality was not an indication that she was less fiery and opinionated; it was a sign that she had become even more stuck in her ways and had withdrawn into her own mad world – a world that would not possibly entertain the prospect of life from another planet.

He folded his arms and did his best not to laugh, or worse, scream and shout at her. He had to marvel at Don's patience as he said, 'A conspiracy, you say? Who is involved in this conspiracy?'

'My bet is on the Chinese being behind it. They've been quiet for far too long.'

'I think that's very unlikely for two reasons; one – they neither have the will or the means any longer. They were badly hit by the Power Wars as you well know. Importantly, China signed up to the global peace accord, along with every other nation. And two – the event last year was most definitely an alien attack. Me, Mackenzie, Major Shaw, plus some two hundred W.F.I. and Southern Alliance soldiers witnessed it. As did you, President Lessey. I still have the footage of most of it. Would you like to see a sample? I can access it via my bracelet.'

Mackenzie had never heard Lessey laugh before. It obviously did not come naturally to her as, what he assumed was a chortle, sounded more like a child practising the violin.

The laugh went on far too long. Eventually, she said, 'I see through them, Colonel. These latest attacks are their next attempt to take control. The Chinese want me to give them my power. This is a takeover bid, put together by people in your organisation and the Chinese. Geron will tell you I'm right.'

Mackenzie and Don looked towards Geron who, in response, gave a nod. There was enough uncertainty in it to tell Mackenzie he would be right to pull him to one side later and try to agree a sensible way forward. For now, to play along with her might be the only way to get information, so he said, 'Why have you asked me and Colonel Berretti to be involved? What do you think we can do about this conspiracy?'

'Because you, my big friend, know all about the quartons.'

Mackenzie raised an eyebrow. 'The quartons?'

'That girl who was on the recording told me about them. They have something to do with the power source at that portal. I want you to use these quartons to threaten the Chinese and then this will all go away. And don't say you don't know anything about them. That MASH machine we were in at the end is something to do with it. It taps into the massive energy source that's already there using these quartons.'

Lessey's reasoning on who was behind the attacks was all over the place, but somehow she had managed to glean some truth out of the situation. Don and Mackenzie had always downplayed the power and influence of the MASH, even to the top brass in the Southern Alliance, fearing that it was a tool that was best kept secret. Chuck and Mackenzie had never intended it to be used for anything other than to nullify the threat from Garial. In the wrong hands – in the hands of someone like Lessey, for example – it was lethal. Although Mackenzie's role since the invasion had been to set up dark energy monitoring stations, some of his time had been spent thinking of the best way to dismantle the MASH, just in case, and put it together again, if there was another threat from Garial. It had not yet been done so the MASH was hidden away for now.

Mackenzie kept his face straight as Lessey finished her theorising. 'You stopped that little show they put on last time, they're trying something new, trying to draw you out into the open, Mackenzie. The Chinese want you and these quarton things. But I think I can trust you two and we can come to a separate arrangement.'

She might be right about him being drawn out, but it was certainly not the Chinese doing it. However, until Lessey accepted the truth about the attack by Arrix and his warriors – and the possibility of more – they were going to get nowhere. He had listened and now he had had enough. He stood up.

'I can't take much more of this. Don, can you try and talk some sense into her?'

Don sighed and nodded. 'Leave it with me.'

As Mackenzie stomped out of the room, he was quite pleased to see Geron get up and follow him out. Hopefully, he could have that quiet word with him that Don and he had agreed on.

Along the corridor, Mackenzie spotted a vacant office on the right hand side and ducked into it in the expectation that Geron would follow him in. Geron did do exactly as he expected.

What he did not expect, as he turned round to face Geron, was for him to raise a gun and shoot him twice in the shoulder.

Arrix

Arrix found their internal dialogues wearing. The constant bickering, the negotiations, the silly comments and point scoring that Klavon seemed determined to throw at him. The situation he found himself in was far from ideal.

He had been in a position to dominate a year ago. The bridge had finally landed and he had had his warriors with him. Klavon, Pella and Rana were about to be finished off, for good, and, most importantly of all, he had the coding. With the portal and Chuck's weapon, the world was at his feet, but it had been wrecked at the last moment by Chuck and Mackenzie.

There had been a few moments when he had thought it was the actual end of everything for him as his body splintered and started to scatter with his warriors and the bridge. But, before he could get too far, he was pulled back by the coding and into the body of the young girl recently killed outside the portal. No quartons were necessary this time to survive and then travel the short distance. A satisfactory outcome, in the circumstances, until he discovered Klavon already occupying the body and in charge of its movements.

Arrix soon resented the transfer. To share the body was bad enough; to be pushed – steamrollered even – into a situation where he could not totally control everything that happened was unbearable. His Grand Plan was no longer grand or a plan. Instead, he felt he was being manipulated by the coding. What was even worse was the feeling of rejection and the resultant shift in the balance of power. Part of the coding was with him – with them, him and Klavon – but much of it was elsewhere. And there were no prizes for working out where, and with whom, the power now almost certainly sat: Rana.

Nevertheless, he was not finished. It was not an outright rejection, just another setback, there to test his resolve. The coding would soon be his again to use and he would own it on his terms. Klavon, although very annoying, had his uses. His blunt style seemed to work with the savages they came across. The mixture of his raw violence with Arrix's cunning would do the job – for now.

They would use what they had around them to rebuild and at the same time lure Rana back to them so she could be defeated. He may not have his warriors any longer, but it was what it was. He was moulding their followers into something special, and there were already promising signs with the likes of Jerome and Odette showing they could be as ruthless and adaptable as any warrior. And when the time was right, he would break out of this unwanted partnership with Klavon and go it alone.

In the meantime, he would just have to sit tight, try to stop Klavon saying anything too stupid and wait.

Waiting was far the easier of the two.

Fen

Initially, Fen thought a bomb had gone off. That, along with the realisation that Taron was probably nearby, threw her into fight or flight mode. With no obvious way out, fight seemed the only option and she found herself semi crouched, arms out in front in a fighting stance, as ready as she could be to take on whatever might come through the opening. Pella was next to her in a similar position, eyes wide, breathing loudly.

After what seemed like an age with no obvious follow-up, Fen straightened and moved towards the entrance to the other room. Dust was wafting past and out through the opening, and she pulled her jacket across her mouth and nose as she approached. Pella grabbed her arm. 'Let me go first,' he said. He brushed past her before she could stop him and put his head into the room, holding up his arm to stop her going past.

'What can you see?' she hissed.

'Hang on a sec. The dust is settling. Something's in the middle of the room. I think it's a body. A big body.'

Fen pushed his arm down and slid round him, saying, 'I appreciate your attempts to protect me but I'm a big girl now. Let's have a closer look.'

It was a Garalian – Taron, possibly, by the looks of the armour and the black visor which had fallen to his side. He was on his stomach, motionless with one huge arm stretched out above his head, the other hidden under his torso. His legs were splayed behind, the extensions at uncomfortable angles. If it had been a human form lying there, a casual observer would have diagnosed two broken legs, but Fen knew how her own extensions had worked when she had been a Garalian. The joints to the upper section were designed to rotate as well as flex. Still, he looked in bad shape, although he was breathing judging by the small, erratic up and down movements of his back.

A light piece of something fell onto Fen's shoulder and she looked up. She tapped Pella on the arm and pointed. 'He's fallen from at least one floor up, judging by the new hole and fresh debris up there. Possibly further.'

Pella nodded. 'That's quite a tumble. Should be un-survivable, even for a Garalian.'

'He's a warrior – the armour would have given him some protection.' She gently kicked the side of his upper leg.

'What are you doing? Are you sure you want to wake him up?'

'Who says he's not awake already? Anyway, I'd rather know what we're dealing with.'

'He was going to kill us.'

'Look. We're stuck here on a planet, far too many miles away from where either of us want to be. Maybe he can help.'

'I'll say it again: he was going to kill us. Our chances are even worse if he decides he's still in assassination mode and we're both dead. You fancy your chances in combat against a Garalian warrior?'

'We've both lived for thousands of years. What have we got to lose? If you didn't realise it before, death doesn't mean death for us. The rules have changed. It doesn't even just mean reincarnation with all this body transference. Look at you.'

It was almost impossible to imagine her Garalian brother, Pella, standing here now as a human man in his early forties. Or, even more difficult, seeing him as Forrest, the young girl of fourteen who Fen had helped rescue in London many years previously. But he had been that girl (plus many other people before that) and should have finally died as her with the last quarton being found in London. Yet here they both were, alive still, and Fen almost indestructible in her current incarnation. It gave her confidence that dealing with a potentially unconscious warrior should not present as big a problem as might be thought.

Fen moved to the other side of Taron, searching for a weapon of some kind. It might be useful if he did wake up and needed a little persuasion. He had raised an arm with something, before they were all whisked away, but there was nothing obvious on or around him now. No doubt they were secreted about his body, inaccessible. Even if she could find them, she would have the added problem of working out how to use them.

60

'I think he's stirring,' said Pella. 'I saw his face twitch a little and, look, he's moving his legs. What now? Watch from a safe distance? Run? Stay and chat?'

There was a low rumbling sound that seemed to come from deep inside his body. Fen returned to her original place next to Pella and watched with a mixture of fear and fascination as different parts of the warrior came to in a sequence, starting from the legs up. A light flashed on his armour in one section, followed by a nearby movement of a limb or section of his body. Fen remembered back to when she had been planning the destruction of the original Garalian Bridge. It had been a topic of discussion amongst the rebels about how many members of the guard were fully integrated with their armour, flesh working with machine as one unit. This appeared to be the case now as the warrior came back to consciousness.

'It's not too late to run,' said Pella, just as the large head moved ever so slightly to one side. One eye opened and glared at them. There was another rumbling sound and then in one incredibly swift movement he was vertical and she was staring into the midriff of the warrior.

They both stepped back and looked up. 'It's too late to run now,' she said.

Fen expected something else dramatic to happen then, but nothing did. The warrior stayed where he was, swaying ever so slightly. Fen and Pella took a further two or three paces back before finding themselves up against a wall. She felt no safer, but it did give her a better opportunity to study his uncovered face. This had to be Taron. Any other explanation did not fit.

She could see now that he had been hurt. Part of the jaw on what would have been the chin had he been human, was missing. It looked like a section had been hewn out of it with one swift swing of a very sharp blade. There was no blood. Garalian blood was the same colour as human blood and just as likely to run freely when given the chance, which led Fen to believe that maybe it was an old injury. She soon had the opportunity to get a closer look as the lower legs suddenly flipped up behind, and Taron dropped down to his non-extended height, over two feet above her head. Apparently oblivious of their presence, he started to sway again. Fen ushered Pella away from the wall, worried he could topple onto them.

There was a double clang as two objects fell from out of his armour onto the floor. One came to a stop at Pella's feet and the other rolled off a couple of metres before spinning into a clump of dirt.

'Grab that other one,' Pella said stooping down for the one nearby.

With a quick glance up at Taron, Fen skipped over and picked it up. Brushing the dirt off, she examined what was a flat, metal ring, the diameter of a drinking glass. Matt grey and perfectly smooth, it felt much heavier than it should have been for its size. She handed it to Pella who was turning over the other identical ring in his hand.

'I remember these,' he said. 'Incredible!'

'What are they?'

'Batteries, effectively. Power sources with huge capability. In the early stages of building the bridge, they were going to be a backup to the quartons in the event of a power boost being needed in the final connection to the target planet. But there were problems over compatibility. They were unstable during dark energy surges. I had a blazing row with the scientists developing these because I thought they were far too dangerous and could end up destroying the bridge, Garial and the target world in one fell swoop. In the end, Arrix stepped in and banned them. Or so I thought.'

Fen had another look up at the warrior, who stood transfixed, his eyes firmly on a spot somewhere on the other side of the room.

'Why would they be on him now?' she said turning her attention back to the discs.

'More's the point, why aren't they on him now? Of all the things to suddenly drop out. I'm holding onto something that could meet the energy needs of a small, fully functioning city for a year.'

'Maybe it's his way of helping us.'

'You're convinced he could be on our side, Fen, aren't you? I can't get the image out of my head of him destroying that blade Larm gave me and then making us wait before killing us.'

'Maybe he had no intention of killing us. He needs our help. I think he might be in trauma.'

'He seemed pretty with it when he came round. The way he jumped up.'

'But not anymore – he's shut down.'

'What do you suggest? I'm not a doctor, neither are you.'

'Judging by the amount of machinery on him and probably in him, I'm not sure a doctor would be the best person for the job. Now, someone technical, maybe with a background of engineering... that would be a different matter.'

'You want me to take him apart? Have you got a tin opener on you?'

'I don't remember my brother being the sarcastic type. All I'm saying is that it's worth exploring. We have no obvious idea what to do next. He might have. He's been on this planet more recently than we have and might know where things are and how things work now. He's probably highly capable. Arrix must have rated him if he chose him to finish us off.'

'I can't believe you want to help him on the basis that he's good at killing people. That's a good reason not to help him.'

'Look, Pella, you'll have to trust my instinct on this.' She ignored his doubtful look and proceeded to examine Taron's armour in more detail. 'Is there any obvious way to get this off? He might collapse without it, but it's a risk we'll have to take.'

Pella sighed. 'I have an idea. But first, let's take one of the rings each and keep them somewhere safe. We might be able to use them at some point.'

Fen took the one he offered and tucked it inside the front pocket of her trousers. With a plan, of sorts, developing, she felt a sudden injection of hope. There was just the small matter now of working out how to revive a killing machine, and then persuade him to do the opposite of what his instincts might be telling him to do.

Mackenzie

There was no sound from the gun – just a 'thud, thud' as the bullets pierced his shoulder. Mackenzie stood and stared at Geron in disbelief, then looked down and watched two large patches of red seep through his green khaki jacket. A second later, an excruciating bolt of white-hot pain scorched through his shoulder and down his arm. He felt himself stumble, caught himself, and then stumbled again, grabbing hold of the nearest thing in an attempt to remain upright. A desk lamp, it was no help and he crashed right though it, tumbling over the side of the desk. He was unconscious before he hit the floor.

Sometime later, Mackenzie awoke in agony. He clenched his teeth and screwed up his eyes as wave upon wave of pain flooded his shoulder and arm. Desperately, he tried to get control of his breathing as he felt himself begin to panic. He used to regularly meditate to help him deal with a back problem – too much time working around heavy machinery in awkward positions. There was something about observing the pain rather than feeling it, 'noticing its shape, texture and colour.' Here it was impossible not to notice it, but he concentrated the best he could on those qualities, trying to detach from what he was experiencing. After a few moments, he began to feel a little relief. Progress, he decided; enough to allow him to open his eyes.

Everything was a blur apart from two stunning blue lakes that shimmered and sparkled, with two black holes at the centre. The lakes disappeared and reappeared even larger and even more enticing. He was distracted from them by a prick at the top of his good arm and he sighed as he felt all the pain begin to melt away. Something damp was placed on his forehead and he closed his eyes again, enjoying the sense of relief.

When he reopened his eyes, the blue lakes were still there but further away and he realised they belonged to a face. It had an elfin-like nose that sat between two high cheek bones below a forehead almost totally hidden by a straight black fringe. The face – a girl's – was quite young but determined looking and intelligent. Seeing he was staring at her, the girl self-consciously tucked back one side of her chin length hair behind her ear.

'Bonjour,' she said. There was no smile, neither did he detect animosity. He grunted a response. 'You have been shot,' she said in an accented English. 'But you will be okay. I have given you an injection. It will help.' Mackenzie was familiar with many French accents having worked with people from all over the country at various stages of his life, pre and post war. He considered himself an expert, but when the French person was speaking English, he often found it hard to tell the difference. Hers, though, had a singsong element to it and he took a punt.

'You from Toulouse?'

She had turned away, then quickly pivoted back in surprise, mouth slightly open. Mackenzie smiled inwardly. He had no clear idea what situation he was in now, but it did no harm to put whoever this was off guard. Just in case. She said nothing.

A short stab reminded him all was not well still. Pursing his lips, he put his hand to his shoulder and drew it away to examine it for blood. There was none. 'You've patched me up?' he asked.

Her eyebrows furrowed. 'Patched?'

'Put a bandage on.'

'Ah, yes.' She finally smiled – a smile that told him if he had had a daughter, he would have liked her to smile like this girl. At

66

sixteen, he guessed, she was young enough to be his granddaughter... at a push. 'No bullets,' she continued. 'They went out the other end.'

'I hope you've bandaged the other side of me as well, then.'

She smiled again. 'Both sides. Four holes. You will be okay.'

Mackenzie looked at her and tried to get his brain to work. As nice as she seemed, things were obviously not right. He had been shot and he did not know where he was or who she was. He lifted his head and then let it go down, immediately feeling sick and dizzy. He started to frame a question in his mind, but it never reached his lips. He soon realised there had to have been something else in the injection because he could no longer keep his eyes open.

When he woke up again, he sensed he was now alone. His head felt clearer, the nausea had gone and the pain was just a dull ache. He looked up and let his eyes settle on a point in the pitched wooden ceiling above, and waited for them to come into focus. When they did, he shifted carefully from side to side and worked out he was on a long bench, barely wide enough for his broad frame. His injured left shoulder had been bandaged into a sling; still he managed to grab the edge of the bench with the other hand and ease himself up without rolling onto the floor. Things began to spin again, so he sat and waited with his head down towards the stone tiles until he felt well enough to look around.

He was in a small room with walls made of wooden horizontal slats. Two pine chairs stood either side of a matching desk against one wall and there was another bench opposite his, this one covered with rather tatty, stained yellow cushions. Above it, were three empty wooden shelves. A sturdy looking oak door in the centre of the other wall suggested there was only one way in and out as the window above his bench had been boarded over from the outside. The only source of light was an old-fashioned bulb hanging loosely in the centre of the room. He ought to check if the door was locked, yet was it worth the bother? It almost certainly would be locked and it would only make him frustrated.

He tried to remember the sequence of events back at the base and what motives Geron might have had for shooting him. If Geron had just had a rush of blood and it was some big mistake, surely he should still be there and Don would be somewhere around. But that girl – as pleasant as she might be – was no army medic and this room was definitely not military. It had more of a cosy log cabin feel to it. All it needed was some new cushions, a stove, a few books on the shelves, and a banjo propped in the corner. A window overlooking snow-capped mountains would complete the effect, of course. Cushions, books, a banjo, for goodness sake – what was he thinking? 'Focus, Mackenzie, you big lump,' he said under his breath – he could almost hear Chuck saying it.

This had the feel of a setup followed by a kidnap, and he needed to do something about it. He would feel stupid if he did not check the door and it ended up not being locked, so he forced himself to his feet and edged round the room, using his good hand to steady himself on the walls. It was indeed locked, but seeing as it was outward opening, he decided that he should go through it anyway. Leading with his good shoulder he took a few steps back and charged. With a tremendous clatter, the door came crashing down on the table where a man and the girl were sitting.

Somehow, he remained on his feet and stumbled to a halt. The two people had been eating, judging by the cutlery they were still holding. Both had stood up as he came through, knocking their chairs to the floor. He recognised the girl straight away as the one who had been looking after him. The man he did not know but, from the size of him, he looked the biggest threat so he targeted him first. His huge hand was round his throat in an instant. He walked the man to the wall and held him there without releasing his grip. The girl moved towards a bag to her right. Mackenzie stopped her with a sideways glance, snarling, 'No! Pick up that chair and sit down.'

Mackenzie turned his attention back to the man who had his heavily tattooed hands around Mackenzie's wrist in a desperate attempt to yank it away. With the man on his tiptoes the two were a similar height, the other slighter, though still well muscled. His efforts to escape were in vain as Mackenzie, his arm locked and his feet in a fighting stance, continued to apply pressure to his neck. His fists fell short as he lashed out and soon Mackenzie felt the fight and strength begin to seep away.

'Florence Nightingale is going to tell me who you both are and why you've locked me up,' Mackenzie said to him, 'and very quickly, I suggest. I reckon you have about thirty seconds before you choke to death.' He glanced at the girl. 'Talk.'

He was surprised by how calm she sounded. That should have served as warning as to what was to come shortly. 'My name is Odette and he is Jerome. We took you from President Lessey's offices after you were shot.'

'Where am I?'

69

'Somewhere near Paris.'

'Where exactly?'

'I cannot say.'

He squeezed the man's neck even harder which drew a desperate rasp. Blue veins bulged either side of his forehead, and his face, already red, turned a bright crimson, a stark contrast to his white short cropped hair. 'Are you sure you can't say?'

'Yes.'

She was a lot cooler than he gave her credit for. He tried another tack. 'Geron shot me. Why?'

'To make you less dangerous.'

'You work for him?'

'No.'

'Lessey then?'

She shook her head.

'You arranged the attacks on the villages?'

She hesitated before replying then looked at Jerome who, with his arms by his sides now, had given up struggling. 'We did.'

'We? Who exactly is *we*? Is it the girl? '

Another voice appeared from the side. 'Yes, it's the girl.' Mackenzie spun round, releasing his grip on Jerome who slid gasping to the floor.

'Ruby?'

'Correct. Odette – you may have said too much and you've tired out our guest. Why don't you arrange for him to have another nap?'

Mackenzie could not react in time. She was already by his side with a needle which she jabbed into his arm. His last image as he slumped to the floor was of Jerome standing over him, rubbing his red neck and shouting what sounded like extremely unpleasant French swear words.

Lessey

After Mackenzie and Geron had left, Lessey and Don sat in silence for a short while. Lessey had said all she wanted to say; now it was down to Don and Mackenzie to see the sense of it and fall in behind.

Geron had done the right thing in following Mackenzie out. He had more of a technical handle on the whole energy quarton angle and could talk specifics with him. Only last week, before all this trouble kicked off, he had been in the south of France at some meeting – one of many he had been having recently away from this, his usual base – where he said he had picked the brains of some of the top scientists in the world who had been working on various theories about hidden energy. What he reported back to her had proved she was right about what had been going on in England last year. There were these sources available and she was convinced the French-Irish Alliance could get control of some of it, once she countered this threat from the Chinese. Getting Don and Mackenzie's expertise on board was a good way into that. She would get them to reveal exactly what was behind the energy sources and quash these outrageous attacks on her people at the same time. It was a win win situation. The attacks could be a blessing in disguise.

Don eventually broke the silence. 'President Lessey... we are prepared to work with and support your organisation's efforts to get to the bottom of who is behind these attacks, if – and only if – you give me the guarantee now that, whatever the result, you accept the findings we present to you.'

Usually, she was not one to accept preconditions given to her, but this was an easy one to go along with. 'Of course, Don – can I call you Don? Don't get me wrong – I know I sound sceptical about the alien theory, but really I am an open book when it comes to this new world we all live in. I only have the best interests of both our alliances – in fact, all of Europe and beyond – at heart. The first stage is to prove the Chinese are behind...'

'President...'

'Correction... find out who is responsible for the attacks and then we can take it from there. Now, I suggest we get straight down to it. I have arranged for our fastest craft to be at your disposal. I take it you will want to visit all three sites, starting at the French one? We can be there in less than half an hour.'

'We have enough data from the Irish and English sites, but a visit to the one over here would be useful. I don't want to trouble you for the journey. Perhaps Major Shaw can accompany us?'

Lessey smiled. 'As you wish.' She tapped her bracelet to call Shaw. There was no need because, at that precise moment, he burst through the door.

'Apologies, President,' he said. 'V.P. Geron and Mackenzie have just left the base in the flyer we had ready to use with two unidentified individuals. The tracking on it has been disabled, but we've sent up flyers to find it.'

Lessey's smile dropped. 'What the feck is Geron up to?'

'This might help explain, Ma'am.' Shaw projected a bird's eye visual of two soldiers just inside the entrance to their building being attacked by a large white-haired male and a smaller female who had appeared from nowhere. A blow from a blunt object to each soldier had been enough to take them down.

'Who on earth are they?' Lessey spluttered. 'Where did they come from?'

'No idea, Ma'am. Presumably, they are the same people who left the envelopes. Security is running through our systems. My guess is that we've been hacked.'

The visual continued, showing the two attackers running down the corridor then, with the help of Geron, dragging Mackenzie out of an office, back along and outside the entrance.

Don was already on his feet. 'Lessey, what are you and Geron playing at? If you're responsible for harming Mackenzie, I'll...'

'This is not my doing, I can assure you, Colonel.'

'No? Geron is your Vice President. How do you explain what we've just seen?'

'I can't... Shaw?'

'One of our corporals spotted the flyer take off from outside the building, with, I am assuming based on this, those four I mentioned on board. The Vice President and Mackenzie are certainly not on the base. I can only conclude that Mackenzie has been kidnapped, possibly with the assistance of Vice-President Geron.'

Lessey was aware her mouth was open throughout this short explanation.

Twenty-three hours and thirty-five minutes later, she was pretty sure she still had not shut it. During that time, they had established that there was absolutely no sign anywhere of the flyer, her Vice President or the man she was relying on to open up the largest energy source ever known on Earth.

Fen

Taron still had not moved. Like all the warriors, he had no hair. It made what should have been an oval face, with the lower section gone, look even stranger, poking above what was a bulky section of armour covering his torso. In the light on Earth, the metallic blue they all wore had been striking. In the subdued light of the complex, lit only by the light from the larger of the two Garial stars at this stage of the morning, Taron's armour looked jet-black, the twists of the helix sections covering the limbs lost in the dark depths.

'We need him to lie down again, preferably on his back this time,' said Pella.

'You're sure?'

'No, but when I was studying engineering, I vaguely remember we had something on the mechanics of warfare. Armour had built-in systems to give basic medical attention when needed. More serious injuries would need the armour to come off, and they would assume they would be down if injured.'

'He was down before. He landed face down.'

'True. I just think we have more of a chance with him on his back. There has to be a release somewhere to enable it to be taken off.'

'Push then?' ventured Fen.

There was no need. The Garalian lowered himself to the ground, his joints in his upper legs almost buckling before he collapsed onto his side and then rolled over onto his back. Still the eyes had not moved.

'Automatic? A reflex of some sort, like when he got up before?' Fen asked. 'Or he's listening and understands English.'

'He'll understand English, I'm sure. Larm tuned into it when we were talking after the bridge landed on Earth. They would all have done the same.'

It occurred to Fen that she had a lot to catch up on with Pella. Their experiences after the Friendship Bridge was destroyed were very different, right up to the point where they had met again in the portal. Yet, though they had taken different paths, they had so much in common too, both still linked as they were to the quartons and the coding.

'Well, if he is aware we are here, he's not trying to kill us,' she said. 'That's a start. Okay, Doctor. What next?'

Pella walked up and down the length of the warrior's prostrate body. 'Nothing obvious. No red button saying, "Press Me". I suggest we run our hands over him and hope.'

'Hope? The scientist that is Pella hasn't disappeared, then.'

He ignored her sarcastic comment and just nodded towards Taron's head. 'You start that side, I'll do this side.'

It took only a few seconds and neither of them could say which part of the armour they had touched did the job, if any. The armour started to peel back in small sections, starting from the very centre all the way down to each leg, including the extensions and the box like boots. The arms did the same until Taron was fully revealed with the armour, unrecognisable as such, in a neat pile forming an almost perfect outline around him.

His body was covered in a simple white cloth, a one-piece that covered him up to his slanted shoulders. Or rather it covered him save for one area on Fen's side below his arm which had a small gap. Through that protruded what looked like the handle to a blade, about fifteen centimetres long. Had Taron been holding it before they were pulled away from the portal? Or was it one of the many weapons which had folded away with the armour and been left? She could not remember seeing him with one before. It was irrelevant anyway as there was no doubt that the other end of it was stuck firmly inside his body, dangerously close, depending on the length of the blade and her sketchy knowledge of her own previous Garalian anatomy, to his heart.

'Did that go through the armour?' said Pella.

'Possibly, although, remember we were literally torn apart and put back together again before we arrived here, as was he. It's a miracle we're in one piece.' She knew 'the miracle' was not quite true, bearing in mind the influence of the coding, but she continued, 'Maybe he had the weapon somewhere on him and it's just not gone back to where it should have.' She looked across at the visor nearby. 'That could have come off at any point. Could account for the injury to his face too. Or maybe he injured himself after he got

76

here. He might have fallen through the existing hole above us or landed on a worn section that could not hold his weight, and stabbed himself on the way down. We won't know until we wake him up and ask what he remembers.'

'No blood on his tunic. But there could be a lot if we remove the blade.'

'What is that round the handle?'

Between the hilt and the skin underneath the cloth was some sort of seal, dark in colour which pulsed gently. Pella took a closer look. 'I reckon the armour has done that to protect the wound. It's keeping him alive. If we take the blade out, that seal will break and it will probably kill him. We need medical equipment if we're going to remove this safely.'

Fen frowned. '7,000 years is a long time. Just look at the state of everything we've seen so far. Would anything we could use have survived and if it has, where would we find it?'

'The medical centre was above us somewhere, I think. They were tasked with adapting technology that could be miniaturised so it could be taken easily to the new world. Some of it was put into armour, like Taron's. They would have worked with portable medical units too like the one Larm put me into on the bridge on Earth. Maybe the warriors reused units from here.'

'On the last bridge landing, you mean?'

'Yes. After you absconded with my daughter...' Pella caught her eye to take the sting out of the comment, '...Larm found me and took me back to the bridge. She put me in a unit. It sorted out the injuries I had left over from the accident.'

'Accident?'

'The one that killed me. In my previous life before Mark, I was Lennie. The real Lennie died and I transferred into Mark from him. It's why I'm so determined to find Ruby again and be with her. It's an obligation in some ways for the real Mark.'

'One of Sal's henchmen was called Lennie.'

'That's him. Or rather that was me. I woke up as him near the Friendship Bridge after the last quarton was destroyed. Became a pilot, then died in the crash with Mark, his wife and baby. Ruby survived and I became Mark.'

A memory flashed into Fen's brain of her driving one of the trucks towards the Friendship Bridge, with Forrest in a confused state beside her. In her haste she had hit a man. It had barely registered at the time. But his face, as he was knocked sideways, was very clear now. It had been Lennie.

'What's wrong?' asked Pella. 'You've gone quiet.'

'I'm trying to get my head round something.'

It took some doing. Forrest, who had been sitting in the truck when Fen had accidentally killed Lennie, was a reincarnation of Pella. When Forrest had been killed in the explosion on the bridge, Pella's life-force transferred into Lennie's body, the person they had not long before killed. How ironic was that? How cruel.

The coding, through the quartons, had often played with their lives. It was not at all uncommon for the four on the original Garial Bridge – herself, Pella, Klavon and Arrix – to reincarnate with one or more of them being related in some way; from parents, siblings, cousins to friends or associates. In the latest chapter of her life, Klavon had come back – a body transfer rather than a reincarnation – as her best friend, Lee. There was always a connection with the coding finding a way to be close by physically at the right time in their lives so they could battle to find a quarton. But it was not just a question of geography; the emotional closeness seemed to be a deliberate attempt to make things as hard as possible mentally. Here was another twist. It was as if the coding was laughing at her, just at a time when Fen thought she was getting control over it.

She shook herself out of her thoughts. Pella was waiting, not particularly patiently. 'Fen? We need to do something about Taron soon if we are going to do anything at all. I doubt that this medical seal is designed to keep him alive forever.'

'I'll stay here. You know where you're going and what you're looking for. Get me a snack while you're out too, if there's anywhere open.'

Pella snorted a laugh, then got up and left the way they had come in. Fen hunkered down next to Taron, hoping Pella did not think she was joking about the snack. She could not remember the last time she had eaten anything or, more importantly, drunk anything. After all she had been through, dying of thirst would be a horrible way to go.

Mackenzie

Sleeping was becoming a habit and not the good kind. It was not as if Mackenzie woke up feeling refreshed and raring to go. Once again, he came to, hurting. His shoulder pain was accompanied, this time, by a thumping headache, one he would normally associate with a good night on the town – if he could remember that far back.

He was sitting on a low chair, so low that his knees were level with his head. It was one of those chairs that needed a good push up from behind using both arms to get out of. Difficult with one arm in a sling; impossible with both arms in slings.

Odette was sitting opposite, fiddling with some things laid out on the other chair. She seemed engrossed in her work, every now and then referring to a data pad attached to her wrist. The door Mackenzie had smashed down had been propped up against a wall and the remains of the table and crockery swept into a corner. There was no sign of Ruby or Jerome.

'Someone has a sense of humour,' Mackenzie said.

The girl looked up. 'Hmm?'

'Very funny.' Mackenzie wriggled the elbow on his good arm. 'Two slings. Hilarious. Very effective though. Bit tight around the neck. You couldn't just...'

'Non,' she said, and returned to her work.

Mackenzie grunted and stretched out his legs. It was at this point he noticed they had been tied together with a rope. 'Bit more standard. Run out of bandages?' He got no reply. He tried to sit forward. 'Extra rope round my stomach and chair too. You are being careful.'

He peered through the gap into the room where he had originally been. The light had been switched off which suggested that was empty. There was another door to his right that looked like an outside exit. Still wooden, it looked more modern and robust, likely sensor controlled for access in and out. A thick looking red curtain was draped across another doorway next to it, through which

Mackenzie could hear the sound of murmurings – several voices, too quiet to hear properly.

'Did I hear your name correctly? Odette?' He spotted her raising her eyes slightly before going back to her work. Nodding towards the curtain, he asked, 'A planning meeting – you not allowed to go to those?'

Without looking at him, Odette got up and walked across to a cupboard on the wall, fully exposing the other chair she was using as a temporary table and the three small boxes on it. Next to them were three crystal spheres standing on small sponges to prevent them rolling away.

'Are they what I think they are?' He could not keep the concern out of his voice. 'Or fakes? Please tell me they are fakes.'

There was no reply. She returned to her seat and pressed something on her bracelet. From one of the spheres, there was a subtlest of tremors.

'Oh, my God. Not fakes – they're what you used for the attacks!'

Detons they were called, short for detonators. It had been the ultimate in warfare technology, short of blowing everyone and everything apart in a nuclear attack. No human involvement required other than to 'set it up and let it loose' which became its catchphrase amongst the hardened members of the military community. Mackenzie's understanding of how they worked was sketchy – he put the technology into his 'dark arts' category. He had watched an instruction visual about them once in his army days, before the Power Wars, which was intended to make recruits think about the value of human life rather than just become killing machines. Detons were very much killing machines. The army visual explained it thus: 'Deton spheres connect to any weapon – repeat, any weapon, friend or foe – in the specified zone and take over control. That weapon then has the capability of being manoeuvred into positions to extinguish life.' The instruction visual had certainly discouraged Mackenzie, so much so that he left the army soon after joining it because of what he had learned.

The detons took all human decision making out of hand-to-hand combat which was why the Geneva Convention was updated to ban their use. It was agreed to get rid of all associated technology – every physical box destroyed, all the data research wiped, everything independently verified by the United Nations.

Somehow this group had got access to spheres – or the rare materials used to build them – and possibly a significant amount of weapons to back them up. Either that or they had access to brand new technology. Odette was working on them right in from him. Her group were definitely ones for sending out threatening messages; this was another one directed at him, telling him they meant business.

'Detons?' he repeated. 'Am I right?' He looked for a reaction. Nothing. He tried a different tack. 'Are you angry with me because I broke the door and table or because I ruined your meal?'

He saw her eyes glance across to the mess in the corner, an indication he was piercing the barrier she had put up around her. 'I'm clumsy, what can I say?' Still nothing. 'Don't you want to know what the others are talking about? Are you fed up at having to guard an old codger like me'

'Be quiet,' she said.

He had her attention. She just needed a bit of winding up to get her talking. 'Is it because you're too young they leave you out? Mind you, that other girl is younger. What is she, ten, eleven? That must be really annoying. Taking orders from a little girl.'

A couple of screws fell to the floor. 'Merde,' the girl said under her breath before huffily scraping her chair back and reaching down to collect them. She sat back on the chair and tapped on her pad again. But Mackenzie could see she had lost concentration on her task. He gave her a few seconds before speaking again.

'Thanks for looking after me. I think you've done a good job on the shoulder. It feels a little better.'

She turned to him. 'Please don't speak. There will be problems for me.'

'Ah, I'm sorry.' He lowered his voice. 'I'm not good at whispering. My mouth is too big.' Her lips twitched ever so slightly and he saw a hint of the same something he had seen in her eyes when he had first come round earlier. 'I swear when things go wrong too, but I use far worse words than *merde*.'

She returned to her work and he decided to push her no further, for now. He put his mind to something equally as pressing as the detons and no doubt connected; the presence of Ruby. Last time he had met her, she had been vulnerable; a little girl searching for her dad amongst the craziness of an alien invasion. But she had disappeared just as he and Don had approached the portal with Lessey, and there had been no sign of her afterwards. The Ruby that had just foiled his attempt to escape was very different to that Ruby. Her brief exchange with Odette and the confidence and sarcasm behind the way she had instructed her to make him 'take a nap' was typical of another character he had met and taken a dislike to: Lee. Klavon had survived in the form of Ruby – he was there, behind her eyes – and was probably in the room next door planning the next move. It confirmed his and Don's suspicions that the threat from Garial was far from over.

Odette seemed far too nice to be wrapped up with such a monstrosity. But he was going to have to be very careful with the approach he took to convincing her she was.

Fen

Fen soon decided that this was a waste of time her standing guard over Taron. She could do nothing for him at the moment and it did not look like he was going anywhere. If he did wake up, what would she do anyway? Pella may not have picked up on her hint to find food and water and, in any case, he had plenty to do finding medical equipment. A search – a scavenge – not too far away, gave her a good excuse not to sit around doing nothing.

Looking outside for a natural source of water might be her best option. Anything stored in the complex would be well out of date, surely. The view she had seen from Pella's office had showed plenty of green and blue foliage, typical of the mountainous areas in this part of Garial; an encouraging sign of regeneration and, she hoped, a source of water nearby.

The quickest way out would have been through the opening, but since that was some one hundred metres up high, she headed back to the concourse again. She had come in from the right with Pella and had not noticed any obvious exit points, so she opted to go left and follow the upward slope towards the top of the building and the mountain. The complex was far bigger than anything she had come across during her scavenging days in London, but it was striking how similar the buildings were, particularly in their ruinous states. There were small and large rooms off the path, corridors, even stairs at one point, and what might once have been central meeting areas which would not have looked out of place in a shopping or office centre in any city on Earth.

She ignored several sections that may have led to other levels and stuck to the main route. It seemed the right decision as the first real piece of luck for some time presented itself surprisingly quickly. She already had the impression that she had climbed some significant metres in a gradual narrowing spiral when she suddenly noticed freshness to the taste and smell of the air. Up ahead was what looked to be a dead-end which, when she followed it, actually became a ninety degree turn, followed quickly by another in the opposite direction. She followed it round until she could see clear daylight at the end of a short tunnel. Between her and the light was a tricky stony section to negotiate, but she managed it without too much trouble and then she was out, blinking into the full glare of a Garalian day.

Both stars were fully out now. The first to appear during most days, Garla, was on the way to setting in the south. Meanwhile, her smaller sister star, Gia, was providing some light as it rose in the northeast. This, Fen recalled from her life on Garial, used to be her favourite time of the day. The mixture of light and combination of shadows could produce a stunning effect. Shafts of Gia's light shone through an adjacent mountain making the overall effect even more dramatic. She walked out onto what might have once been a viewing platform, jutting out past the building. Like everything else, it was badly decayed with no barrier in place along its sides, but it was large enough for her to stand on and take a moment to wallow in the warmth and magic of a perfect day. The red and yellow in the striations on the rocks to her left faded gradually into mauves and greens and then to the deeper purples of the vegetation to her right. She gulped in every outline and shade, mesmerised by its beauty. For a few moments, everything she was, everything she had done was forgotten. Her worries, her hopes, even Sam and Martha were at the back of her mind. She was just there, on Garial, the planet where she had been brought up, the planet she had fought so hard to save. Here it was; strong, healthy, alive and thriving. All the things she had wanted it to be.

So engrossed was she that she nearly failed to hear the gentle trickle of water just below and to her right. The sound provoked a sudden raging thirst which she had to satisfy straight away, so she edged her way over to the side of the platform towards the source of the noise. The drop down was not as sheer as the one from the previous view inside the complex, but nevertheless tumbled ominously into the valley far below where a river snaked its way along the bottom, feeding the flora – and, no doubt, fauna to the east. There was a section of the platform missing and a gap of a couple of metres with a drop onto rocks below, but she could see the source of the water – a gentle waterfall – not far away on the other side. She figured that there would have been steps and a path leading to it at one stage providing a welcome break into nature for the workers at the complex. Overgrown by spindly vegetation, there was no path or steps to use now, but she was confident she could make the jump onto the ledge on the other side of the gap and pick her way through from there. She very nearly misjudged it and landed awkwardly. The jolt served as a timely reminder that not only was she suffering from dehydration and hunger, but that her body probably needed more time to adjust to the slightly higher gravity on Garial compared to Earth.

Rubbing a new tender spot in the back of her thigh, she walked across towards the waterfall. It was not at all far. The water poured over a ledge only a few metres above her head into an almost perfectly oval shaped small pool she had not seen from the platform. She could wait no longer and immediately knelt down to scoop up handfuls of water over and over, until she had to stop to catch her breath. Impulsively, she dipped her whole head and held it there for a few seconds before coming up for air again. It was one of the most wonderful sensations she could ever remember. The mountain setting, the light and warmth from the suns, the pool, the satisfaction of quenching her thirst. She rocked back onto her haunches and pulled her soaked hair back tightly behind her head, enjoying squeezing the drops out of it and feeling them run down her back. For a moment she felt happy.

Which made what happened next all the more shocking.

There was no warning. The familiarity of where she was and what she was doing hit her. Everything she had done now, she had done before. This spot, this view, the pool, even dipping her head into the water, she had lived these experiences before. It must have been when she was Rana and had worked in the complex. She had come out here during a break, taking the opportunity to get away from the stress and worries of working with Arrix.

No, she realised quickly, it was not then. She had never stepped out of the complex in her short stay there, other than to leave at considerable haste when she discovered what Arrix had planned. Yet she knew she had been here before... she most definitely had... but – and it took her a few moments to process this – not as Rana. She felt her stomach flip once and she gasped. It continued to spin over and over as if she was plummeting from the edge into the valley way below. Thrusting out a hand, she grasped a large rock nearby to steady herself.

She tried to force her mind to take that in: *Not as Rana*. That was not possible. If not as Rana, then who? She had lived so many lives on Earth but only one life on Garial, the life that had started it all and the one that had made her Fen, the person she was today. Yet even that incredible, crazy, impossible fact was not the whole story.

Just as she was a reincarnation of Rana, so too was Rana a reincarnation.

It was all too much. She put her hands up to the sides of her head, clutched her hair and screamed.

Ruby

'Vice President Geron. You have completed your side of things well.'

'Thank you.'

'Jerome, you have been careless. Mackenzie is dangerous.'

88

'I am sorry. I did not expect him to recover quickly.'

'I do hope he is secure at the moment?'

'Very.'

<It is not all his fault, Klavon. The size and strength of him for an Earthling is impressive. You had dealings with him on Earth. More precautions should have been taken. If you are going to be our voice, use it well. I can't be there for every decision.>

I had hoped that Geron shooting him might slow him up a little.

<Don't hope. Plan and do. And watch out for Odette. She is competent, yet I detect weakness in her.>

You are not my master, Arrix. Don't lecture. Let me handle this.

'Are Lessey and the others rattled, Geron?'

'Rattled?'

'Worried. Scared. Unsure.'

'Lessey is. She is not the same since the attack last year. She is weaker, but she still wants to hold onto power. You can use that to get what you want.'

'To get what we all want, Geron.'

<Well said, Klavon! You are learning that it is not all about using the stick. A carrot is effective as well. Keep them thinking we want them and that they are useful.>

I prefer the stick. Still...

'So, we go to phase three now of our operation. Our people are spread widely across the major cities in Europe. Mackenzie will be watching Odette work as we speak and will know what those detons can do. He will know who I am and what threat I pose. Now we show him how serious we really are. Jerome, the detons?'

'They are ready. The detons and weapons have been planted and our people have moved to outside the cities.'

'Geron, you have set up the message to be released from Lessey? The Southern Alliance and the governments concerned will be convinced it came from her?'

'I have used her codes that Odette obtained. They will be convinced.'

'Good. So, we go ahead and show the world what we can do and what more we are capable of. Mackenzie will have a choice – see the world at war again, or he gives us access to the MASH, the portal and everything else that he and that stupid, annoying Chinese man...'

~Stay in control, Klavon. Don't lose it. Insults show weakness.~

'... that he and the Professor had access to. Shall we join Mackenzie next door for the entertainment?'

Ruby led the way through. She was pleased to see Mackenzie looking very uncomfortable, trussed up like a turkey on the chair. Odette stopped her work and looked up somewhat nervously. Jerome nodded at her and she fiddled with her bracelet until a 3D projection appeared on the opposite side of the room. Ruby sat down while the others stood around to watch. She said nothing. The pictures would speak for themselves.

Jerome spoke a simple command into his bracelet. 'Allez – go, go, go!'

The image split into two. In the absence of many useful landmarks these days, each picture was helpfully titled with the name of the city. The first two to come up were Paris and Edinburgh, both cities which had started to rebuild well, post the

Power Wars, both with increasing populations. Ruby alternated between watching the screen and watching Mackenzie's reaction. The Klavon side of Ruby took particular satisfaction from his pain.

His face, normally grizzled and hardened, crumpled and collapsed as the scenes played out in front of him. Twenty seconds passed showing Paris and Edinburgh before it switched to Warsaw and Milan, Vienna and Madrid and then back to the first two. As the visuals moved through the locations, the action was much the same: images of unmanned guns roaming the streets and picking out targets to shoot at. People going about their daily business were struck down, shop windows destroyed, monuments flattened, entire city centres devastated by the ghost like attacks. The sounds were the worst part. Parents pleading for their young children's lives, ear piercing shrills of anguish, the sound of footsteps stampeding through narrow streets, glass smashing, wood splintering, and all the while the regular thud thud thud of rounds of ammunition. In some locations, police responded with their own gunfire, but with no one to shoot at they were ineffective and most of the time they became victims too.

At first, Mackenzie seemed too shocked to say anything. Then he turned to her: 'For the love of God, make them stop,' he pleaded. 'Stop!'

Ruby looked away and back at the images which were from the perspective of snipers in high vantage points picking off targets in the squares below. Any people that escaped or tried to hide were swept up by weapons on the ground. Klavon and Arrix were used to high-tech weaponry from Garial controlled by thought. Here they were witnessing something raw, like facing an opponent in the

91

traditional, ancient method of combat their ancestors used. It was very one-sided, but both were impressed by the fact that humans had produced such a cruel and clinical way of killing. No wonder it had been banned.

Ruby became aware of Mackenzie again as he bucked violently in his seat in a frantic attempt to get up and make them stop.

Jerome grinned at Mackenzie and snorted, 'You are like a little feesh on a hook.'

<That's enough.>

A little longer, Arrix. Come on, this is good to watch.

<Give the order. He has to know that we will give him what we want if he gives us what we want.>

Spoilsport.

'Enough,' said Ruby.

Jerome repeated the command into his bracelet and all at once the noise of gunfire stopped. The screams did not. Shortly afterwards, they and the images faded and disappeared. Mackenzie was left rigid, staring into empty space.

'Send the message on behalf of Lessey, Geron. Let's have a listen.'

It was an automated voice, but the source code left no doubt as to where the message came from.

'Message from the headquarters of the French-Irish Alliance from President Moira Lessey to all international governments and the Southern Alliance. You will have seen the images from the six European cities we have attacked. You should know that we have acquired numerous units of the illegalised detons. These have been set up in seventeen other European cities and tuned in to significant stocks of armoury. We also have access to your existing hardware which means your weapons can be used against you. We have the capability to attack cities beyond the European borders too.

Our demands are that every European power surrender to us. Each of you will send your leading ambassador to Dublin by seven pm tomorrow where they will be given further instructions. That is all.'

'Perfect, Geron. Jerome, too, you have redeemed yourself.' Ruby turned back to Mackenzie. 'Look at me.' He lifted his head up and turned his eyes towards her. They seemed dull, lifeless almost, just how she hoped they might be. 'Now, I have something I need from you.'

Lessey

Lessey had remained at the base, leaving Don and Shaw to investigate the site in northern France where one of the initial attacks had taken place. In the absence of any news about Mackenzie and Geron, they had agreed that it was, at least, something to be doing. Shaw had already messaged in saying that there was not much to report, although Don had contacted her separately to say he had a theory he wanted to discuss with her when they got back.

She was surprised at how hard she was finding it to think about taking decisions without Geron there. It left her twiddling her thumbs, intrigued by Don's message but powerless –or worse, unable, to act at the moment. Everywhere around her was unnervingly quiet as she waited for them to return.

And then everything went absolutely crazy.

The first thing that happened was a notification on her bracelet that the verbal message she had apparently recorded was ready to be sent. Before she could check what that message was and who it was going to, she had another message confirming that it had just gone to the inboxes of every world leader. She opened the message and listened in horror while the automated tones of a female speaker set out conditions on her behalf. A check on the verification codes confirmed that it was sent from her outbox. In response, some one hundred plus notifications appeared from world leaders and ambassadors demanding her attention, all of them headed 'urgent' and all of them mentioning the word 'atrocity' 'retaliation' or something similar. Just as she started to plough through them, Shaw came through on her direct line via her bracelet sounding incredibly shocked and asking as politely as possible, 'Without wishing to overstep' his authority and making it clear he was 'enquiring on behalf of Colonel Berretti too', whether there was anything he should know about the attacks that the French-Irish Alliance had carried out on the six European cities. At that point, Lessey had swiped on the images that had already played across the world.

She could not bear it for long and soon pressed stop. Her first inclination was to find a dark room and sit in it. But she straightened her back and searched inwardly for some of the fight and tenacity she was famous for. She found enough of it to give her brain space to work out what she should do, starting with finding out how she had ended up being in this dire situation.

She revisited recent events. Don and Mackenzie had been called in to help her deal with the attacks on her territory on the basis that they knew something about the tremendous energy source she knew was out there. Just as she was making inroads into them agreeing to assist her, Mackenzie had been kidnapped by her right-hand man. In the meantime, someone had turned the tables totally on her. Rather than her being the victim, she was being made out to be the aggressor, and on a huge scale. All of this had been done using technology and techniques she had no idea about.

Revisiting what had happened may not have provided any answers, but she was now angry at the injustice of it all. She always worked better when she had fire in her belly.

She started to scribble out a statement which she would personally read denying any involvement in the attacks and putting the blame squarely back onto the Chinese. She would stop short of admitting her systems had been hacked because that would show weakness. It was a risky strategy since she had no evidence to back up her theories about China, but it would have to do for now. She had just composed herself and was just about to record her message when Don came through the door.

Startled, she looked up. 'Where's Major Shaw?'

'Busy dealing with a queue of flyers, manned by very irate representatives from half the governments around the world. Apparently, you're not replying to their messages.'

'I'm about to if they give me a chance.'

'I'll let you do that, President, but first, why don't you tell me why you've carried out this attack.'

'It's not come from me!'

'No? Are you sure?'

'Course I'm sure.'

'What can you tell me about detons?'

'Detons? They were banned years ago. No technology exists any longer to use them. No one on this planet would dare use them, not even us.' In her haste, Lessey had not taken in how the attacks were being done. It had been enough that they were being done and she was being blamed for it.

'The attack on the village in France and, I suspect, in Ireland and England had all the hallmarks of deton use. You've seen the images from the six cities. What do you think that was?'

'You're saying they were done by detons?'

'Yes. The technology was lost, eradicated, yet here they are, back in use.'

'Not by me.'

'I agree that you would not use them, Madam President.'

'It was the Chinese. Had to be.'

'No, not the Chinese. You yourself said that no one on this planet would dare use them. Well, how about someone from another planet?'

Fen

'Fen! Fen, are you alright? Where are you?'

It took a moment to realise that Pella's voice was coming from somewhere above her. She was kneeling next to the pool with her hands still holding onto her hair, but she had stopped screaming. How long she had been there, she had no idea.

'Fen!' Then louder: 'Fen!' There was the sound of panic in his voice. She managed a response.

'I'm down here, outside near a waterfall. Where are you?'

'I see you now. I heard a scream. Are you okay?'

'Yes, a bit surprised by something that wasn't actually there. I'm being silly.' She tried to sound upbeat. 'I've found lovely fresh water.'

'Good. Stay there, I'll come to you. I've found something too.'

She took another drink and tried to collect her thoughts. Should she say anything to Pella about what she had just experienced? She was conscious that, already, she was not being totally honest with him by not sharing how she believed she could control the coding. Why was she doing that? Was it to do with protecting that knowledge, protecting herself, or more to do with protecting him from something? She knew power could do bad things to people – look at Arrix – yet she was reluctant to share what she knew with someone she should be able to trust. If they were ever going to be able to get home, surely they should be open with each other. This additional knowledge that she had lived a previous life before Rana – and the more she thought about it, the more certain she was that it was knowledge and not something she just imagined – had to be relevant. Everything connected to the coding was relevant. Maybe Pella should know.

Before she had reached a conclusion, he was calling to her from the viewing platform. At least that put off her decision for the moment. As she got closer, she could see his face was full of concern.

'Are you sure you're okay?'

'Really, I'm fine. Can you make that jump over to here?'

'For fresh water right now, I'll jump over anything. Here, catch!'

He threw over several small containers with carrying straps on and then took a few steps back. 'Where...' she began before deciding she ought to let him concentrate on the jump. He made it with ease and then almost fell headfirst into the pool in his haste to get some water. While he rehydrated, she started to fill up the four containers he had thrown over and then took another slug of water from the pool for good measure.

'That's much better,' he said wiping water away from his mouth with his sleeve. 'I found the containers... and something more. Come on: we need to get back to Taron.'

They were able to swing the containers over to each other and negotiate the jump back safely before heading out the same way Fen had come. Close to the exit to the platform was a large box. 'Grab that end and I'll take this end,' Pella said.

'What is it?'

'It's a medi-chamber.'

'You're joking!' she said. It's enormous. Must weigh a ton. How did you get it here?'

Pella pulled out a small stone like object from his pocket. 'Remember these?' he said. 'Data droplets. This one is connected to this thing and there's still power from somewhere.' The chamber suddenly rose up several inches and started to move away at quite a speed. 'Come on,' Pella called chasing after it. I've not quite got the hang of driving it properly. I zigzagged my way down from one of the upper slopes to get here. Hopefully, it will be worth the effort.'

Fen set off at a jog after Pella and the chamber. Still not feeling quite with it, she found herself lagging behind so by the time she arrived back in the room where Taron still lay, Pella had already got the chamber close to the warrior's body. One of its long sides was open.

'It sensed him, Fen,' Pella said as she arrived. 'As soon as we were close by it was already hooking up to him. There must be something in the armour or within him that connects the two.'

The space inside the chamber was considerably smaller than the outside, yet there looked plenty of room for Taron to fit inside for treatment. A lot of action was happening on the shell of the container, inside it and on parts of Taron's discarded armour, especially on the area that had been close to his wound. Lights of varying colours wove around and across between them, presumably downloading information about his condition, before coming to an abrupt stop.

'What now?' said Fen.

'I guess we get him inside.'

That task was not straightforward. Taron was heavy, even without his armour. They managed to clip up his leg extensions and then it was a question of together easing one end of him over the outline of the armour, moving to his middle section to do the same and then his legs, all without disturbing the wound. It took a while but, eventually they managed to get him into the chamber. As soon as they pulled back, the open side closed off and the light show started again.

'We leave them to it, do we, Doctor?' asked Fen.

'What other choice do we have? You hungry?'

'You bet! Something dehydrated, I'm guessing.'

Pella smiled and produced two silver packs from his back pocket. 'Dehydrated and only past their sell by dates by 7,000 years. Based on the fact Garalians aimed to live on Earth, I assume their digestive systems are similar to ours. Do you want to risk it?'

There were risks, for sure. Would whatever was in the packets have survived that long and would their human stomachs take it? There was only one way to find out – once they worked out how to get the packets open.

As Fen ran her fingers along one side looking for an opening, the other side peeled back and all the contents spilled to the floor leaving a small pile of white powder.

'Damn!' she said, frustrated at her clumsiness.

'We've got the other one.'

'Where did you find these things?' Fen asked.

Pella explained that he had headed in the same direction as Fen had gone and ended up not that far away from where she had been on the viewing platform. He had gone up a steep slope, missing out the first two floors because he could not get onto them. On the next floor, he had just walked around until he stumbled upon a medical bay.

'I found the data droplet on the floor,' he said. 'When I touched it, this chamber came to life. I reckon every floor or area has a medical bay like that. Obviously built to last. The packets of food slid out that side bit there.' He pointed to a panel. 'I'd just manoeuvred it down when I heard you screaming. Fortunately, you're okay. All a bit lucky, I guess.'

Fen was starting to doubt how much luck was involved in all of this, but she was hungry and keen to sample the contents of the one remaining packet, so she tried again, hoping she would not spill any. This time she held the packet over one of the water containers as she touched along one edge. Fortunately, it opened the right way up and she poured the powder in. Immediately it solidified into a soup like substance, giving off a surprisingly pleasant smell.

'Meat?' she offered as a suggestion. 'A stew of some kind.'

'Who knows? I'll try it.'

'Are you sure?'

'Sure. I'll just have a sip.'

He took the container and gingerly put it to his lips, wrinkling his nose as he did so before tipping it up.

'Well?'

'I'm not dead. A good sign.'

'Let me try.'

It tasted okay and seemed to go down easily enough. After only a few mouthfuls, she was beginning to feel a lot less hungry. 'Time will tell,' she said handing it back to Pella, 'but I think that's half decent. Must be powerful stuff.'

Pella nodded as he took his own fill of the substance which, like Fen, was no more than a few gulps. 'Water, food, medical supplies. We're doing well. Just got to wait for our guide to wake up now and we'll be on the next transporter home.'

Fen could not manage to laugh at his light remark. So far, so good, yes, considering the dire straits they were in. Yet it was all turning out to be a little too convenient. The feeling she was being manipulated from one place to another, one experience to another, was too powerful to ignore. Had she found the pool only so that she could discover something else?

She looked across at Pella who was drinking from one of the water containers. This was a lot for him to take on, yet he seemed to be taking it in his stride. He had always done the same as a child on Garial too. Their father said it was the scientist in him – the ability to step back, analyse information and accept it for what it was. She had always been the more emotional of the two, passionate about causes, opinionated about everything.

He became aware of her staring at him and returned the look. 'What is it? What are you thinking now?' he said.

'Pella...' It felt the right time to share all her feelings and experiences. 'I have something I need to tell you.'

And she felt she would have if the wall to the chamber had not suddenly dissolved away. Taron's head snapped towards them and his eyes opened. There was a clinking sound behind them and Fen turned to see his armour unfurl and start to take on its full 3D form.

Taron's mouth rippled and a low hiss came out of it. His eyes locked onto hers and the sound was repeated.

'I don't understand,' Fen said in response.

His breathing flap fluttered and his chest went up and down, then he tried again. The hiss was louder this time, but still not understandable. She looked along his body where the knife had been lodged in him. The knife was now beside him on the floor. Where the wound was, there was a patch of the similar substance that had been around the hilt.

'Talk to him,' Pella suggested. 'English will be in him somewhere, as I said. Start saying things and he might pick it up.'

'What should I say?' The clinking of the armour continued in the background. It was a half formed shell now, ready for Taron to lie back into and use, if he was able.

'Anything. Tell him he was injured and we've been helping him. Tell him where he is. Just talk.'

Fen looked back at Taron. Brushing away a few loose stones, she lay on the floor next to the chamber so that her eyes were just a metre away from his. It felt the right thing to do, to be on the same level as him, less threatening maybe. Although, she did have to remind herself that she was dealing with a warrior here, nearly twice her size, and one who had a piece of armour close by that was equipped to take out a fighter jet.

The hissing stopped and his mouth returned to its natural pencil line position. She had forgotten Garalians had no eyelids so she was initially surprised to see a film of water appear and rinse the yellow eyeballs. The excess water ran down his face and onto the pad he was lying on. It could be a good sign he was functioning better than he had been.

She lay there for a moment feeling strangely at ease, breathing in time with his breaths. He seemed to notice as his eyes moved down to note the movements of her chest before settling back on her face. She started to talk. She told him they had found him here. She told him about the knife stuck in him and how they had taken his armour off to assess the injury. She told him about her search for water and how Pella had found the medical chamber that he was now in. She said that they hoped he was recovering well.

103

Out of ideas, she turned her head towards Pella. 'Is that enough?'

He shrugged. 'Look, he's trying to say something.'

His lips began to move again, this time they opened and a grunting sound came out, still not clear. 'Try again,' Fen said. They waited.

The next time he spoke, he was understandable. Unfortunately, what he said did not take them a lot further forward.

Mackenzie

If Ruby's plan was to scare Mackenzie into doing whatever she wanted him to, then it was working really well. Even after the visuals had finished, he could hear the screams in his head. The one he had seen in the army all those years ago had been bad enough, but at least they had used virtual humans and animals. This one had been the real thing and he felt wholly responsible for what might happen next. He knew what Ruby was going to ask him, and he knew that the lives of thousands, possibly millions, of people hung on his response. He was not given very long to think of a suitable answer.

'Do you remember me? I'm Ruby.' She pulled her chair close to him, almost within reach, but he could do nothing, even if he had decided he wanted to. It would have taken a crane, to get him out of the chair. He was also conscious of Jerome standing to the side with a gun.

Mackenzie looked directly at her. 'You're not Ruby.'

'No? Are you sure? Look at me,' she said using her finger to draw an oval around her face.

There was nothing remarkable about her at all; she looked much the same as she did when they had last met. She was wearing a simple dark grey hooded top with a white zip and thick black leggings. Her shoes were also black, plain and practical, and her brown hair was tied back in a ponytail with an elasticised hair tie. But it was the eyes that distinguished her. There was a depth and complexity to them which did not sit right on a ten year old girl. They were eyes that had seen and done a lot, ones that were incapable of showing hurt, sorrow or compassion. He had seen these eyes before – on Lee. Yet, there was another aspect to them he could not quite pinpoint.

'You're not the Ruby I met. She was a little girl. What happened to her?'

She ignored the question. 'Are you going to be well-behaved? No more jumping up and blundering into doors?'

'Is Ruby dead? Tell me. Is she dead? Have you taken over her body?'

'Shh, shh, my oversized bearded friend. None of that should concern you. What should concern you is what might happen next if you don't cooperate. Would you like to see more?' She pointed to the wall where the visual had been projected. 'I expect there may be one or two survivors we've not got yet. I must say these detons are rather good. Easy to switch on and off and, as you can see from Odette's handiwork, we've got plenty more we can send out.'

Mackenzie shook his head. 'Don't. I'm listening to whatever you've got to say.'

'That is good news. But first I want you to understand exactly what could happen next. A world view might make clear exactly the extent to which you are going to help us.' She leant back in her chair. 'Vice President Geron?'

Geron stepped forward. 'After many years of peace,' he said pompously, 'the world is about to go to war. President Lessey will try to persuade the world that the French-Irish Alliance is not responsible for the attacks, but she will fail. Her reputation for wanting to grab power is such that she will not be believed...'

'And to make doubly sure,' Ruby interrupted, 'the flyer that you three and Geron escaped in will be programmed to crash into the North Sea with no survivors. The flight data will show an encrypted conversation between yourself, Vice President Geron and the President – deciphered by a programme Odette here has uploaded to the Southern Alliance – where Lessey instructs you to go ahead and liaise with her friends in China to arrange the next set of attacks. Geron, please carry on.'

'It will be worse than the Power Wars. Lessey is already on the record showing her distrust for China. China, with support from France and Ireland, against the world. No nuclear weapons this time, but still war.'

'All of that just to persuade me to do something you want? Why didn't you just kidnap and threaten me?'

'You have no family, Mackenzie,' Geron continued. 'No one close we could hurt. And you are strong. Difficult to break down.'

'And a little disorder in the world might just suit our interests,' said Ruby. 'There is also the fact that what we are asking you to give us has a high price attached.'

'You want the MASH?'

'Yes, we want the MASH and the precise locations of all the places in the world which are potential dark energy portals.'

'What makes you think I know?'

'Jerome. Give the order again.'

He swiped his bracelet and was about to speak before Mackenzie stopped him. 'Okay, okay. I understand. The dark energy portals.'

'In exchange, there will be no more deaths other than the fake death of Geron in the flyer. He will be blamed for all that has happened – a rogue member of the French-Irish Alliance. He doesn't mind. He will be rewarded in other ways. There are plenty of quiet places he can retire to on the other side of the world.' Mackenzie glanced across at Geron who raised his eyebrows in response.

'That's agreed then. I'll give you ten minutes to organise your thoughts about the locations of the dark energy and how best to get the MASH to us.' Ruby pushed back her chair and started to get up, then lowered herself down again. 'Oh, there is one more thing.'

'That's not enough?' Mackenzie growled.

'Not quite.' She leant forward again. This time Mackenzie thought he recognised the something else in her eyes that he had not been able to identify before. Or rather the someone else.

'Arrix?'

Ruby smiled. 'You've seen both of us?'

He could not respond.

'Yes, I see you have. So you realise what you're up against. So the other thing is: tell us where that fragment of quarton is that you and Chuck kept back.'

Fen

It had sounded like: 'He promised us everything,' before Taron had lapsed into silence again. Despite their prompting, he would not – or could not – repeat what he had just said.

When she was a Garalian, Fen would have been able to read the slight movements or changes of expression that her race used. After so long as a human, it was much harder. His apparently expressionless face was giving no clues. Nor did she feel any physical connection to him like she had with the warriors when they had been close to Earth. Deliberately, she moved her fingers round to the small of her back where a tiny fragment of quarton was embedded. The lack of connection suggested there were no other quartons nearby, possibly none on Garial at all. Yet Arrix had got back to Garial from Earth by quartons connecting. It gave her a glimmer of hope for getting back.

'He promised us everything.' Pella repeating Taron's words shook her out of her thoughts. 'He, being Arrix?'

'Got to be.'

'What does it mean?'

Fen sat back up, her eyes glued to the warrior, urging him to say more. He stared back, his mouth firmly closed. His chest rose sharply before setting back to its former rhythm. 'Something's stopping him talking. Maybe he's in pain.'

'He shouldn't be in pain if the medi-chamber is doing its job.'

On an impulse, she pulled out the energy ring he had dropped earlier. 'Where's yours?'

'Here,' Pella said handing his to her.

'We can't wait much longer,' she said to Pella. 'We have to find out if we can get back and we're pinning all our hopes on him at the moment. Maybe these might prompt him. She put the rings down in Taron's eye line. 'Taron, we need you to tell us. Come on. You gave us these. Why?' His mouth twitched and there was another deep breath.

'He pr... promised...'

'That's it. Go on.'

'He promised...us... everything.'

'Arrix?'

'He lied.'

'He knows Arrix well,' muttered Pella over her shoulder.

'How did he lie, Taron? What did he promise?'

'Life. Forever.'

'Eternal life. Familiar story.'

'The coding,' said Pella.

'Yes!' Taron's eyes widened. 'The coding. He said we will live forever. He lied.'

Taron was right: the warriors would not live forever. Not when they had been split into billions of pieces and dispersed throughout the galaxy.

'The energy rings, Taron. Why did you give us the rings?'

'I trust you.'

'Did Arrix know you had them?' said Pella.

109

'No. He did not want them. Too dangerous.'

'But you had them anyway? Against his wishes. Why?'

'I had to.' Taron lifted his hand up to touch his face.

'What happened to your face?' asked Fen. 'And the knife wound – when were you injured? Do you remember?'

'The knife – an accident when I fell to here. The face – you have forgotten?'

'Forgotten?'

Taron rolled over onto his uninjured side facing them and moved his legs and arms as if to try to get out of the chamber.

'Wait,' said Fen. 'We will help you, but tell me first. I don't remember anything about your face. We found you here after you fell.'

'The face is an old injury. You did it.'

'Me?'

'Perhaps as Rana?' offered Pella.

'No,' said Taron. 'Not as Rana. As...'

And before he could finish, she instinctively knew. They had met before.

More than that, they had loved before.

A special love: a mother's love for her son.

She was alone, staring at the waterfall which was barely a trickle at this time of the cycle. The hot period with no rain dried up its source. But she had visited before when it had cascaded down in such quantities that it was almost impossible to hear herself think. Whatever the time of the cycle, she loved this spot in the mountains. She used to bring Taron regularly, when he was growing up, to

110

swim and play, then they would hover over the waterfall in their bubble, enraptured by its movement. It was never the same from moment to moment. It was different again on this occasion – still it gave her comfort to be there. She could remember the good times. So much of her life these days was spent remembering the bad.

The bad... Taron would never forgive her for what she had done. She had tried to explain that it was an accident but, injured, he had gone away from her, forever. The last she had heard of him was that he was on the other side of the planet, doing all the wrong things, making all the wrong choices in his life. Yet it was her fault because she had fired the weapon. She had risked her son's life, for the future of the planet. She had to take the one shot she had while Arrix was still young and before he could do much damage. She missed and hit Taron instead.

The memory of that day was vivid. Her son's young, innocent voice as he announced he was home with a friend. The feeling – the knowing –that his friend was the one who had taken the coding from her in an earlier life. The scrabbling around for a weapon, then taking aim as they both came into the room. The firing of the weapon as her son started to introduce him. 'This is my friend, Arr...' The scream of pain. And Taron's face would never be the same. Their lives would never be the same.

Every time she came to the waterfall now, she would vow to search for Taron and save him from the desperate life he had to be living. She never did follow through on that promise. All she had left were the memories of this place. As for the coding, her link was weakening and there was a risk she might lose all connection.

Access to the spot was difficult now that Arrix's science complex had been built. She was not supposed to be there but that had not stopped her tackling the long climb up from the bottom. She stood on the edge, closed her eyes and made her vow again. So wrapped in her thoughts was she that she never heard Arrix arrive. She had time to turn to face him; not enough to avoid the kick that launched her from the top.

Fen understood. With that life went the last strong piece of coding she had kept since Arrix had claimed overall control of it from her in a previous incarnation. He stripped it from her as she clattered into the rocks below. Every digit, symbol, twist of the helix, every strand that she had clung onto over the last few lives, hoping she could yet get control of it back, left her mangled body and wound its way up into that of Arrix. Every last piece, save for one tiny extract of code which, like a seed on the wind, floated away to become part of the DNA in Rana.

No wonder the coding felt so good, so right, so much like it belonged to her. It did belong to her. It had been hers from the start.

Arrix had stolen it from her. She was just claiming it back.

Lessey

The spectacles were not needed, but it was part of the personality Lessey liked to project. Eyes, ears and her voice had always been her strongest attributes, and she had made sure that these had special attention at rejuvenations and follow-up appointments. She peered over her half-moon glasses now as Don, hands on her desk and leaning towards her, waited for her response.

She had to admit, there was part of her which was starting to enjoy this turn of events. Never one for avoiding being the centre of attention, she certainly was that now. She had not been feeling herself at all in recent months – a little low and lacking motivation. This crisis – and especially the fact that the whole world seemed to think she could be capable of such barbarity – had given her the boost she needed. Maybe without that simpering fool, Geron, interfering in things, she could make the tough decisions she was famous for. The situation could be turned to her advantage, if she played it right.

'Colonel Berretti,' she said. 'You asked me to keep an open mind about the existence of aliens. I am a woman true to my word. And if it gets all these feckin leaders off my back, to be frank, I'll believe in anything.'

'So talk to me then, please, President.'

'Happy to, Colonel. The Southern Alliance is the world's police force at the moment. You know I have had nothing to do with this act, so tell your superiors that too. Get them to issue a statement saying that the French-Irish Alliance is the victim of an alien attack and that President Lessey will open her doors to full scrutiny by the Southern Alliance. You and it will have full access to all our systems and data.'

'It's a start.'

'In return, we will, of course, need access to all the data the Southern Alliance has about the alien threat so that we can take steps to prevent any such attack on our systems again.'

'You wouldn't be trying to see this as a way of accessing information that you think is being hidden from you, President, would you? For example, this claim of yours that the Southern Alliance is making up the whole thing just to keep you from accessing an energy source?'

'Colonel Berretti!' She did her best to show surprise, a very slight raise of the eyebrows which were permanently etched high above her eyes. 'What are you saying? This is a serious threat from an extraterrestrial source. We need to keep our eyes focussed solely on that – no other distractions. Now, are you prepared to do what I suggest?'

Her own face might not always be capable of showing expression but Don's was, and she knew what scepticism was when she saw it. However, he nodded and straightened up. 'I'll get a statement out straightaway.'

'Give me two hours to arrange the necessary access to our systems.'

'I'm sure that you won't need that long, President Lessey. Shall we say an hour?'

'An hour it is.'

'The Southern Alliance statement will be through in a couple of minutes, if I can get hold of the right people. You should get some relief from the calls and messages.' With that, he turned and left.

The door closed and Lessey, ignoring the urgent flashing on her bracelet, opened up a secure link to her military commander, Reeve Barrow, in Dublin.

He looked extremely stressed. 'President Lessey, I've been trying to get hold of you with some urgency. Do you realise...'

'Of course I realise, Barrow. We're up Shit Creek, but don't worry because I've found us a paddle. Now, I want you to do something for me. We will soon be opening up all our systems and data to the Southern Alliance. In return, they will be sending us information on these mythical aliens. I want your tech guys to get off their arses and do some work for a change. They have less than an hour to come up with a patch that uses that short gateway when they plunder our data to go in under the radar and search theirs for any reference to the energy source at the Severn Bridge. Is that clear?'

'President, that is some ask. An hour?'

'Fifty-eight minutes to be precise. 'Don't let me down, Barrow. I'm looking for a new Vice President; you could be it.' She broke the link and sat back, putting her hands behind her head. It had been a difficult time but there were positive signs that it could all work out well.

And she might even find out the source of those detons and how they got onto the market. They could be very useful in the future.

Mackenzie

They left Mackenzie where he was. No doubt, Jerome would be keeping a watchful eye on him from somewhere, though, even if he could escape, what could he do? This was not about his safety – he had the lives of hundreds, possibly thousands of people in his hands. If he gave Ruby what she wanted, the consequences could be even worse for the entire planet. As for the fragment of quarton Ruby spoke of, he had no idea what she was talking about. As far

115

as he was aware, the entire piece he and Chuck had worked on was destroyed in the experiment they had done which, in practice, had proved the undoing of Arrix at the end. Ruby was under the impression a fragment had been kept back. It was not kept by him, so maybe by Chuck? Whether it had or it had not, he could, at least, pretend he knew where it was and buy some time to come up with a solution.

To do that, he needed to understand the full extent of the problem and he was not sure he did. The threats were real; there was no doubt about that. These people were capable of carrying out horrendous damage. But had he fully established exactly who they were and what they were capable of? He went through them, one by one.

First the easier characters – Geron, he knew, sort of. He was capable of violence as demonstrated by using the gun on him, but it did not seem natural to him. He seemed weak, easily led, and his judgement had to be in question. He suspected he was not all that intelligent, although that was just a hunch. Mackenzie did not view him as a massive threat on his own.

Next there was Jerome – angry, violent, strong too – he had felt it in their encounter earlier. He detected a blind loyalty towards Ruby, the type that would walk through walls for her. A lot about Jerome scared Mackenzie, and he was not a person to be easily scared. One to watch, for sure.

Then there was Odette – very intelligent, wanted something, he was sure, that she could not get from a normal post-war society, which had made her turn to whatever it was Ruby was offering. She was complicated and possibly wrapped up in something she did not know how to get out of. He had seen kindness there which he hoped he could tap into

And there was a whole host of people involved he did not know – an army of them, maybe – who had already carried out a bunch of bad things. They were likely being dragged along with the promise of a better life than they currently had. How many there were, he was not sure.

Finally, the most dangerous of all: Ruby. As he and Don had thought, Klavon was in her, at least in part of her. He could see it in her manner and in her actions. She spoke like Klavon (like the Lee version of him) and she had showed ruthlessness that was typical of what Fen had said about him, and what Mackenzie had seen. The little girl he had met before was gone, leaving only a shell to be used, actually by two people. Ruby had been right when Mackenzie had detected something else in those eyes. Klavon spoke, but Arrix was definitely there in the background. Mackenzie had no idea how that was possible, just like most of what he had witnessed since Chuck had first spoken to him about the presence of aliens and a powerful stone that tapped into dark energy. Having the two most evil people rolled into one complicated things enormously. They were a formidable force. On the positive side, at least Mackenzie knew where they both were. Beat one of them and they both go down.

Which brought him onto the most worrying aspect of all of this: how could a being, capable of reincarnation and transferring into bodies, ever be beaten? It was a depressing thought... but it led him to a potential source of help that might lead to a solution. It involved enlisting the services of someone else who, seemingly, could never be beaten. That tiny fragment of quarton Ruby wanted, if it did indeed exist, could well be the key.

He was suddenly just as keen as she was to find it.

Ruby

<Klavon, I've been over this with you so many times now. It is starting to become more than tiresome.>

Don't patronise me, Arrix. You might think you can control me, but I am our voice and legs. You can do nothing without my agreement.

<I may put that to the test one day, Klavon. However, I will, in the interests of team spirit, explain again why finding the fragment of quarton is so important.>

The fragment that we cannot be sure exists.

<Indeed, but you saw Mackenzie's reaction when you mentioned it.>

Yes. He said nothing.

<Which means he knows something. It does exist and he will lead us to it.>

And it will help how?

<My fragment of quarton was destroyed by Chuck with my body. The coding has found a way to keep me... and you... going. We are being tested, Klavon, as much as I hate to admit it. We have a challenger, a strong one at that.>

Rana.

<Rana, Fen, whatever you want to call her. She will have found a way to survive and, as you pointed out, she has a fragment of

quarton inside her. That means that if we have the other fragment, she can be found and then we can destroy her. She will come to us.>

You're sure of that?

<The quartons are linked. Either directly or indirectly, they will bring us together. She also has a daughter who she will want to see again.>

Ah, yes, the daughter. So sentimental, these humans.

<True – but that's how the coding works. Through the quartons and that attachment, she will find her way back. Until she is back and we have destroyed her, we won't have full control and without full control we cannot guarantee we can live forever.>

Forever, together.

<I do hope not. That would be unbearable. But we will come to an arrangement, I am sure of that.>

Well, I'm so pleased to be in such good hands, Arrix. I trust you to be fair and honest on that point.

<Sarcasm is an unfortunate human characteristic, Klavon. It does not suit you.>

Really? I would never have guessed!

<Let's just agree that we are on track to get the three things we need – the MASH, access to as many dark energy outlets as we could possibly need, and the last two pieces of quarton in existence.>

The last quartons? Are you sure? It feels like we've been here before.

<Indeed it does, Klavon. Indeed it does.>

Fen

Coincidence, perhaps, yet, on Garial, at more or less the same time, similar thoughts were running through Fen's head concerning the quartons.

She touched the area on her lower back again. She had not even been aware of the quarton until Lee had pointed it out to her in those last few minutes at the portal on Earth, but it had been in her since the last quarton had been destroyed on the Friendship Bridge in London. 'Last' quarton? There was nothing accurate about that word 'last'. All those lives spent working towards an aim, a purpose, even if she had not always been aware of it at the time. The battle for the quartons seemed never-ending. And now, as she tried to think through the importance of what Taron was saying about Arrix's promise for eternal life, she could not help but question her own mortality. Both Lee and Arrix had seen something different in her – she was the only one who had survived the explosion on the Friendship Bridge in her own body. She had also recently survived the apparent destruction of the warriors and Arrix on Earth, again in her own body. Now she had discovered that she had lived at least one previous life before she had been Rana on Garial. When did it all start? When was it ever going to end? Immortality was not an attractive proposition, yet she seemed stuck with it.

It was really Martha that was keeping her going now. Trillions of miles away, yet she felt she could still get back to her. The coding was a means to an end and she had just had an idea as to how she could use it to get back to Earth.

120

'Taron, do you want to come out of the medi-chamber? Are you well enough?'

The fact that he immediately began shuffling over was a good sign. The side of the chamber closed down once he was out and with Fen and Pella's help, he was soon sat up so he was leaning against the side of it.

Pella pulled up a couple of rocks for him and Fen to perch on. 'Water?' he offered.

'Yes.'

Pella handed over the container and they watched as Taron drank greedily from it. 'We can top them up again,' he said. 'How do you feel, Taron?'

'I feel better. Not strong, but better. I can talk more.'

'We might need you to, Taron,' said Fen. 'That's if you're willing to help us?'

'Yes, I will help. So, you are Pella? Rana's brother in your last life on Garial.'

'Yes.'

'I'm Fen now. I've lived many lives since I was Rana.' And more before it, apparently. She was sorely tempted to pursue that relationship with Taron, but she was also desperate to get moving, so she floated her idea to Pella and Taron. 'I have part of a quarton in my back. You won't be able to see it because it's not active at the moment. The reason it's not active is that it has nothing nearby to connect to.'

'Makes sense,' said Pella.

'Help us understand why that's the case, Pella.'

'The quartons were designed to interact by capturing dark energy through the exit point at the end of the bridge and ramp it up by travelling up and down the line of quartons set along the bridge. As you know, they help provide the enormous power required to span the vast distance to Earth. From what we've experienced, that connection can carry on over greater distances, even when the quartons are separated.'

'Even from trillions of miles away?' asked Fen.

'The more quartons you have and the closer they are together, the more powerful they are.'

'However, there was a strong enough connection to enable Arrix to jump into his body double here because a piece of quarton was left with it.'

'That is out of my area of expertise. Something to do with the coding, right? Our life-forces jumping around. Not your usual science.'

She nodded thoughtfully. Pella was right: throw in the coding and its apparent desire to live forever and the rules of science tended to bend somewhat. Live forever... was it actually alive? She still did not know whether the coding was organic, inorganic, a mixture of both or neither. There was a lot she felt she should know, wanted to know.

'So, I have a quarton here. There should be a link to Earth if there is a quarton on Earth.'

'*If* there is a quarton, that is feasible. But I should point out that it's not a scientific link I understand. Do also remember that I was a scientist a long, long time ago.'

122

'Somehow we got here, physically got here. That means we can get back. Maybe we can use the link between two quartons, if, as you say, there is one left on Earth.'

'Okay, but unless you can snap your fingers...'

'Snap fingers?' said Taron.

'It's an expression to show magic,' Pella explained.

'Magic?'

'Anything that can't be explained by science. I mean to say that unless Fen can do some magic to get us back we are stuck here.'

'I can't do magic, but I do know we can use the coding. It helped get us here. It doesn't want us – me, at least – dead. There is unfinished business on Earth and it will want us to go back.'

'Well, if you can't do magic, then give me a load of quartons, a link to the dark energy on Earth, thousands of Garalians to help with labour and I'll build you a bridge. Although, it might take a while. Strangely, I think I could remember how. It must be the Garalian air.'

'We might already have a bridge.'

'Hasn't that been destroyed? Wasn't everything else connected to the quartons destroyed, or so you said?'

'That's what I think happened. But isn't it worth checking?'

'I guess so. Maybe there will be quartons on it? No, no – we would feel the connection to them. Without quartons, how will we generate enough energy?'

Saying nothing, Taron stuck out a hand and drew the shape of a ring in the air.

Fen looked at Pella and raised her eyebrows.

'Okay, the rings you gave us,' said Pella. 'That may not be enough power, but it's a start. We know there is plenty of dark energy available in the universe and we have some sort of link to Earth with Fen's and if there is a quarton there. We might have parts left in the bridge, if that's back. Lots of ifs – but, maybe... Perhaps... right... leave it with me... this needs a lot of thought.'

'You're a lousy doctor but a great engineer. I will leave that with you, as you suggest. Taron – the bridge location is a long way from here, as I remember. Can you get us there?'

'Yes. But it may not be easy.'

'Do you know what? Somehow, I never imagined it would be.'

They helped Taron to stand. There was no need for his legs to be extended because, even without the extensions and still not one hundred percent fit, Taron's natural stride took him off at speed, something they found out as they headed up to get more water from the waterfall. By the time they arrived, both she and Pella were breathing heavily.

Fen was desperate to make headway quickly, but she was also hoping that with both she and Taron at the spot where she had been killed in that incarnation, some other useful memories might come to her. However, as they waited for Taron to take his fill directly from the pool near the waterfall, she felt nothing. Taron remained silent on the subject too.

They filled up the water containers, and looked expectantly at Taron, awaiting directions.

He took their cue. 'We need transport. There is none here. We stripped the building when rebuilding the bridge.'

'We were lucky to find the medical equipment, then,' said Pella.

Luck? Fen was seriously starting to doubt whether luck played any part in this epic she was living. 'How far are we from the city? Walking, I mean, Taron.'

'Several cycles if we do not stop. We may find some transport once we get out of the mountain area. We may not.'

'Okay. Let's get going. Which way?'

Taron put his arm out towards the valley below. 'That way is quickest.'

Pella took a couple of paces forwards and peered over the edge. 'Directly down?'

'Yes, we follow the river for a while before we travel over and out of the mountain area.'

'Because of the Brack?' Fen said. Where did that name suddenly come from? Having been overloaded with thousands and thousands of names of places and people in her lives, she did not think her brain held on to many. She had been trying to remember the name of the science complex they had been in since they arrived with no success and had stopped even trying. Yet the Brack had jumped straight in. Why?

'That's the name of the marshes and swamps the river here used to lead into, right?' said Pella.

'Correct,' said Taron. 'Inaccessible without transport. Quite dangerous to walk through.' There had never been a need; people had always flown in and out. 'But the river will lead us close to the end of the range. Before the Brack, we will get out, find a way up and out of the mountains, and then it will get easier.'

125

The Brack... The Brack... It kept going through Fen's mind now. There was a reason for everything she was going though now. The return to Garial with Pella; this waterfall they were standing next to and the memories it brought back; finding and helping Taron, now their guide; and heading for the Brack. Something very important happened there, but it looked like she might have to wait to see what it was when they reached it.

'Are you sure you're fit enough to do this, Taron?' Pella asked. 'It looks dangerous going down.' He and Fen began looking for a possible route amongst the boulders and screed. Taron turned to them and gave them the only facial expression that worked across both races: a smile.

'We will see.' And, with that, he leapt over the side and hurtled directly down the mountainside. They watched in amazement as he skilfully wove his way down avoiding major rocks and mini cliff edges, until he was out of sight.

Pella turned to Fen. 'Well, that's one way to do it. But it's not my choice.'

'Nor mine.' She could have added that she spoke from experience after remembering her encounter with Arrix in that earlier incarnation. 'I favour the cautious zigzag approach, preferably with a big stick for support if we can find one. Come on; let's see what we can do.'

It took quite a long while, many scratches, bumps and bruises, and hearts repeatedly leaping into mouths, but they eventually worked their way to the bottom, by which time Fen had realised that what had looked like a gentle meandering stream from the viewpoint high above was, in fact, a thunderous, boiling torrent.

They spotted Taron busy putting something together on a clear patch of ground further along by the river. From the way he was laying out branches, it looked ominously like he was preparing something to be used on the river.

'Did you know the river was as wild as this, Taron?' Fen asked.

'Of course.'

'You meant it, then, when you said we would get out of the river before the Brack. We're actually going on it.'

Without looking up, he replied. 'My language is not yet perfect, but I understand that you have to go on a river before you get out of it.'

'Or in it,' said Pella with a nervous glance towards the water.

'Yes, or in it,' Taron said.

Fen hoped his reply was an example of Garalian humour, and he actually knew what he was doing. Still, even if he did have any advice on dealing with the relentless twisting and crashing of the white riders that pummelled the rocks jagging above the surface, she very much doubted she would be able to hear him.

Mackenzie

'You're thinking time is up, Mackenzie.'

'A child's voice,' Mackenzie said, 'but not a child within. Are you happy to take advantage of little girls in this way, Klavon?'

'What do you think?'

'I think that you are, but you shouldn't be.'

'The girl was already dead. This is a way to keep her precious memory alive.' Ruby clutched both hands to her chest and lowered her head solemnly.

'And what about Arrix? What does he think? Or can he not speak for himself?'

Ruby lifted her head. 'Leave us for a moment, Jerome and Odette,' she said, her eyes firmly focussed on Mackenzie.

Mackenzie waited until they were gone before asking, 'So they don't know everything about you? '

Ruby walked across to the table and perched against it. There was a fruit bowl with one apple on it which she took a bite out of and then gently lobbed it at Mackenzie. It was a weak enough throw for him to have time to move his head to the side so that it bounced harmlessly off his shoulder and rolled onto the floor.

'Not hungry?' she said.

'They obviously know you are unusual and you seem to have enough in you to persuade them a little girl has some power, otherwise they would not follow you.'

'Correct.' She bent down and picked up the apple which had rolled back towards her, took another bite and threw it at Mackenzie again, this time with more force so it hit him on the side of the face. It was not hard enough to hurt, but he could see the game Ruby was playing here, much the same tactic she might have used with her followers.

'Behave in a slightly quirky way but don't give away too much. Make them feel scared of what they don't know.'

'A man with brains.'

'Do they think you're possessed, a ghost of some kind?'

'Yes, no, maybe. It doesn't really matter. They do what we want them to do, that's the main thing. Just like you're going to do what we want you to do. You know who we are so that means you also know what we are capable of. You've seen that already through the entertaining show we laid on for you earlier. You've had time to think?'

'Yes. I know I have no choice.'

'That is a given and was not what you were supposed to be thinking about, as you well know. We're more interested in the how and where part.'

'Colonel Don Berretti will be able to download all the locations where dark energy is most concentrated. The MASH, I can take you to...'

'And the quarton fragment?'

'Is – or rather was – in the MASH. I think.'

'Explain.'

'Chuck talked about him needing something to attract enough energy to the MASH or to the portal for it to be a threat. It needed to go through a focal point first – that point, I think, had to be in the MASH, not in the portal, to carry out the counterattack at the end on you. Thinking about it, I reckon that must be the fragment of quarton you are talking about.'

In reality, Mackenzie had no idea whether that was the case or not. He was having to think on his feet, all of it made-up (as far as he was aware), but it had to make some sense from a scientific point of view. In a way, it did. He had no idea what technical expertise Arrix or Klavon had – the likelihood was that, since they were from an advanced race, it was going to be a lot higher than his

– so he was counting on their interest in the MASH. Something about it was new, unknown and intriguing and, if that was the case, it was a potential blank sheet for him to wing it... providing he did not overdo it.

It looked like it might be working when Ruby warily asked, 'So, to confirm, the quarton is in the MASH.'

'I wasn't even aware of the possibility of the quarton until you mentioned it. Now, it makes sense that it had to be there. However, maybe it's not now. Everything Garalian was destroyed, wasn't it? Present company excepted.'

There were a few moments when Ruby said nothing and, instead, just stared blankly at the floor. Mackenzie wondered whether some sort of internal dialogue was going on inside. He liked to think it was a full-blown argument, bearing in mind the characters involved, and he had a fleeting, but not very optimistic, hope, that it might be so heated that it would result in Ruby combusting before his eyes... as unpleasant as seeing a little girl exploding might be.

Eventually, she looked up at him again. 'What you say is possible. But if you are wrong, more attacks will be carried out. You will show us to the MASH, we will secure it and examine it for the quarton. In the meantime, you will contact Berretti and give instructions to download the information about the dark energy concentration points to us. Odette will talk you through that. Where is the MASH now?'

'At a secure location in London. Because of its enormous capability, only me and the Colonel know exactly where. There are systems in place to transfer responsibility to others in the Southern

Alliance should anything happen to either of us. I need to let them know I'm alright for them not to do that.' Mackenzie was quite pleased with that quick piece of thinking which should be another reason to keep him alive for longer. In fact, seven other members of the Southern Alliance command knew where it was, but it did no harm to double up with more safeguards.

Ruby nodded her agreement. 'If the quarton is not with the MASH, Mackenzie, we will kill more people.'

'I don't doubt you will. I hope as much as you do that it is.'

Ruby called through to Jerome and they were joined by him, Odette and two other large men Mackenzie had not seen before. The security was not needed; he had no intention of putting up a fight – not just at the moment. He had achieved what he wanted and created some breathing space. Chuck had always said that Mackenzie was good at finding reasons not to do something, often delaying things until it suited him. 'You've bought enough bloody time to set up your own clock factory,' he remembered his friend saying – a rare joke with a serious message behind it to tell him to get on with some job or other. Well, he had bought time here. The question was whether he could think of anything useful he could do with what he now had.

Lessey

For the first time since she had arrived at the base, Lessey stepped outside into the sunshine. It had been fifty minutes since she had first spoken to Barrow, and Don had already been in with an update to say that the Southern Alliance were ready to share their information about alien threats. Lessey just needed to open up their data so their non-involvement in the attacks could be confirmed. She had pushed back on him and said she needed the full hour. But her impatience waiting for Barrow's hack into the Alliance's systems had got the better of her and she had left her office.

She pulled out a cigarette from the small gold box she liked to show off in meetings before subjecting attendees to the liquorice flavoured brand she enjoyed these days. She lit it and took a few drags before throwing it to the ground and stamping it out with her foot. It seemed less fun with no one else around to blow the smoke onto. She would have called Barrow herself but even she knew she had given him an almost impossible task in the timeframe and did not want to take out precious minutes. A mixture of impatience and excitement at the prospect of being able to finally get some hard information on the energy sources she so craved got the better of her and she took out another cigarette. She was just about to light it when her bracelet showed an incoming call from Barrow.

'Hang on,' she said and scuttled back to the security of her office. She did not want to risk anyone listening in, particularly Don who might be around nearby.

'Well? Well?' she said as soon as the door shut.

'We've got something, President,' said Barrow. 'We can get all the data we need during the transfer but they'll pick up the hack within seconds.'

'How much data?'

'"Heaps," as my techie said. But they will know we've done it. We couldn't find a way to conceal it.'

'That won't matter. By then, we'd have proved to the world we had nothing to do with the attacks. The Southern Alliance will be fed up we've double-crossed them, but I can live with that. They'll almost be expecting us to do it. Berretti said as much, and they will be prepared. Can you get round that if they try to block it?'

'Our whiz kid can get round anything. He's confident that they won't be able to stop it and, anyway, they're not as secure as they should be. They're set up to assist other countries – maybe they're just too kind-hearted.' He chuckled.

'I'm actually happy they'll know we've done it. They've been of no practical help so far, other than stupidly offering this opportunity to us. Are you one hundred percent sure you're ready?'

'Yes, President. Ready.'

She closed the channel and called Don. 'Colonel Berretti,' she said as politely as she could. 'Are you nearby?'

'Just on the other side of the base. Do you have news?'

'Yes. Our data is your data. Help yourself and thank you so much for your assistance.'

'Just on the hour, President. I must remind you again that there are many lives at risk here, including that of my good friend, Mackenzie.'

'I am very aware of that. You are helping us out and I appreciate it. Reeve Barrow's team are ready to hand over our data. Sending you his link now.'

'Received. We'll get right on it. We had a positive response from the other countries following the statement we put out, but they will be assured by your evidence and openness.'

'I'm sure they will. Thank you again. Colonel Berretti.'

'I'll be in touch.' He closed the link.

Lessey sat back in her chair and put her hands in her lap. Calmness flowed through her, a feeling she had not had for a long time. Berretti would be through the door in a few minutes, she had no doubt of that. But that did not worry her in the least. She was much more her old self now – in control, busy deceiving those around her and, crucially, on the attack.

It was as good as things ever got.

Fen

Taron fashioned a raft – of sorts. Without his armour and the weapons within, he made do with his hands and brute strength. The extent of that strength became apparent as they watched him wrench thin trees from the ground with one hand and then strip the branches off by pulling them through the narrow V-shaped branches of a larger one. He then tied them all together with twine from a plant he scooped out of the water. It did not take long to complete a raft which looked big enough (and, she hoped, stable enough) to carry the three of them. All accomplished, Fen reflected, with a hole in the side of his body.

She trusted the big warrior, but still she was unsure about the raft. Pella obviously felt the same.

'Looks quite strong, Taron,' he shouted above the noise which had, impossibly, got even louder as they waited. He examined the raft at length, nervously switching his attention back and forth to the river. 'Do you have a lot of experience of travelling on fast flowing rivers?'

'None,' replied Taron in a flat tone. 'And it's the first time I have built a boat. Find your own... what is the word...?' and he picked up a small stick and motioned with it.

'Paddle?' Fen offered.

'Yes. Paddle.'

Taron searched amongst a pile of nearby driftwood and quickly found a large, fairly flat piece of wood. He swung it back and forth to test it using the arm on the uninjured side. Fen searched for a smaller piece, as did Pella. She soon found two pieces which looked suitable for them both.

'Once a scavenger, always a scavenger!' she said, handing one to Pella and then copying Taron's method for testing which seemed to involve swinging his piece in ever larger circles. 'I've found a lot of wood in my time.'

'I will do this paddle on one side of the boat,' Taron said, 'you two on the other side. It will be dangerous, so be careful.'

Fen could not take her eyes off the water. The violence and intensity of it as it surged by was hypnotic. 'This is definitely the best way?' she said.

'As I said: it will be quick. Ten times quicker than humans can walk. Don't worry. I am a warrior and you are strong.'

Fen did not feel it as they hauled their water containers over their shoulders, grabbed their paddles and helped Taron push the raft into a calmer patch of water protected by rocks and out of the direct path of the torrent.

'Let the water do the most of the work. Hold on and use the paddles only when you need to,' said Taron.

'He's not very specific, is he?' said Pella. 'How do we know when to use the paddles?'

'When you feel the raft capsizing, I guess. I can't feel anything below my waist, can you?'

'Not much. We'll be fine as soon as we get up onto this cosy, warm boat.'

They clambered on one side into a kneeling position as Taron did the same on the other. Fen found herself towards the front of the raft which suited her just fine. She would rather have a clear view of the obstacles and be in a position to react to them rather than follow Pella's lead. She searched her brain for any nuggets of experience which might help her deal with the wild ride ahead. As Fen, she had mainly steered clear of water in her life, but she had had a flashback to a life as the teenager, Jeanie, when her mother had forced their car into a lake. She had survived that ordeal – up until the quarton was found at least – so she could survive this.

There were several places where the twine Taron had used on the raft stuck up enough to get her hand underneath for a grip. She checked Pella behind and noted he was checking for the same. He returned her reassuring smile. If her attempt was as nervous looking as his, he would take little confidence from it.

'Hold the paddle between your teeth,' she joked, but she suspected it was lost in the roar as Taron pushed them off and out into the chaos of the main part of the river.

Immediately, she knew the paddle would be of little use. As a very young girl, she vaguely remembered seeing canoeists on a telecast using them to steer their way through similar situations, but, because their craft was flat and she would need both hands, she had no way of staying on board and paddle at the same time. Somehow, she wedged the paddle into a groove between two pieces of the raft and then clamped one leg over the top to keep it in place. She hoped there would be calmer waters ahead when she could use it. For now, it was just a question of clinging on for dear life.

Taron, she noticed, was using his paddle. He had jammed the lower parts of his legs into the grooves, allowing his upper legs and body to swing and sway in almost perfect time with the erratic motion of the rapids. Skilful manipulation of the paddle seemed to give them some control as they bounced between the rocks and fallen trees. It allowed Fen to concentrate on just holding on. Pella kept shouting – she had no idea what he was trying to say but took comfort from the fact that it meant he was still on board.

She had been scared many times before, but this was a different kind of terror. Water came at them from all directions and she struggled to keep her eyes open. When they were open, the view was not that appealing. As they hurtled down the river, rocks leapt out at them from nowhere and overhead branches threatened to decapitate them. White water that glinted invitingly in the distance threatened to engulf them as Taron tried to find a path through. They were thrown from side to side as the raft careered one way then the next. Several times Fen was launched into the air, her grip on the twine broken, only for her to miraculously land back down with a thump followed by a frantic scrabble to latch onto the twine again. On one section, she felt like a character in a cartoon, with the villain swinging her backwards and forwards over his head and slamming her down either side, as the raft nosedived into one wall of water after another. And all the time Taron kept his nerve and concentration, working the paddle to steer them clear of clusters of rocks that would signify the end, were they to hit them. She could not worry about Pella or do anything to help him. All her efforts were given over to staying on the raft.

Eventually, through the mists of boiling water, she caught sight of what looked to be a calmer section ahead. Pella spotted it too, a string of expletives signifying his relief. There was one last chicane to negotiate through some rocks which, compared to what they had been through before, looked straightforward. She reached down for her paddle which, to her great surprise was still there, stuck as it was between the wood. It had almost become a permanent part of the raft. Somehow, she yanked it out and used it to help Taron through the last section into the smooth water below. Pella had lost his paddle but did not seem overly concerned as he let out a whoop of joy, before collapsing flat out next to Fen.

She joined him there for a couple of minutes, their chests heaving and bones aching. Taron, apparently untroubled by the experience, adjusted his position slightly so that he could paddle on both sides and they continued on. Fen wanted to help but she could not move. Lulled by the gentle sway of calmer waters, she could have slept. She turned her head to watch scenery pass at a good, yet much more pleasant pace. The mountains, now hills, which flowed down into expanses of woodland and grassy areas, invited her to sit up and look around properly. In the far distance, she could just make out a silver dot which had to be the complex they had travelled from. Taron had been right to say it was a quick way to travel; they were miles and miles away from where they had started.

'You are recovered,' said Taron – a statement rather than a question.

'I think so,' said Fen.

'I'm not,' said Pella who was still on his back.

'Well done, Taron,' said Fen. 'For someone who has no water experience, you sure know how to pilot a raft.'

'I am a warrior.' It needed no further explanation. Indeed, it served to reinforce what Fen already knew which was what a formidable force Arrix and his warriors would have been on Earth had they prevailed. She was pleased they had one of them with them and on their side now.

But the moment of self-satisfaction was short-lived. Her head snapped to the left at the sound of a deafening roar. Whatever the source was had moved incredibly quickly as all she saw was a huge grey tail covered in scales slip into the water before disappearing under the surface.

Mackenzie

For the second time in the space of twenty-four hours, Mackenzie was bundled into a flyer. This time he was fully awake which made the experience all the more unpleasant. Jerome had it in for him and with two burly assistants for support was going to make sure that Mackenzie knew that. All three landed punches while he was strapped into a seat at the back of the hover with his hands tied behind. As Mackenzie, winded, doubled over, one of them shoved him back up again, thumping his injured shoulder. He was determined not to let them know how much it hurt, so he just clenched his teeth and waited for the pain to ease. It did not, much.

The seats were arranged in two rows facing each other and his assailants sat down in ones close by, but not directly next to him, he noted with just a tinge of satisfaction. The caution in their eyes betrayed their bravado. They were joined by two more men – obviously there for added muscle – and Odette. A blond, short woman in her fifties opened a door at the front and sat in the pilot's seat. Ruby was the last to get in and she took a seat near the front behind the woman. She nodded curtly as she walked past him, said nothing.

Before they had boarded, Mackenzie had spoken to Don using an anonymous link on a bracelet. His own had been taken off him, but he knew Don's pass code by heart and he was soon through. His friend sounded mightily relieved to hear his voice but, with a gun at his head, Mackenzie had no time for chitchat. He had been given a script which he read out directly to Don:

'I have been kidnapped by the organisation that carried out the attacks in the cities earlier. Make your way directly to the location of the MASH – alone – and we will meet you there. You will make no mention of this conversation to anyone else at all, otherwise more attacks will be carried out.'

Don had tried to ask a question. Predictably, he was cut off. Now, Mackenzie was on his way back to London, tied up, tired, in constant pain from the gunshot wounds, and very hungry. None of these things were likely to put him in the best of moods, yet he was not as angry as he might have been. He had had a short time to think and a plan was beginning to take shape. However, it relied on two things he could not control:

One: that there was a piece of quarton somewhere in the MASH.

Two: Fen being alive.

He was all too aware that both these things being in place was very unlikely. There had been nothing whatsoever connected to Garial left after the MASH had destroyed the bridge. On the other hand, he also knew that both Fen and the quartons had proved very resilient.

Plan A had to be viable because there was no plan B.

Actually, that was not quite true – plan B involved him somehow breaking his security straps and causing as much damage as he could to those around him, with the possible exception of Odette... whose eye he was trying to catch now. Getting her attention was proving difficult since she had spent the first ten minutes of the flight staring out of the window from her seat, two down from Ruby.

Mackenzie was very conscious that someone might have their eyes on him too at any point. He did not want to get the girl into trouble but, similarly, he needed to know whether she had any sympathy for him and the situation they were in. If she did have, she could be approached, given an opportunity. She was the technical brains behind much of what was going on – that could prove extremely useful if the other parts of his, now he thought about it, rather loose plan fell into place. He picked a moment when he was as sure as he could be that no one was directly looking at him, and then deliberately glanced over at Odette. He was in luck; her eyes flicked towards him, held his for a split second and then looked away. It was not conclusive, but Mackenzie thought he had seen enough there to suggest she could be swayed, at least. The question was which way: towards him or even further away. It would need careful handling, and he was not renowned for his light touch.

The local authorities would be on heightened alert after recent events, and airspace would be monitored. He guessed the flyer had some sort of cloaking device to travel from France across the channel and all the way to London without being detected. He was aware, through his military experience, that technology had been developed to make craft undetectable to heat sensors, as well as visually and sonically. He was sure that Ruby's organisation would well have made good use of such developments, especially with people around like Odette.

It was not long before Mackenzie's stomach told him the flyer was losing altitude. Ruby moved down to sit in a seat opposite him and addressed him for the first time in the flight.

'Be clear, Mackenzie. If Berretti has let on to anyone that we are coming, we will know about it long before he will be aware we do. That will result in another city being attacked. I hope your colonel has the brains to appreciate that.'

'Don't worry on that count. He knows who he's dealing with.' There was no use pretending that he did not, despite the statement Mackenzie had read to him not giving a name. Ruby might just as well have started it with, 'Klavon and Arrix have kidnapped me.'

'He will be alone,' Mackenzie added.

Ruby fiddled with her bracelet and tuned it to the pilot's visuals. 'Good. Guide us in, Mackenzie.'

A screen popped up in front of him. They were hovering over the Thames, approaching from the east, near what used to be the Thames Barrier. The city was vulnerable to tidal surges since the barrier had been destroyed in the Power Wars. As a result, the few new buildings that had been constructed were placed on higher ground. Mackenzie had been to London several times before, the last time with Fen and Sam. Little had changed since then, from what he could see. In truth, it was no longer a city and had not been for some time – just a collection of spread out buildings. Most of the ruins that had remained when Fen had been a scavenger there post-war had been cleared underground. But there was one small area that Mackenzie indicated for the pilot to hone in on.

'Coordinate D7C5,' he said. 'You can probably see the entrance to the building out the window.'

Ruby was watching intently. 'Really, Mackenzie? It's in there?'

Mackenzie nodded. 'Out of the way of prying eyes.' As the flyer got closer, he said, 'There's plenty of space to land, as you can see. Sod all round here.'

'Mackenzie,' said Ruby, 'you are full of surprises!'

'You know this place?'

'Possibly, Big Man. Just possibly.'

Ruby

<I've been here once, Klavon. Briefly. As have you.>

It was a department store. My previous body, Lee, lived here with Fen and the Westsider Scavengers. Run by a vicious man: Sal.

<Vicious, like you. I thought he was you.>

143

I remember. That was amusing.

<Don't gloat. I had many victories over you.>

But not the last one. I won the keystone, Arrix.

<May I remind you that it was not the last one? This goes on and if you want to go on too, I suggest you work with me. Now, I recognise the other entrance further down. It was an alternative route into the store where they lived. I came here looking for the real Lee because she knew where the keystone was. She hid it on the Friendship Bridge and showed me to it from here.>

Then you killed her.

<Correct. And you jumped right into her body. These coincidences of place, people and time are not coincidences, of course. This is where the keystone was hidden by Fen before Lee moved it. Mackenzie may not know of the connection, yet he chose to hide the MASH here.>

A good sign.

<Yes. This is where it will happen. This will be our base, right under the noses of these stupid humans. We will find that piece of quarton, and Fen will come. If she is alive and the quarton piece is here, she will come. Then we can have the final test, a last confrontation. We will have everything we need to win it – the weapon to destroy her, as much dark energy as we could possibly need and, of course, the coding. With her demise, the coding will be ours.>

Is this the point where you do your evil laugh, Arrix?

<No. You're the show off. I'll leave the theatrics to you.>

Part 3

Fen

Taron had spotted it too. 'That's not good,' he said.

'What do you mean, it's not good?' said Pella who, moments before had been on his back, was now on his knees, eyes wide, head turning from side to side.

'It's a Laric,' said Taron. 'A river dweller. Feeds on meat. A big one. They're all big.'

Fen had, instinctively, adopted a crouching position. 'Where is it now?'

'Under the boat. It will want to play first.'

'Play?' said Pella. 'What do you mean, play?'

'Five of our warriors explored this area before we came to Earth. One came back. I saw most of the attack afterwards.'

'It killed four of your warriors,' said Pella in disbelief, 'and you thought this was a good way to travel?'

'I said the journey was quick. I also said it would not be easy.'

'How does it attack?' asked Fen.

'They flew low over this river several times, searching for quartzite in the valley. It tracked them and could have struck at any time. It was playing. It waited, and then jumped out, pulled the craft down. After that, we're not sure. The surviving warrior was too badly injured to explain.'

Fen shifted uneasily. She caught sight of a shadow several metres below. 'I see it. How long did it play before it attacked?'

'Long enough for them to think it would not attack.'

'Suggestions, Taron, please,' said Pella. 'As quick as you can.'

'We attack it.'

'Wh... how?'

'You've lost your paddle, Pella?' said Taron.

'Yes... sorry.'

Taron leant back and undid the clasps on his leg extensions. The lower legs were no longer wedged between the wood of the raft and he started to flex them up and down, loosening them. He then placed the larger piece of wood he had used as a makeshift paddle on the joints between his upper and lower legs.

'I will try and make it a clean break. Be ready to stop the pieces going overboard and don't fall off as the raft shakes.'

With that, he took a deep breath and whipped up the lower legs. The momentum pushed him forward and he let out a grunt as his arms took his weight. The raft did rock, but not as much as Fen had expected, and the wood snapped into three pieces.

'Take the smallest one, Pella. Both of you, paddle to the shore as quickly as you can. That side.' He pointed to the opposite side of where Fen had, moments earlier, been admiring the scenery. The other side was a mixture of thick growth and sheer rocks, but Fen spotted a possible flat area that they could get out onto. 'Go as high as you can. Larics can move on land but cannot climb well. If you get to the top, look out for a mountain with ridges that go down like steps. That is your direction.'

While he was talking he had grabbed the two remaining pieces of wood and extended back to his full height. The process took some practice for young Garalians to master, but on land, it was

146

straightforward for adults: unclasp the lower legs, then push up from the upper legs (which had the small joint halfway up, precisely for this purpose) with one, almost violent, thrust upwards. It was the equivalent of a human doing a standing jump. The muscles were strong around that joint and warriors' ones would, no doubt, be especially strong. On a raft that wobbled, and under pressure from a possible attack, it took some doing. But Fen was not surprised to be looking up at Taron, still in his white garment which was soaked through from the recent exertions, looking as intimidating as any warrior she had seen, especially so with the two pieces of jagged of wood clasped in each hand.

Pella had already started to paddle with the piece of wood Taron had left for him and Fen joined him from the other side. She pointed out the possible landing point which, on this wide stretch of the river, was a good thirty metres away.

'What are you going to do, Taron?' she shouted over the noise of their paddles beating the water.

He did not reply. Instead, the raft lurched to her side. She turned round to see Taron midair, his leading arms about to hit the water.

'What's happened?' said Pella who was still frantically paddling.

'He said to attack it. I guess that's what he's gone to do.'

Neither pieces of wood were ideally shaped for paddling, yet they thrashed their way to safety. Soon they were close to the shore, so close Fen was debating whether she could reach out to one of the overhanging trees and haul them in for the last part. The water was no longer calm and they were, once more, buffeted by water, enough to suggest that there was a great deal of movement below the surface. At one point, Fen caught another glimpse of the tip of the Laric's tail, further back from where they had come. Of Taron, there was no sign.

Fen reached up to grab the branch when a sudden wave knocked her off balance. She was only saved from going in by Pella's quick reactions. He caught hold of her arm, in the process losing his paddle again.

'What is it about me and paddles?' he groaned as the wood floated away from the raft.

'Thanks,' she said. 'Just a bit closer and I think I can reach the branch.'

'Swap and let me try. You keep us steady with your paddle. Try and turn us... that's it. This way. Keep going... Got it!'

They were soon close enough to jump off. As Pella hauled the raft onto the small pebbly beach, Fen looked out onto the river in the hope she would catch sight of the warrior. The river was relatively calm.

She felt a nudge on her arm. 'You heard what Taron said: we need to get as high as possible.'

'We can't just leave him.'

'Think about it, Fen. If he's survived he'll find us. If he hasn't, we are that thing's next meal. Come on.' It was a harsh side of Pella she had not seen before, but he was right. Reluctantly, she started to look for a way up.

There was no path, not even a section where the undergrowth was vaguely lower or flatter than anywhere else. They had no option other than to head up what looked like the least difficult route.

From the start, it was tough going – a scramble over slippery, mossy stones hidden below the growth on the lower section, followed by rubble underfoot and tougher vegetation that did not give way much as they forced their way higher. Ten minutes or so of hard graft and they felt safe enough to stop to take a breath... and a drink. Fen had barely noticed her container was still strapped on. She wrinkled her nose at the first gulp and quickly realised she had the one with the stale tasting, added nutrition. Fortunately, Pella's was pure water, and she gratefully took a few mouthfuls when he offered it to her. He did the same from her container before swapping back

Fen shivered; the night was drawing in. She was still wet – a mixture of the soaking she had got on the river and sweat from the exertion of the climb. It would get much colder later and they would need some shelter before long. Thick bushes, some of them covered with thorns the size of hunting knives, surrounded them. Above them, rose tall palm like trees. There were no branches, but right at the top, massive orange leaves hung down like giants' tongues. The bark on their thick trucks was a blue-grey on the outside where still attached and a darker flecked brown where strips clung on. The flora was so like Earth in many ways, yet in others totally different. For some reason, the similarity bothered her.

'What now?' Pella said. It seemed a familiar, overused question.

'The only way we know which direction we're going is by continuing up. Taron had said we needed to get out the...' And she suddenly stopped. She could not say it: *The Brack*. She had felt a connection to it when they had talked about heading towards it

149

earlier, but had put it out of her mind. Now it was firmly at the front. These marshes Taron had warned about would be avoided if they continued up and they found a way out. They might even be lucky enough to see the mountain ridges which would guide them to the where the bridge could be. Yet...

'There's something I need to do,' she said, 'at the Brack. I need to see the Brack. Be there.'

'I thought the whole point was that we didn't go close to the Brack. Too marshy, inescapable, no way through. Dangerous. Mind you, everything's dangerous round here.'

'Pella, there's a lot I need to tell you, most of which doesn't make sense. I thought it was starting to, but now, for some reason, it doesn't. It will, if I can get to the Brack.'

He looked at her and she stared back. He was sodden, exhausted, scared, confused, everything she was. Yet, she could see in his eyes that he trusted her. And she trusted him.

'So that means...'

'Yes. We have to head back down to the river and continue along until we reach the Brack.'

'And what about the Laric?'

She smiled. 'It's not invited.'

Lessey

Had Lessey known that Ruby and her people were so close to the location of the MASH, she might have been feeling less smug than she was, as Don slammed her office door open. He stood at the entrance, glaring at her.

Lessey could do 'glares' well herself, but instead she smiled knowingly at him. 'Can I help you, Colonel?'

He advanced purposefully towards her desk. However, rather than staying on the other side of it, he walked round, spun her chair ninety degrees and pushed her on several metres, at speed, towards the window. Her arms and legs flailed helplessly, her stomach flipping, as she braced for impact. He was either a good judge of force and distance, or it was pure luck, since the chair slid to a halt, just short of the glass. Shaken, she put her hands on the arms of the chair and tried to stand, but he had already followed up and was standing right over her. She sunk back into the chair.

He took a couple of steps back and waited, fists in a ball, face crimson.

Lessey coughed and brushed away some imaginary dirt on her trousers then straightened some loose hairs on top of her head. Deliberately, she reached round to a hair grip at the base of her bun and adjusted it, all the while avoiding direct eye contact. Eventually, she looked directly at him.

'I'm not accustomed to being pushed around my own office in such a manner, Colonel Berretti. Do you have a reason for such violent behaviour?'

His calm voice belied his apparent fury. 'I thought we understood each other, President Lessey. I suggested that you did not take advantage of the Southern Alliance. Our role is as peacemakers. We – I – am here to help, to caution, to advise. I was open with you, hoping you had genuinely changed and you could be trusted. Deep down, I did not believe you had but, in the interests of peace, I had no real choice other than to share with you

151

the information we have on alien attacks. I did it in the hope you might, finally, have come to your senses about what is going on here.'

Lessey interrupted. 'And I am very grateful. I'm sure we will find it all very... educational.'

'It's not just supposed to be educational!' She noticed the slight crack in his voice. 'Every other nation in the world has seen that data. Ever since the incident by the Severn Bridge, your organisation has refused to engage fully. As soon as we agree to let you see every aspect, you take advantage and send your tech guys on a hunt for sources of dark energy.'

'Energy sources that the Southern Alliance has kept quiet from us. I can't help ask myself why that is.'

'Because they are not energy sources to be exploited for your personal gain – or ours, or anyone's. Don't you see? This is an alien driven attack. You are being deliberately short-sighted.' He shook his head and stretched his fingers before tightening them up again. It was pleasing to see him struggling to contain himself, although she did not much fancy another roller-skating trip round her office on her chair.

She struck a soothing tone. 'We had nothing to do with those attacks on the city and we have been open in sharing our data to prove that and help keep the peace.'

'And we've done our part by supporting you. What you've done here is disgraceful. Lives are at stake. Yours included.'

'Mine? I doubt that. Was there anything else, Colonel?'

'Plenty... Just a second.' He stopped and looked down at his bracelet. 'It's Mackenzie.' He took the call via his earpiece, a source of frustration for Lessey who was keen to listen to what was being said at the other end. Don said very little. 'Mackenzie! Where are you? Are you alright?' After that he said nothing and the call ended.

He looked up at Lessey. 'I need a flyer.'

'What for? What did Mackenzie say?'

'Nothing that should bother you.'

'He was kidnapped by my former Vice President. I think that should be of concern to me.'

'I need a flyer, President. I have a meeting.'

'With Mackenzie?'

'Do you have a flyer I can use?'

She sighed and then flicked her own bracelet. 'Shaw? Arrange a flyer for Colonel Berretti, will you?'

'Thank you. I'll be in touch.' Don turned on his heels and left.

She watched him go and then continued on the open link to Shaw. 'You will track it, won't you, Shaw? Let me know which direction he heads in and get another flyer ready. I fancy a little jaunt out of the office.'

Mackenzie

'Won't someone see us?' said Mackenzie. Intrigued by whether their flyer did have a cloaking device, he was fishing for information, but he was ignored. 'I'll take that as a no.' Either that or they were so confident, they did not care whether they were spotted or not.

They landed on a patch of concrete in a large bleak area of wasteland. This part of London had once been a thriving centre of commerce. Now it had an eerie, hopeless feel to it. Mackenzie half expected to see tumbleweed ghosting across the dirt, bumping over the small piles of rubble dotted around. They were metres away from a short ramp which led down to a set of thick grey metal double doors. This was the vehicular entrance situated at one end of the department store which provided access to the loading bay several floors underground.

Having been built mainly below the surface, the bulk of the store had withstood the blasts during the Power Wars and had subsequently become a safe haven for Fen and the other Westsider Scavengers. The little above ground that had survived the missile blasts had since been flattened, along with most of the rest of London post-war, as part of the English government's 'Clean Sweep' initiative.

Don had asked the Prime Minister to keep some Southern Alliance equipment in London, in case it was needed at a later date. Grateful for Don and Mackenzie's assistance to thwart the alien invasion and also prevent Lessey from gaining more ground in the west of England, the English were happy to oblige. It had proved a very secure place to keep the MASH.

Don had insisted on extra security to the doors – a seven digit pass code known only to him, Mackenzie and certain members of the Southern Alliance leadership team, plus handprint recognition requiring two of that number to be present. Mackenzie explained this as they approached the doors.

'The Colonel is on his way,' Jerome said. 'Do we wait?'

'No,' said Ruby. 'Odette: get us in.'

'Give me a minute,' Odette said, unhooking a bag that was slung over her shoulder. She examined the lock with the pass code then unscrewed the cover for the pad which verified the handprint. 'I need Mackenzie to put in the code first.'

'Don't you need his handprint?' said Jerome.

'No.'

'Mackenzie?' said Ruby. 'The code. And remember...'

'No funny business. Yes, I know.'

He had committed the number to memory, and said it aloud as Jerome tapped it in.

'Code accepted,' came a crackly automated voice. 'Hand authentications required.'

'Over to you, Odette,' said Ruby. 'Do your trickery.'

'Of course,' she replied and pulled out a hammer from her bag. She swung it hard at the centre point of the pad and the gates swung open. There was a snigger from a couple of the men in the group, quickly stopped by a glare from Jerome.

'I'm so glad we have your high-tech skills with us today.' Klavon's sarcasm cut through Ruby's comment. 'Okay, Mackenzie – lead the way.'

Jerome posted one of the men just inside the entrance and the pilot stayed with the flyer. The rest of them trooped inside and further down the slope. Lights flickered on as they walked and their footsteps echoed against the narrow concrete walls. There was a musty smell, not as strong as Mackenzie remembered when he was last here eleven months ago. The store had been closed off for many years prior to that visit and the smell then had been positively

155

rancid when they had got out of the MASH. He remembered feeling quite relieved when they had walked back up the ramp into the fresh air.

No one said a word until they were close to the bottom. The silence was broken by a loud beep on Jerome's bracelet. 'The Colonel has arrived at the top,' said Jerome. 'He seems to be alone.'

'Confirmed,' said Odette referring to her bracelet. 'No other air or land craft activity detected. Although...'

'Although what?' snapped Ruby.

'There is another flyer that has just left the other side of the channel about ten minutes behind. It followed a similar route over France. There are another two behind that one which have gone round and look like they might arrive from the east. They won't be the only flyers around today, but it's suspicious.'

'It's probably Lessey,' said Ruby. 'Send the details to Jerome to keep an eye on them. I'm going to need you and your magic hammer focussed on other work shortly. I do hope Colonel Berretti is not playing games with us.'

'He wouldn't do that,' said Mackenzie.

'Well, if the man who tried to end my life says that, who am I to argue? Send Colonel Berretti down, Jerome.'

They continued on until they could go no further. They had reached the loading bays where goods in were received by the store pre-war and where the scavengers used to organise their finds ready for dispatch out to their contacts. Mackenzie was not to know the importance of this area for the previous occupants. However, he was very aware of the importance of it now as he gestured to where the MASH sat underneath a tarpaulin in one corner of the large space.

'She's under there,' he said.

'She? You humans use the funniest of terms.' Ruby's slip of the tongue drew a puzzled look from Odette, Mackenzie noticed. He had been watching her closely for any signs of opposition towards Ruby. This was the first real hint that maybe she was not comfortable. Two of the men jogged over to the MASH and started to remove its cover. Jerome and the other man stayed firmly put next to Mackenzie.

The soldier in Mackenzie was nagging away, urging him to make a move. He might be able to deal with Jerome and use his weapon on the others, but the scientist and engineer in him told him to hold back. Crucial to all of this was that there might be a quarton on board so he would stick to his original idea and wait. Don would arrive shortly and that might give him another option.

Don's presence suddenly bothered him. Ruby could have got Don to send on details of where the dark energy sources lay without actually being there. No doubt, he already had. Was he there as another hostage, perhaps? Possibly or, more likely, he was there to be used by Ruby as a go-between.

'It really isn't that much of a looker, is it?' said Ruby walking around the front of the vehicle.

Mackenzie said nothing. On the face of it, it was ramshackle. The shell of an old hover truck with a gun and turret welded into place on top, it was never designed to invoke feelings of fear, but he had been at the controls when it had made a whole army of warriors, countless alien ships and a massive bridge disappear. He was only too aware of what it could do, which was why he would do anything to keep it out of Ruby's hands.

'Bring him over,' Ruby said, and he was pushed forward. 'Open it up, Mackenzie.'

'It's not locked. Side doors are easiest, although you can get in through the back.'

He looked up at the turret and gun and those last moments in the battle came to mind – hundreds of Garial ships circling above like a murder of crows, a suitable plural name if ever there was one for what Arrix had planned. His best friend had been taunted and abused by one half of the creature inside of Ruby and murdered by the other half, Arrix. Part of him would not hesitate to kill her, given the opportunity. Yet he knew that would never be enough to finish it. If he were to avenge Chuck's death and protect the future of this planet, it would need more, much more. It was a huge risk he was undertaking but a necessary one. He just prayed the quarton was somewhere on board the MASH.

If, at that moment, he had looked closely at Ruby's eyes, he would have seen a tinge of green light in them and realised that his prayers had already been answered.

Ruby

I can feel it.

<Of course you can, Klavon. It's metres away. I felt it as soon as we landed. It's not big, but it's definitely in there.>

You are a sensitive soul, aren't you?

<We're all connected, Klavon. It's just that some are more connected than others. Feel that?>

No.

<A touch... lighter than the hair on a feather.>

And you mock humans – stop talking like one with all these needless words.

<Their language to describe things is attractive... The coding in the quarton is not strong but it is there. Enough to draw her to us.>

What about Pella? We have spoken little about him. Is he a threat?

<He is weak. I'm surprised you lost so many times to him.>

Don't, Arrix. You push this partnership to its limits. Anyway, he was your man. You chose him. He must have uses.

<He does. If he is with her, he will help bring her to us from wherever she is. He will be no threat. But it is necessary that we will all be together at the end.>

How do you know all this?

>My instinct is rarely wrong.>

I could challenge you on that. However, in the spirit of teamwork, I will set an example and just urge caution. You are overconfident.

<Not over – just confident. Both of us are. That is why we do what we do and why we will be successful.>

So, what next? Wait?

<Yes, we wait here. It feels right. It's where it started.>

No, it started much earlier, in the Savannah on Earth... I remember. A painful memory. Most of them were.

<Yes. That was a good one, in the heat and dust of the desert. Your first loss. It helped shape you and gave you the motivation to do what you do so well: provide anger and cruelty. I did you a favour.>

I was motivated before that.

<True. Do not hold it against me. Yes, I killed your Garialian family, but you have to see the bigger picture.>

Eternal life.

<Exactly. Together we will have it.>

What did you mean it started here?

<For Fen, it's where it started. I should have guessed this was where they hid the vehicle. She kept the last quarton here and she will be drawn back to here. This tiny piece from that quarton is the key. Part of the keystone.>

You make no sense.

<Trust me, Klavon. I do know. We wait here.>

Well, if we're going to be waiting here for a while, I suggest we have a bit of fun.

<With the detons, you mean? I see no harm in that. It will keep everyone on their toes.>

'"On their toes" Arrix? I hate to say it, but you're becoming more and more human with every sentence.

<Don't worry, Klavon. I'll never forget where I came from. I can't.>

Fen

They tried to follow the route they had taken in reverse, but the vegetation had sprung back up into position, something Fen was pretty sure Earth plants did not do in such a short space of time. It made her much more wary of the plants than she had been on the way up, concerned they might exact revenge for the trampling they had received and were about to receive again. More than once, her foot got caught on something she could not see, raising her heart rate several notches. The loose rocks and slippery patches of mud they had fought through hampered them further, balance being the sticking point going down. Then the second star disappeared completely and it was only its sister's much further away and lower in the heavens which provided any light at all.

'This is hopeless,' Fen said. 'Maybe I was a bit hasty in saying we go back down straight away.'

She could not see Pella's face, let alone his expression, but his voice sounded weary. 'You did what you felt was right – and it still might be. But I've no idea how far away from the river we are.'

'Nor me.'

'Do you think Larics can see better in the dark than we can?'

'What am I thinking of? This is mad. I'm shattered. We both need to rest.'

'I could quite happily collapse right here.'

'Maybe we should. The ground feels soft enough underfoot.' She squinted in the darkness, willing her eyes to milk every precious drop of light available. 'We're in a clear section, I think.'

She reached down and felt the ground. 'Feels like grass, slightly damp...'

'Just like the back of a Laric is when out of water.'

She snorted a laugh. Her brother was good for her. He always had been. She needed his humour and positivity. She needed him and, she knew too well now, always had done. They may have had disagreements in the past and been on opposite sides when searching for the quartons, but they were destined to be together. Pella knew it and she knew it.

'I kind of feel it would have got us by now if it wanted to,' she said.

'Or it's just waiting for us to get closer.' There was no humour in that statement. That could be true. 'I think we have little choice. We're tired and we can't see much. We could go a little higher up to be sure?'

'I can't hear the river or smell it. Let's just risk it. Shifts?'

'You sleep first. I'm okay to keep an eye out... or rather a nose and an ear out.'

'No, I...'

She felt his hands on her shoulders gently pushing her downwards. 'Take a swig of drink and food, if you can bear it, then sleep. I'll wake you when I can't keep my eyes open anymore.'

She tried to argue but could not stop her knees buckling under his pressure, and she sank to the floor. She was vaguely aware of him offering something to her lips, yet she was too exhausted to even open them. After that, she was dead to the world.

She woke up to a musical trilling from all around that gently massaged her ears. It was beautiful and almost lulled her straight off to sleep again.

'Morning.' Pella's voice close by made her open her eyes. Bleary-eyed, she sat up. He was sitting behind her happily munching away on something. 'Don't know what's singing away, but it's rather lovely, isn't it? These are great, by the way.' He opened his hand. 'I've no idea if they will kill me but, to be honest, I don't care. I'll die happy... and with a full stomach.' On his hand were three small yellow melons – rather, they looked like melons, mini versions of the ones she and Sam used to grow in their garden in Australia. They always needed plenty of water, she recalled, something she felt guilty about using in a dry part of New South Wales. Fen wanted to be more careful with the precious resource, a habit from her scavenging days, but Sam always said that, because their water came from a natural spring nearby, it would just flow past and would be wasted if they did not use it. Sweet and delicious, Martha soon took to them when she was old enough to try them, by which time Fen had convinced herself it was virtually the same as drinking the water, they were so juicy.

'Try one,' Pella said. 'They come from that weird plant over there.' He pointed to what looked like a stick with Christmas baubles attached. About Pella's height, there were no leaves, just fruit. It bent downwards at the top where the stem was thinner but the fruit was no smaller.

'What made you eat one?' she said picking one up and examining it cautiously.

163

'I think I've had them before. Anyway, we're busy taking risks at the moment, aren't we?'

She took a sniff and before she knew it, it was in her mouth. The texture surprised her at first. It was chewy on the outside, and then there was a burst of paradise as the liquid centre bathed the inside of her mouth. She looked at Pella and he grinned. She too had had them before on Garial, on a trip out to the countryside with her big brother in a bubble. They had stopped by a stream that ran through a glade and had had more or less the same conversation as they were having now. She could see his Garalian face now willing her on, daring her to eat them.

She swallowed the remaining pieces in her mouth and immediately reached out for another one. 'Can't stop once you've started, can you?' he said. 'Go ahead, eat your fill.'

'I will.' There was nothing about them that said that they would do any harm. In fact, they seemed to have the opposite effect; she felt awake and full of energy.

It was early. The light was dull, not helped by the cloud cover she noticed as she looked up. She was still damp from the previous day but, strangely, not at all cold. She had slept all night which meant that Pella had not. That bothered her.

'You should have woken me.'

'How could I when I was asleep myself,' he said sheepishly. 'I tried to stay awake but couldn't manage it. He held up his non eating hand in apology. 'I would have taken full responsibility had we both been eaten during the night.'

'We can add guard to the list of jobs you can't do, along with doctor and oarsman.'

'Hey! Who got us onshore at the end?'

Fen stood up and looked around. Through a gap in the vegetation, she could just about see the river. They were high enough, probably, to avoid the clutches of the Laric, but goodness knows what other dangerous animals lurked round these parts. They had taken a risk – as Pella had said – and got away with it. Now they had to take advantage of their luck.

'What's the plan to get to the Brack?' he asked joining her on his feet. He wiped his hands, covered in juice, on his trousers. 'I know I keep asking about plans, and I realise you might not have one, but in case you do, what is it?'

'We get to the riverbank and turn left. Stay on land as much as possible. Where we can't, we go in and wade or swim. When we reach the marshland, we stop.'

'And we pretend we haven't seen any river creatures that can take out Garalian cruisers?'

'Yep. We have no choice. Do you still want to come?'

'Try and stop me.'

They stuffed their pockets with more of the tiny melons and set off, steering in a diagonal direction to the left of the river (when they could see it) to cut the corner. As they neared the water, the nerves started to jangle and they were both on heightened alert. They took it in turns for one of them to lead the way and choose the path, while the other kept an eye out for danger from behind, paying particular attention to the river. It was reckless – Fen knew it – but necessary. She kept having mad visions of coming across Taron, sitting casually on a stone by the river, a trophy head of the Laric slumped in the shallows at his feet. It was unrealistic because

165

the odds of survival were hugely stacked against him. Yet, she could not feel sad – by no means had she written off the warrior.

For the large part, their luck held. There was no path, but the vegetation gave way as they ploughed their way through. Where the terrain became too difficult, they had to make a decision whether to cut inland or to step into the river and it seemed their judgements were good each time. There was one particularly tricky situation when a fast flowing stream which ran through a gully and emptied into the river blocked their path. It ran through at such a pace it would have meant them swimming out quite a distance into the river to avoid being caught up in the turbulence. Neither fancied that, yet there was no easy point for them to wade through further up stream because of the steep sides of the gorge, and it was just too wide to jump. The drop into it was less than two metres; not one she fancied.

Fen could not help but be impressed by Pella's casualness in dealing with it. 'If we can stand up that old tree trunk on one end then push it down across the gorge, we can crawl across it. See those two rocks there on the other side? Aim for the gap and it will help to hold it in place. It might not work. But we have nothing to lose.'

He was right; there was nothing to lose and everything to gain, particularly when, miraculously, the log fell into position first time. Fen kept her eyes firmly on the other side as she straddled the log and hauled her body across the small gap. Pella had a more difficult time of it, the log rolling slightly from side to side with no one on the departure side to steady it, but they were soon safely over and could continue their journey.

After a while, they lost track of how long or how far they had walked. With both Garalian stars covered by cloud and no obvious change in the quality or direction of light, their progress could only be measured by the aching in their feet. There were plenty of opportunities to drink fresh water and they found more of the same fruit which gave them enough energy to keep going. It was plentiful, as were other types, but Fen did not want to take the chance of trying something else that could badly affect them. If luck was indeed with them, why risk doing anything too stupid to change it?

She soon realised that luck had nothing to do with it.

Because of a particularly open stretch of water, they decided to take a diversion further up the mountain that they had been skirting. They had been under the cover of trees for most of the day and this route was taking them through a particularly overgrown section, away from the river. The atmosphere around them had become heavier. It was muggy, sticky and breathing had become more difficult. More importantly, there was a danger that they might lose the river so Fen was relieved when she spotted a clearing and the potential to check their position. As they stepped out and looked down, there was no sign of the river at all. They were in a totally different valley, one where the fast flowing river was replaced by marshland.

Any thought that she had any control whatsoever of the coding was immediately crushed. If she was the one who was actually calling the shots, she would have known how she was going to feel when she arrived at what she now knew was the marshlands of the

Brack stretching out before them and she would never have gone there.

She soon realised why she had not been able to remember much about this place. She had blocked out what had happened here for a very good reason.

Lessey

Lessey rubbed her eyes with both hands and then looked down at the sea. It used to be the busiest shipping lane in the world. Now hardly any sea traffic used it. It would take decades to build up that level of trade again after the Power Wars. There were not enough people in any of the European countries left to need it.

She lost herself in the greenness of the water for a short while. She needed a break before turning her full attention onto what Don was up to, having spent the last twenty minutes taking calls from leaders of various nations demanding why she had stolen data from the Southern Alliance. Most of them were questioning the evidence she had provided that she had nothing to do with the deton attacks on the basis that, if her organisation was capable of theft, it was capable of falsifying evidence. She had said more or less the same to each: that she was as shocked as they were about the attacks, that detons were vile weapons which the French-Irish Alliance would never use and that she was only seeking the data that had been wrongfully withheld from her in the past. And no, she did not believe aliens were involved. The attacks had been conducted by another nation, which made the conversation with the Chinese Ambassador considerably more awkward than with the others.

The water below was called the 'English Channel' by the English and 'La Manche' by the French. Typical that the English had to claim it in their name. The French were a little more laid back about it and had called it 'La Manche' for centuries – 'The Sleeve' – because of its similarity to that part of a garment... apparently. She had never quite got that based on the maps she had seen. Although her native country of Ireland was aligned with the French, she had never been able to understand them. It did not matter much, providing they did what she told them to, which they did... mostly. Geron had been an exception. He had double-crossed her and he would pay for that, eventually. But she was not after him now; he did not have the brains or the balls to be any real threat.

She was focussed on Don who had taken the call from Mackenzie and gone to him. Whoever had Mackenzie was not only behind the attacks; they also held the key to unlocking this huge energy source. Yes, she had the locations now – how to tap into it was what she needed. Don would lead her to the people that could do it. Backup, if required, was not far behind her flyer, taking a different route to London, Don's obvious destination.

'Not long now, President,' said Shaw from the pilot's seat in front of her. 'Berretti won't be aware we are following as we disabled his tracker, although the English will know, of course.'

And no doubt whoever held Mackenzie captive, she thought.

She was not worried about the English tracking them. They were weak and unimportant. Mackenzie's captors were the concern – exactly who they were, needed pinning down. Her theory that the Southern Alliance was leading on this seemed less likely;

169

kidnapping one of their own and involving Geron just did not hold water. They were unwitting partners who were not driving this. The Chinese Ambassador had seemed genuinely shocked by the deton attacks but that did not mean they were not involved. There was the possibility that it could be a group working within China, outside of the Chinese government, or even working across governments. Lots of possibilities and she was getting closer to the answer. She could feel it in her old bones.

Shaw interrupted her train of thought. 'He's on course for the old centre of the city, President.'

'What's around there?'

'Nothing much. As you know, the PM has set up his headquarters in the north part of the city. There are medical units dotted all round with supporting admin, accommodation and other facilities in various pockets, but nothing within a few kilometres of the centre.'

'How far behind us is the backup?'

'Seconds, if we need it. We've been cruising.'

Lessey looked down again – even at cruising speed they would be over London shortly. Already the sea had been replaced by what the English were hoping would once again be its 'green and pleasant land'. It was heading in the right direction, although habitation was still low south of London.

'Let me know when Berretti has landed.'

Shaw glanced down at his controls. 'He's coming down now. Circling... circling... Okay, he's taken a holding position... just in the old Soho area. Dropping... and he's down. I've sent you the exact location.'

Lessey remembered that area well from a long time ago. It used to be very popular, packed with bars, restaurants and shops. She had had many an enjoyable day, and night, there in her youth. It was a great place – providing you had plenty of energy, and deep pockets. She had splashed out a fortune on one trip during a spending spree. What was the name of that store she had gone to? It would not come to mind. She did remember it had been very happy to take the money of a teenager with an eye for fancy clothes.

'Are we close enough to get a visual on him?'

'Not yet. With nothing else round here, he'd see us too.'

Would that really matter? Surely he was not fool enough to expect they would not be following him.

'Any response to us from the English?'

'Nothing aerial yet. They're probably tracking from the ground. Hang on. I have spotted something though.'

'What is it?'

'I'm not sure. Launched from the south, from our unit in Calais. It's one of our missiles.'

'One of our missiles?' The French-Irish alliance was not blessed with much military hardware – no nation was, or should have been. Lessey, however, had insisted on maintaining a very small stock of precision, medium impact missiles, just in case.

'Got it now. It's heading east, on course for... for... no!'

'What?' Lessey unbuckled from her seat and hurled herself forward so she was bent over Shaw's shoulder looking at the same visuals he was. She was just in time to see one of her flyers, in a holding position just off the east coast, before it disintegrated into an orange and white ball of flame. 'No!' she shouted.

'It's gone.'

'Patch me through to the other one.'

'I can't. It's blocked.'

'Well, get me Barrow.'

'Everything's blocked.' Shaw had one hand up to his ear while the other frantically swiped and pushed across his control panel. 'Nothing.'

'You must be able to get hold of someone.'

'I can't get any communication link out. We're on our own.'

The girl's voice came into her head again. The voice that sounded like a young child yet spoke like Lee. No, not possible...

Not expecting her major to answer, she expressed her frustration and uncertainty. 'Who is doing this?' Detons, her own missiles taking down one of her flyers... this was some organisation she was dealing with. She needed to regroup. 'Get us home, Shaw, and fast.'

'Yes, President. Ah, I've got a connection now. An incoming call...'

'Who from?'

'I'm not sure.'

'Put it through.'

There was a high-pitched tone and then a voice. 'President Lessey?' The girl sang her name. 'Can you hear me?'

The girl. She half expected it, yet she was thrown. 'What do you want?'

'What do I want? Oh, nothing much, really. Just a bit of fun... while we wait.'

'Fun?'

'Yes, fun. Byeee!'

Shaking now, Lessey turned to Shaw who was struggling with the controls. 'I've put it on manual, but it's not responding.'

'You have to get us out of here, Shaw, now!'

'I'm trying, believe me, I'm trying.'

She could see he was, yet she could also see there was little point. On the visual to his right, two small dots appeared on the map. One headed east and then quickly changed direction to the north. The other headed directly north, adjusting slightly as it moved so it was heading straight for London.

She did not need three guesses to work out who was the target.

Ruby

<Fun?>

Yes, Arrix. As I said, just a bit of fun.

<You're wasting missiles. We might need them.>

We won't need them. You've got it all under control, remember? You know what's going to happen. In the meantime, I thought I would play. Why waste the time Odette took to hack into Lessey's systems?

<It took her five minutes, two weeks ago. We shouldn't be drawing attention to ourselves with explosions.>

See them as distractions.

<I thought you were going to play, as you put it, with the detons. We still need President Lessey. She has done a good job of stirring things up in this world. I don't want to dispose of her yet.>

Are you sure? That's a shame.

<Yes. Bring her to us.>

Can I still blow up their other flyer?

<I can see no harm in that. I guess it might make her even easier to handle. Just do it quietly.>

You're too kind. I'll leave it to the last second before I give her the good news that she's been saved.

Fen

Same place, different view. Different time. Fen knew all this, yet she was living it now.

The marshes had not yet been formed. The landslides that would block the entrance to this valley and take the river on its modern course were events of the near future. For now, the river flowed gently through the valley, feeding crops and livestock for the farmers to benefit from. As on Earth in the earlier centuries, Garial was clean, fresh and under populated for the resources it gave up.

Fen watched her former self perform the everyday chores expected in the small community, one of the many that shared the bounty along the valley. She saw similarities and experiences to lives she had lived on Earth; everyday ones like washing, tending to animals, doing the hard graft of digging, ploughing, picking produce, as well as the gentler, more enjoyable pleasures like talking, sharing food, swimming and, of course, loving. A simple life. Her first life. She was not Rana, nor one of the ten or fifteen that preceded Rana. Not the one that gave up the coding and handed it over to the soul that would become Arrix. This life she was watching started as a life that would end forty or fifty orbits in

174

the future – just as it should do. Just like everyone else's life should do. A good, long, healthy and happy life.

But the decision she took at the waterfall that day changed everything in ways she could not have possibly predicted. How could she? Hindsight, as they say, is a wonderful thing. Now she could see the misery her decision would bring, not just to her and not just to the three other souls – Arrix, Pella, Klavon – who would suffer with her. The misery it would bring to her planet, to Earth and possibly to more planets. It all came down to the decision she took on this day at the Brack – her community, the Brack. She was ultimately responsible for the destruction of that too – much later – as the sea put down a marker for one of its claims and turned it to marshes. If she had gone down a different route, she would not have been so connected to the souls of Arrix whose greed and hunger for power would ruin the environment in her world.

Fen could not change the decision, just as she could not change anything that happened in any of her other past lives. She wanted to shout to her old self: 'Don't! Don't!' But it would do no good; she was not there. She had to just watch and endure the agony of the choice she made that day and live forever with its consequences.

'Fen! Fen!' She was aware Pella was shouting close by. She was stock still and he had hold of her arms, shaking them hard. As his face slowly came into focus, she could see panic in his eyes.

'Thank God for that. You're back with us. Here sip this.' He held the container to her lips and poured, but the water seeped down her front as she kept her lips firmly shut. He stopped, slung the container over his shoulder and, with both hands still on her arms, guided her to a fallen tree trunk where he lowered her down.

'You were gone,' he said. She could hear his words, see the marshes in front of her, yet could not respond. 'You just stood there, frozen. Your eyes – they went all strange. Blank, nothing behind them. Then you started talking. I couldn't understand a word or bring you out of it and then, suddenly, you were back. Here...' With one arm still holding her steady, he reached across for the container. 'Drink something, please. Show me you're with it again. That was just too scary.'

With enormous effort she moved her eyes towards him and nodded. She opened her lips, hoping to convey to him that she was ready for a drink now. He understood and held up the container again. This time she took several mouthfuls – a raging thirst suddenly all over her. He poured until she finally tilted her head forward so that he would stop.

'Better?' he asked.

She nodded again and followed it with a quiet, 'I'm okay.'

'You said you needed to come here. Is that what you expected to happen, whatever that was?'

She started to form a reply, but was violently overcome with nausea which hit her from nowhere. There was a great heaving in her stomach and she was spectacularly sick. A brief pause, and then, she was sick again and again, each retch seeming to produce a bucketful of grey coloured vomit. With one hand, she squeezed Pella's, desperate for relief. But, even with nothing left inside her, she continued to convulse, her body apparently intent on dispelling every last drop from within. Her muscles around her waist cried out in agony and still it went on until, just when she could bear it no more, it stopped, leaving her drained, shaking and covered in sweat.

She was aware of being lifted and carried a short distance before being placed carefully onto something soft. She lay there, breathless still, her stomach, at last, was easing. Her head was aching though – dehydration, for sure – and she knew she had to get some water into her, if at all possible. She tried to lift her head, grateful that Pella placed his hand underneath for support. 'Water,' she managed to croak, but he was already there with the container once more at her lips.

'Little sips,' he encouraged. 'Don't want to see much more of that stuff. I wonder what caused it. Hope it wasn't those melon things.'

She knew it was not anything she had eaten. That had been her body reacting to what she had experienced, an attempt to dispel the guilt and shame she held inside of her. But it was nothing like enough. Whatever she did now, however hard she tried, it would never be enough to make up for what she had done at the Brack. This journey back to Martha, to be with her and to be a good mother could not possibly compensate for that choice she had made on that day. No amount of right choices now – saving Martha, saving Pella, Taron... even saving the world could not put it right. For it had not been a choice between good and evil. Not at all. It had been a choice between having the coding and not having the coding.

She had chosen to have the coding.

And she had chosen to kill her family to get it.

177

Part 4

Mackenzie

'Show Odette how it works,' Ruby said. 'Don't go in and don't touch anything. Just explain.'

'Alright,' said Mackenzie. 'I can do most of it from the driver's door at the front then talk through the workings if you open up the side panel. I suggest you don't try to operate from down here in the loading bay. It can be done in enclosed spaces, but accuracy is better if you are out in the open.'

'You wouldn't just be saying that to make us go up top where we might be more of a target, would you?'

He was, partly because he did not feel at all safe down here with these people. 'No. The MASH draws on the closest dark energy source, plus the more pure it is, the more powerful it is. It operates better in open space. Next to the portal was ideal. Nothing to get in the way.' He looked for a reaction from Ruby and Odette to the lie he was peddling about the purity. It was well-known that dark energy was all around and could be extracted from anywhere. The concentration points, one of which was the portal near the Severn Bridge, acted like magnets, attracting huge amounts of dark energy from all around. Chuck had never worked out how or why they did that; it was enough to know that they did and Mackenzie had since been able to identify other similar points worldwide.

'Do you have the locations of the other dark energy concentrations from Don yet?' Ruby stared blankly at him. She was giving nothing away. 'From memory,' he continued, the closest point of decent concentration – not as strong as at the Severn Bridge – is east of here at what was Tilbury, the old docks. There's another one north of London, a long way up on the Yorkshire Moors somewhere and quite a few offshore in the Atlantic.'

'You are being very cooperative, Mackenzie,' said Ruby. 'Should we be suspicious?'

'Isn't this what you wanted? Complete submission from me in exchange for saving lives?' The anger in his voice was not forced.

'True... Okay. Well, the information about this place, Tilbury, and the northern location fits with what Berretti has sent through. So we need you now to explain to Odette how it can be accessed.'

'You do realise that Chuck set up a lot of equipment to allow the Severn Bridge one to be used efficiently? We needed to be close. I'm not sure how well it will work from here to Tilbury, say. It must be twenty kilometres from here. It might not work at all.'

Mackenzie was pushing the boundaries of how much he would be believed. Yes, the marriage between the MASH and the portal at the bridge had been very efficient, and it was more so because they were right next to each other. Chuck was able to easily get the two machines to talk, allowing control to be switched back and forth. That was partly why they had taken the MASH directly to the site. It was harder to draw on dark energy remotely; easier to get the best use out of it if the natural magnet was monitored and controlled by the equipment that Chuck had installed. Harder at their current location but not impossible.

Unfortunately for Mackenzie, the Arrix within Ruby knew a little about that. She indicated for Mackenzie's two minders to push

Mackenzie down onto the floor so that he was sat, legs outstretched, his hands still behind his back. She ushered the others away and then walked behind Mackenzie. Even with him on the ground, she had to stand on tiptoes to whisper in his ear. 'Mackenzie... Arrix has a message for you. He wants me to tell you that he knows you are not being totally honest here. He remembers, long before you humans had developed so much as a grain of intelligence, his scientists being able to tap into that portal without any machinery from trillions of kilometres away. I believe this Tilbury place, twenty or so kilometres is considerably closer than Garial. Correct?'

Mackenzie had realised he had not played this as well as he could have done. He tried to backtrack. 'Correct. I'm just saying it would not be as straightforward.'

'Oh, now I see. Not as straightforward. That's not the impression we got. I think you are delaying things, trying to make it more complicated than it actually is.

There was a moment when Mackenzie could not see Ruby or hear her, and then she whispered in his ear again. 'The Klavon within me did not need an excuse to have more fun with the detons, but he's just been given one. Do you know anyone in Lisbon?'

'Don't. Please don't. I am cooperating. I'm doing what you want me to.'

'This is just a little reminder that we mean business. Jerome, hook into our colleagues outside Lisbon, will you? '

Lessey

Lessey sat back down in her seat behind Shaw and puffed out her cheeks. She had given up; told herself she had lived a long life, tried to convince herself she had done her best throughout and if she died now, so what? The 'so what?' part she did not feel happy about. 'So what?' suggested she did not care if she died now or not. That was not true; she did very much care. Despite her old age, she had a lot more living in her and, specifically, something to finish off. The missile heading for her flyer now was not going to let her do that and that made her feel angry. Life was not fair.

She glanced at Shaw who had not given up. He was still intent on trying to work out how to evade the missile. He was surrounded with visuals – communication links that did not work, flyer controls that would not respond and a mini weapons system onboard that was probably better at scaring sheep than it was at destroying missiles.

Would she be remembered fondly? Did she care if she was or was not? No and no were the answers to those two questions. Lessey sighed again – it was pointless, yet there was something beautiful about her last act as President being blown up by one of her own weapons.

The look on Shaw's face as he turned round suggested that he definitely did not want to die. 'This is it!' he said, and then he did something she had not seen anyone do for a long time: he closed his eyes and prayed. There was nothing more to be done. Lessey grabbed hold of her armrests, hunched her shoulders and closed her eyes.

181

But the impact did not come. She stayed frozen to the seat, her white knuckles shaking uncontrollably. A few more moments passed and she could bear the tension no longer. Surely it should be over by now? She opened one eye. Still the end did not come. She was startled by the noise of Shaw pushing some manual buttons above his head.

'Where is the missile? Why aren't we dead?'

'I've no idea. It should have hit us a minute ago. I still have no communication links and no power to make us move.'

'They've changed their mind. They've realised how important I am and decided the fallout internationally will be huge. They've lost their bottle.'

'You might be right, President. Thank God for that.'

'It's not him you need to thank... it's me. I...'

She did not finish, there was a sudden thunderous whooshing noise, a second's pause and then an enormous bang.

Ruby

<That is such a childish trick to play, Klavon.>

We're supposed to be a child, aren't we? Anyway, you can't stop me. I'm going to scare the life out of them, and then I'll check what's going on in Lisbon.

Ruby adjusted the output volume on her bracelet to full, made a loud whooshing sound into the microphone then put her bracelet hand next to the MASH and thumped the side of the vehicle with her other hand. There were two loud screams that echoed through the large room.

Come on, Arrix. You have to admit that was funny.

<Get Odette to bring them in before Lessey dies of a heart attack.>

Okay, will do. Can I tell Lessey where the missile actually went when she gets here?

<With one other flyer in the area? I think she will have worked that one out already.>

Fen

Fen claimed another log at the other end of the small clearing, away from the mess strewn all over the ground. She would welcome some rain to wash away the dirt and smells. However, the sky was clear and the Garalian suns were performing the last stages of their heavenly dance, signalling the end of the day.

With traces of vomit still, her mouth tasted foul, even after swilling it with water and spitting out. Not even a mouthful from the container with the taste of the out of date nutrients made a difference to the sick that felt like it was seeping into her gums and rotting her teeth. She could not face eating yet so passed on the fruit that Pella offered. At least she was feeling well enough to think about how to improve how she felt. A few minutes earlier when she was doing her devil child impression, she would have gladly taken death. Yet death had not been on offer, and nor would it be for a while yet, she suspected.

She was definitely feeling a little stronger and less nauseous, although she had spent much of the recent hour or so with her head tucked between her knees. Pella had waited to one side, picking leaves from a thin broken branch and throwing them aside while he gazed into the distance. Every now and then he would turn around and check on her, smile sympathetically, and then return to his study of the marshlands. He did not press her. He was the big brother she knew of old – considerate, caring, and loyal, always with time for her – only with a different face. He had been more than patient. She had promised she would tell him some things when they reached the Brack. Well, they had reached the Brack and now she knew enough – not everything but enough – to give him the explanation he deserved. She took a deep breath and beckoned him over.

She began slowly. 'Pella. You and I are Garalian siblings.'

'Yes. Rana and Pella – the dynamic duo,' he said smiling broadly as he approached. 'And we've stayed connected on Earth.'

'Yes. Sometimes close, sometimes distant, but always connected, even if we were on different sides.'

His face clouded over. Throwing the branch to one side, he took a seat on a stone opposite her; his hands clasped together, his face serious. 'Yes, that bothers me, a lot. I don't know why I always did what Arrix wanted.'

'You had no choice.'

She had had a choice, though. Right at the very start, she had made her decision, long before the Garalian Bridge and the quartons had taken them to Earth. She reached out for his hand, squeezed it gently and then tapped it before moving her own away.

'You know how it works? How we're joined and how we keep living?'

'Through the quartons. The coding in it links us together. How, I've no idea.'

'I can explain some of the how parts. At least, I'll do my best to make sense of it.' The 'why' was the real tricky part. She took a deep breath. 'The coding is a living thing... sort of. I found it here... at the Brack. Somewhere down there, in fact.' She pointed in the direction of the marshes. 'I can't say exactly where as it's all changed. This didn't used to be marshland.'

'Wait: you found it? What do you mean you found it? When?'

She dipped her head down and found a patch of ground to look at. 'A long, long time ago.'

'How long?'

'Thousands and thousands of orbits ago.'

He leant forward and gently lifted her chin up with his fingers so she had to look at him.

'Thousands of orbits ago. As Rana?'

'No, before that. Long before that.'

He put his hands on his thighs, shook his head and stood up. She watched and waited. She had hoped she had been able to tell him the whole thing in one short narrative, but it was not working out that way. Her hesitancy annoyed her, and she could not find the words she needed. Pella took a couple of strides away with his back to her, turned round and then sat down again.

'I don't understand, Fen. All the reincarnations happened when we were on Earth. Maybe you are getting confused with the lives we led there. Maybe you lived somewhere like the Brack on Earth.'

'I'm sure I did live somewhere like this. I'm not getting confused, though. Look, Pella. I didn't know this until we got back to Garial. It's come to me slowly, starting at the waterfall by the complex.' She knew she had missed out a lot – about how she felt she could control the coding, how she had been responsible for bringing Pella and Taron to Garial with her. How she felt that she might be almost invincible now. It was relevant but not as important as the story she was trying to tell. 'I lived many lives before I was Rana. My first life was right here, at the Brack.'

'I thought this hell we keep living over and over again all started when we went to Earth.' He picked up a stone and angrily launched it over the edge of the clearing onto the slope below. She heard a clatter as it hit something and rolled away.

'In some ways it did. That was a new phase, based all around Arrix's control of the quartons.'

'You're not making much sense, Fen.' He picked up a couple of smaller stones and rubbed them anxiously between his palms.

'You lived before, too – you were reincarnated before you were Pella, just as I was,' she said.

'Not possible. I'd have remembered something before now. I remember quite a lot from my past lives on Earth so why wouldn't I remember about lives here?'

'You still might.' But not too much, she hoped. Not all of the detail about what happened here. Knowing what she did would be more than enough.

'So if we're both these super beings, capable of reincarnation over and over again on different planets, who else is? Arrix, Klavon, I presume? Anyone else?'

'Arrix and Klavon, yes. No one else.'

'How do you know that? Why have we got the rights to this special skill and no one else has?'

'Because no one else has the coding. We do. You've felt it?'

'Well, yes.'

'It's in you, like it's in me and Arrix and Klavon.'

'But no one else?'

'No.' She knew he needed more information. The scientist in him demanded more: evidence, facts. He needed to know how it all began. She could tell him that. As painful as it was, she had to.

'We were a family, living a similar life to the one we had in the stack as Pella and Rana. We had a mother and a father and you were my brother. We were in a community leading a simple life. No technology to speak of and then...' She hesitated. Was this why she did what she did? Had she seen it as a chance to improve things for everyone around? Was she just thinking of others? No – her decision came from a much darker, purely selfish, place. '... and then I found the coding.' Pella opened his mouth to interrupt, but she carried on, afraid that if she stopped now, she might never say everything she needed to. 'It was behind a waterfall, just there, leaping between rocks. Green threads, jumping around. I'd never seen anything like it before. We had no power sources to speak of – just fire, water, air. This was something very different, something special, maybe something we could use in some way.' Why did she follow through on that justification for her actions and continue that lie? 'I was high above it, desperate to get down and take a closer look, but it was too dangerous. I rushed home and told you all, virtually pulling you back up there with me. I could tell as soon you got there that I had made a mistake. All three of you were as taken

187

by it as I was. More than that, I could see that you wanted to get it. I couldn't have that. I couldn't share it, not with anyone. So, while you were all looking over the edge trying to figure a way down, I pushed you off... one by one. I pushed our father first, knowing he would be the strongest to resist, and then pushed you and our mother. I felt it wanted me, so that gave me the strength I needed.'

What she was saying was terrible. Yet, now she had started, it was surprisingly easy to say. This had been in her forever and now it was a relief for it to be coming out. She stared through Pella, unaware of his reaction. It was just as well as she would have hated the look of hurt and disbelief.

'I found a way down and claimed it. By being ruthless, I had proved myself to it. I didn't know what it was, but I didn't care. I didn't know that parts of it migrated to the three of you until much later in our reincarnated lives.

I left the community and lived for a little while, a long way away. Then I died. Can't remember how. It's not important. I lived more lives, not really aware of being reincarnated and not knowing you were doing so too. I began to change and started to care for other things – family and friends, compassion, all became important. The coding detected this, I think, and went to someone stronger, more selfish, more ruthless.'

'Arrix.'

Fen looked up in surprise. She had almost forgotten Pella was there. She nodded. 'The incarnation that became Arrix. 'What I did at the Brack was wrong – very wrong. I have a chance to put that right.'

She focussed on him. He had not changed position. He was just staring at her, now with a neutral expression on his face. 'Say something, Pella. Please.'

He looked away and then back at her. 'So you killed your family to get the coding. After that, Arrix's earlier incarnation took it away from you. Since then... what? Are you trying to get it back again?'

'Yes. This body is different, Pella. Finally, I've got a chance – it's nearly mine again. I have control – some control – but it's not over yet. Arrix is still a threat.'

'What will you do with it if you get it all?'

'Destroy it.'

'How? You say you have some control, but it doesn't look that way, not from where I'm sitting. You've not been in control from the start. It made you kill your family. How can you destroy something that can make you do such things?'

'Don't you see? The coding did not make me do that. I chose to do it. I chose the coding over my family. That was wrong. Nevertheless, it was my choice.'

'Really?' Pella swept his hand round. 'Look at where we are! We're back on Garial now because you chose it? This journey we're on – your choice? Taron, almost certainly dead in the river, eaten by a monster – your choice? Leaving your child in Australia – your choice? Making me leave Ruby. How far do you go back, Fen? The battles we fought over the quartons – you chose all those outcomes?'

'I'm not saying I did but...'

'You chose for this body I'm in – Mark's body – you chose for him to die, did you?' His voice got louder as his anger increased. She shook her head vigorously. 'You chose to kill your own family at the Brack to make sure that every life after that would be hell for them too. Just when I had a sniff of happiness – Ruby, a daughter I could call my own – you chose to take it all away and bring me here.' He was filling in the gaps for some of the parts she had not explained – correctly as it turned out – but not the way she wanted him to see things. 'If you are in control and calling all the shots, I have to say that I'm not much impressed at the moment with your choices.'

She watched the anger drain away from his face to be replaced by something far worse: disappointment. Before she could say anything else, he strode towards the path they had trodden on the way in and he was gone.

She wanted to cry. But no tears would come. So she just sat, clueless about what to do next. She had found out what she had needed to find out at the Brack and she shared it with the one person in the universe who she hoped would understand. That was foolish of her. How could anyone understand why she did what she did? She barely understood it herself. Now she was alone – for how long, she did not know. Perhaps Pella would change his mind. If not, she would be left to find her way back to Earth, Martha and, in all likelihood, Arrix, on her own. It was an unenviable prospect.

Pella was right: she absolutely had no control. If she did, he would still be with her now.

She had no idea how long she sat. It was quite dark when she eventually got up from the log. She had decided that she had no other option than to find a route out of the Brack – if that was possible – get to the top of the mountain range and, from there, pick up the trail via the mountains with the steps to whatever fate awaited her. It was something to aim for, but her enthusiasm had waned and she had begun to wonder what the point of all this was.

The moment she had found the keystone quarton, scavenging around the rubble in London, she had been on a voyage of discovery. With the exception of a few happy years with Sam and Martha in Australia, it had not been a pleasant trip. She sensed she was coming towards the end of it now and she had severe doubts that it would end, like the films she watched as a young kid, with a happy reunion. There might be a reunion, yes, but it was odds on it would be with the likes of Arrix and Klavon rather than with Martha. Still, she had to carry on, so she grabbed a container that Pella had left behind and walked out of the clearing, heading in what she hoped was the right direction for up.

Surprisingly, the going was easier than before and she did not feel that tired. The time she and Pella had spent at the clearing had been emotionally draining. However, physically it had allowed her body to rest and take away some of the aches she had had from earlier. Like the previous day, the problem was going to be the decreasing light. However, yet again, her luck was in. Garial was at the start of a period when there was a longer gap than usual between the setting and rising of its two stars. It coincided with clear skies, so she found herself walking in constant twilight. As before, there was no track to follow, yet, with little vegetation, she was able to pick her way quite easily up the mountain. The mud became drier the higher she climbed and with occasional rocks embedded in the ground, in some places she was almost able to step her way up. Her spirits lifted as she looked back down into the Brack and was able to see the progress she had made. In the far distance she could see the part of the river they had travelled along and where it continued its journey away in a loop around the Brack. Her current course was taking her in an adjacent loop on much higher ground. It felt like the right direction and made sense. The Great Garial Bridge had originally been built by the sea. If it had been returned to its former place, the river would lead her to the sea, at least, and she still had the mountain steps as a reference point; providing she could get high enough to see them.

The problem with walking in mountainous areas is that more mountains can be hidden behind the mountains being climbed and Fen realised this as she approached what she had thought was the top. It was not, and now she had a choice to make: take the more direct route down the other side and then face a steeper climb up the next mountain, or take the flatter, longer route along the ridge which ran round and joined the same mountain about halfway up. Despite the low level of light, she could see a path, of sorts, along the ridge. Down was the darker and less appealing option so she set off along the ridge, hoping it was not going to be too narrow for the entire way.

Concentrating on not falling either side took her mind off her worries for a period and stopped her thinking about how far she still had left to go. As the ridge widened and the incline steepened, her thoughts returned, yet still she trudged onwards, convincing herself that this next mountain would be the significant one that would give her some idea of the magnitude of her journey. Taron must have thought it was possible on foot, even if it would take a long time.

Taron... Taron... Her son, Taron. He had known who she was before she had realised it – how? Perhaps Arrix was aware of the connection and told Taron? That was unlikely; Arrix had never given any indication that he knew her from her a life before Rana. Or maybe while they were being returned to Garial, Taron had picked up the connection through the coding? Whatever it was, she was kicking herself now: if she had actually asked him, she might have gained more of an idea how the coding worked, crucial if she was going to use it effectively to destroy Arrix.

The more she found out about the coding, the more confusing it got. Losing people who might be able to help her understand it – like Pella and Taron – was maybe not the wisest of tactics.

Mackenzie

Mackenzie was unsure what was going on. Whatever it was, Ruby was enjoying herself. After she had made the strange noises into her bracelet and banged on the MASH, she and Jerome had withdrawn to the other side of the loading bay. He was just hoping they were bluffing about the attack on Lisbon with the detons. It seemed a forlorn hope.

He had been hauled to his feet by the two henchman – not easily done because of his size and weight and he was in no position to help with his hands behind his back – and been walked over to the passenger door of the MASH. Inside, Odette was sitting in the driver's seat examining the controls, most of which were virtual. Already she had proved her prowess by working out how to skip the security code to switch those on. Chuck had equipped the vehicle with a power pack that would run the internal systems for days without topping up, although moving the vehicle long distances would require a boost without access to solar energy.

Mackenzie was left standing there, his bodyguards slightly behind and to the side, while Odette's eyes swept over the array of lights, visuals, buttons and slides that made the MASH work. She started to focus on two sets of buttons and slides, the important ones. After a couple of minutes, she looked up at him.

'I've seen how the dark energy goes through here after it is caught and I can see how targets are chosen. I'm halfway to understanding how it finds the energy and – how do you say in English – attracts it...' She flicked up another visual and studied it for a few seconds. 'Correct that – a half and a little more. There's one thing I'm not sure about.'

'Just the one? It took Chuck three years to design this and another three for both us to build it. You seem to have worked out one of the most sophisticated machines ever made by man in less than ten minutes.'

'Less than eight, actually. What does the gun do? I can't see why it is needed.'

'You're right. You don't need it. It points in the general direction of the target, but it's more for show really.'

'For show? To show off?' She shrugged, got out the seat and clambered into the back to study the various circuits and wiring. A minute later, she popped her head out again. 'The quarton piece – where is it?'

'I told you all – I don't know exactly. I really don't. I didn't know there was one here until it was mentioned.'

'I'm surprised you don't know.' She stood upright and clicked open the latch to the opening in the roof then climbed a few steps to look through the top. She spent a moment examining the gun barrel, shrugged again before going back down and closing the latch behind her. 'Are you sure, Mackenzie? It will save some time.'

He shook his head.

She had a quick scan around the cockpit then sprawled across the passenger seat with her legs kicking up behind and her head dangling over the edge. She wriggled and twisted around to take a good look under the seat and in the well. There were no frills to the MASH – no glove boxes, dashboard, rear-view mirror, sun visors. It had a steering wheel on the driver's side with manual controls on it for heat and headlights, pedals like a traditional vehicle and that was about it. Mackenzie and Chuck had not even bothered to hide any of the wiring that ran through the front, although an effort had been made to clip sections back where access in and out was needed. Odette flipped onto her back and Mackenzie watched her eyes roam across the flat roof between the windscreen and the opening she had just been looking through. Like most of the rest of the MASH, the roof was made from steel. There was no soft lining to it as there might have been on most vehicles. It was just grey and very ordinary, yet Odette was paying a lot of attention to it.

She tilted her head back a fraction so she was looking at Mackenzie – upside down. 'Another question,' she asked. Mackenzie was convinced her French accent – strong at the start – was getting stronger every time she said something. 'Does the shell of the MASH act as a conductor?'

'If you mean, does the dark energy go through the shell of the MASH, yes. It goes through mostly everything.'

'That's not the same, as you well know, Mr Mackenzie.' Her slightly playful tone surprised him. She turned back over, knelt on the seat and ran the palm of her hands along the roof, walking them over every part of it, including the driver's side as she shuffled over.

The roof was a single layer of steel throughout the MASH. It was part of the shell which had no particular purpose other than to protect the machinery inside of it from the rain and allow it to be moved from A to B. Yet Odette seemed very interested in it.

'The shell is the first place where the dark energy enters the MASH. It would make sense to put the quarton there, maybe, so it could be used in some way?'

'I moulded the shell myself. As far as I know, there is no part of a quarton in the shell.'

She sank back onto her haunches, tilted her head to one side and addressed him again. 'Tell me more about what the quartons do.'

'Hasn't Ruby told you that already? She's the expert.'

'No.' She leant out the window and said something in a language – possibly a dialect of French – to the two guards which

196

Mackenzie could not understand. The taller one to his left replied and Mackenzie turned his head to try to pick up some clues about what was being said as a short conversation started between them. Both men kept glancing across at Ruby and Jerome and at one point one of them put his bracelet to his mouth ready to speak into it. Whatever Odette said next reassured him as both men stepped away several metres, out of earshot, placing their hands very obviously onto their holsters.

Odette motioned Mackenzie forward, forcing him to stoop a little so he could still see her through the passenger door. 'I've told them to shoot you if you do anything naughty,' she said.

'Nice. Thank you.'

'So, will you tell me some more things?'

It was time to take a risk. There would not be a better opportunity than now to find out whose side she was, or could be, on. He started by telling her briefly what he did know about quartons. He told her that his understanding was that they were made up of a very powerful compound, made largely from quartzite. He told her that Chuck had located a quarton block which had been later stolen from him and destroyed in London and Chuck had kept back a small piece which he and Mackenzie had, many years later, tested. He gave some detail about the experiment, including the fact that the piece had vanished when they had tested it, but also that they had discovered it had unusual properties, one of which was its ability to store and spit out energy in huge amounts. The MASH's use of dark energy was developed, as far as he knew, without using quartons. Although Mackenzie had helped build the MASH and he knew how to make it do the things it did, the finer scientific and technical details were always Chuck's area of expertise. The rest of it... well... Even if his friend was still around, he did not think he would ever fully understand.

He did not mention aliens. He wanted to know what Odette's view on that was.

She listened carefully, still on her haunches on the driver's seat, her hands clasped in front of her. When he had finished, she unfurled her legs and sat with her hands at the wheel, staring through the windscreen. 'Dîtes-moi,' she said. 'Sorry, tell me... do you believe in phantoms?'

He shook his head. 'Ghosts? Not really.'

'I don't. They say that Ruby is a phantom. They are all scared of her.' That answered one of his questions about how she had developed such a following

'Are you scared of her?'

'Not really.'

'Odette?' She turned her head towards him and raised an eyebrow. 'Why do you help her do these terrible things? At this very moment, she is with Jerome, letting off more detons, killing more people.'

Her face hardened. 'That is your fault. You did not help enough.'

'This is not my fault.'

'It is not my fault, too.'

'What about the detons?'

'I do not want them to use them.'

Encouraged, he pushed her harder. 'They are forcing you to help, aren't they?'

'No.'

'Then what is it? Have they threatened you or your family?'

'No.' She sounded irritated. 'The others are stupid to think Ruby is a phantom. They believe it because she has skills which make her special. She can make people do things they don't really want to do.'

'So don't do those things, Odette. This is evil.' She lowered her eyes. 'What is special about Ruby?'

'She is an alien.'

'You know?'

'Yes. It is simple to see. You used the MASH to stop aliens last year. Not everyone believes it in the French-Irish Alliance, but that is because of the stupid president. However, I saw it on visuals. And then Ruby arrives and she is... different. There are no such things as phantoms so she must be an alien. It is logical. Others think she is a phantom.' She nodded slightly upwards and tutted. 'That is up to them. I know what she is.'

'You saw the attacks last year. You saw how dangerous they were to our planet. Why help someone who wants that?'

'Because I am curious. I want to find out more about aliens; girls that can lead hundreds of people to do bad things; technology like this MASH; quartons. It is exciting, no?'

'No! It's dreadful. Innocent people are getting killed.' His hopes of finding an ally were fading. 'Odette, you have good inside of you. Don't let them carry on with this.'

'I have started. Now I cannot help it.'

'You can, Odette. You know this is wrong.'

'Perhaps... It is confusing. I do not want people to die, but there is something about Ruby and all of this...'

Finally, a chink of light – a hint that he was getting through. 'I'll help take this vehicle apart to help you find the quarton, but you'll have to say you'll help me. We'll give them what they want to stop the killing now, then together we can work out a way to defeat them.'

'I do not know.'

'Odette... please!'

She glanced nervously at the guards. 'I am worried. If Ruby finds out...'

'I know that it's a risk, but it's the right thing. You know it is.'

'Okay...okay... What do you want me to do?'

'I think we can use your knowledge of technology to disrupt their plans and then turn the MASH against them. Tell them I am cooperating but it might take some time, and get them to stop using the detons now. We will look for the quarton and while we do that, we can work out specifically how we can turn this round.'

'Okay. I think I have an idea how to break their technology, but we will need to act quickly. The quicker we can get the quarton, the better the plan will work. I think I am right about the quarton being put into the skin, yes?'

'I don't know. I keep telling you that.'

'It is the first place dark energy hits. It makes sense. It will be too small to see so we would need to know exactly which part and we can cut it out. We have the equipment in the flyer to do it. We can melt the steel. It is strong the quarton. Heat will not damage it.'

Her urgency sounded suspicious. 'Odette... I...'

'You have to say which part! Where is it? I cannot help if we do not find it soon.' Her voice went up slightly in volume and pitch and he detected a hint of anger and frustration. It was at that point that Mackenzie realised he had got it all wrong. He was being played like a fiddle. She had no intention of helping him – it was all an act to make him reveal where the quarton was. It was a massive disappointment and he nearly challenged her on it. But he felt Chuck in his ear, urging him not to jump in. Without Odette's support, he needed to move to another plan. It would have to involve Don who should be there any moment. How much time could he buy and how could he limit the amount of damage being caused by Ruby and Jerome with the detons?

If his hands had been free, he would have held them up in mock surrender. Instead, he tried to make his voice as convincing as possible to show he had been fooled by Odette. 'Okay. I haven't been totally honest with everyone. You understand why, don't you?'

'Of course. So you do know where the quarton is?'

'I can't be sure, but I think so. You will definitely help me, Odette? This isn't an act to make me tell you where it is?'

Despite the slight slip up with the voice just now, she was a reasonable liar, he decided. 'No. You are right about the badness of this. If you tell me where it is, I will tell Ruby and she will stop the detons for now. I know how all the technology works so while we get the quarton, we will work out the plan to mess her up.'

'Ok, I'm going to trust you. You were right about it being in the shell. It's tiny, no bigger than a grain of rice. Chuck got me to put it into one the plates which were added on for extra waterproofing under the vehicle.' The lies were coming thick and fast and he had to be careful not to overdo it. 'There are four plates, two at the front and two at the back. It's in one of the front ones, driver's side.'

He looked at her. This was the last chance saloon. If she did not believe him, he would probably be disposed of straight away. If she did believe him it might buy another hour or so. Then all he had to do was speak to Don and come up with an alternative plan to save the world.

Simple.

Lessey

After the near miss with the missile, Shaw tried everything to wrest back control of the flyer but without success. All the while, Lessey sat in the back, waiting for the thumping in her chest to ease. Near death experiences when she was at an age when she was quite near to death naturally should be avoided where possible. She had survived the scare, although the short period when they had been waiting for the missile to hit had tested her heart to its maximum – or so she had thought. The whooshing sound and subsequent bang that Ruby engineered had shown it still had another level it could go to.

She just about had her breathing under control by the time their flyer landed next to the craft that Mackenzie had arrived in, when a wobble of the wings – no doubt done deliberately – set it off again. As the door opened, Shaw grabbed his gun, but he was met by Ruby's pilot with hers.

'We can shoot each other,' she said, 'but that won't help your president. I suggest you drop it.'

Shaw looked at Lessey. 'Do it,' she said and rose shakily to her feet.

Don had been held at the gate at gunpoint. If he was surprised to see her, he gave no indication. Instead, he looked impatient and barely gave her a second glance as she and Shaw were escorted towards him. Her knees felt they might give way at any moment, yet she kept her head high and tried to keep her dignity as she stood there waiting for the gate to be opened.

The guard grinned at her. 'How was your flight, Madam President?' he said, motioning the three of them in front with his gun. She ignored him, instead taking her place between Shaw and Don. She was a good two feet smaller than both and was tempted to change position so she would not feel quite so ridiculous. She thought better of it and they were walked down the ramp. Feeling ridiculous, she decided, was the least of her worries.

As they approached the bottom, she caught sight of the MASH and she was transported back to that day when she had sat inside it with Don and Mackenzie. She pushed back on the images of tall strange looking figures and her soldiers scattered all around. Instead, she said one word to Shaw out the corner of her mouth: 'Situation?'

She just caught his hurried whispered reply before the guard told them to shut up. 'Target vehicle on left by loading bay, girl plus one on right. One more guard patrolling.'

The girl was Ruby, for sure. She nodded and there was a grunt from Don to her right. 'No sign of Mackenzie,' he said. 'If he's been killed because of your stupid...'

The guard behind barked louder. 'Quiet!'

As they neared the bottom of the ramp, they had a better view round the corner of the bay. Mackenzie was standing to the side of the MASH with two other men nearby. There was someone inside.

'He's there. You needn't have worried, Berretti,' Lessey said, drawing another reprimand from behind followed by a shove to her shoulder. She stopped, turned around and glared at the man who met her with a defiant look of his own before raising the gun to indicate they continue down the last few metres.

Ruby watched them take the last few steps, a sly grin on her face. Lessey took an instant dislike to the other man she was with, especially when he looked up and laughed out loud to something she said to him. Their guard indicated for them to sit down on the floor to the left of the bottom of the ramp. Don and Shaw did as they were told while Lessey held her ground as the girl and the man sauntered over.

'I'm not used to being told what to do,' she said, 'especially where little girls are concerned. Last time I saw you, you were looking for your daddy.'

The guard stepped forward, his arm raised. 'You dare touch me again...' she said.

Ruby put up a hand and the guard moved back. She stood directly in front of Lessey and eyed her up and down. She was not a lot smaller than Lessey, but Lessey found she had to avert her eyes as Ruby's settled on hers.

'Can't look at me, President?' she said. 'What is it you see that worries you so much?'

Lessey thought she had done well to recover her poise since the scare in the flyer. However, she found her confidence being sapped by this – this what? Nine year old, ten at the most? She coughed. 'You have no right to hold me here.'

Ruby looked away and nodded to no one in particular before staring at Lessey again. Lessey tried to return the gaze but found she still could not. The girl made a sound that could have been a laugh. If it was, it was not like any laugh Lessey had heard from children she had come across before. Not that she was much of an expert. So far in her life, she had managed to largely avoid contact with them. This one in front of her gave nothing to suggest that habit was going to change.

'We've downed your other craft. If anyone else comes looking for you, we will do the same to them. We have lots of weapons and are very good at using them.'

It was a blow, yet no more than Lessey had expected. She was alive; for the sake of the French-Irish Alliance, that was the main thing. 'What do you want?' she muttered.

'That's a deep and complicated question, but I'll answer it. I'm like you – I want control of this planet, and a little more besides.'

'Who are you?'

Don spoke up from the floor. 'You still don't get it, Lessey, do you? After all that's happened, you still refuse to accept what's going on here.'

'Is he right, President Lessey? You still don't get it?' The girl came right up close, her face inches from hers, and then whispered

205

in her ear. 'I heard that you don't believe in aliens.' She pulled back, watching for a reaction. Lessey was doing her best not to give her one.

'Why am I here?'

'So many questions. I thought you'd be happy with me saving your life. That missile was meant for you to start with, but I changed my mind. I thought you, and Colonel Berretti, might come in handy, though I'm not sure we need two high ranking military men here.'

The smirk reappeared and Lessey looked down at Shaw. She had to give him credit. He had looked like he would fall apart when the missile was about to hit and who could blame him for that? Since then, he had held it together and he did again now as Ruby made her threat. He stared straight ahead, not a flicker of emotion showing.

'We'll see how that goes.'

This girl treated people worse than she did. It was mental torture. It would be impressive if she was not on the receiving end of so much of it.

'So, you're wondering why you're here? Well, we're expecting a very important visitor in the next day or two. Once we've dealt with her, we want to take over the world. Now, we don't want everyone in the world killed, which would be the easier option if I was being honest. We are going to need some manpower – or woman power, we're not fussy – to do a few jobs around the planet. That will be so much easier to arrange if all the countries are having their own squabbles. Divide and conquer is the expression, I believe. You know what it's like with world domination – or maybe you don't. Anyway, I did have a powerful army until the Colonel here stopped me with his brick wall like accomplice. My new friends, some of which you've met already, are very good, but we're going to need help. We like people that stir things up and you're doing a good job of that. I take it, President, you'd like to have a little more power than you have at the moment?'

She was right about that, at least. Lessey did want more and it sounded like she was being offered the beginnings of an arrangement which might help her to get it. This girl was an interesting person to deal with. How she had so much power at her fingertips was particularly intriguing. When she had heard her original message back at her base, Lessey had detected something in it that reminded her of the Lee she had known. She hated to admit it but Lee had scared her, and Ruby did the same which was an extraordinary skill from someone so young. Lee had double-crossed her and she would need to be careful it did not happen again. But, she reminded herself, she was only dealing with a girl. If there was any double-crossing to be done, Lessey was sure she would be the one doing it.

'I can help you,' she said.

'Go on.'

'The Southern Alliance has given me access to all the places in the world where they are hiding massive sources of energy.'

'Goodness, hiding things? That is naughty.'

'I can tell you where those places are.'

'I know where they are. Colonel Berretti is about to go through that with us.'

Lessey's heart sank; still she recovered quickly with another proposal. 'Oh... well, you're still going to need someone to talk to the other world leaders. They will listen to me as they suspect I am behind the deton attacks.'

'They suspect you're behind them? Well, that is so unfair. Are you sure you won't get into a lot of trouble?'

Lessey ignored the sarcasm. 'I have influence.'

'Hmm, well, I suppose that could be useful, although Jerome here,' she pointed to the man she had been talking to earlier, 'is quite fluent in three or four languages and could contact them. I'm only a little girl so they wouldn't believe me.'

'It's about speaking to the right people. With our resources combined, they will do whatever we... you... want. And then you're going to need someone to help out afterwards.'

'After what?'

'After whatever you're going to do next. More deton attacks or using the MASH thing over there.'

'What do you think, Colonel Berretti? Can I trust her?'

He ignored the question. 'Mackenzie said that you wanted me here. I'm here. Now what?'

'Now you're asking questions too! Well, look, President Lessey, you give me that list of your contacts. That's a good start. I've prepared another little speech that you and Colonel B are going to give to the world. We'll get that done first and then see how things are after that. Fair?'

Lessey was about to say it was fair, providing she had some assurances about her role in the future, when one of the guards who had been by the MASH came running over.

'Odette is close to finding the quarton,' he said, addressing Ruby. 'We need cutting and heating tools.' Lessey's ears pricked up at the sound of that word again: quarton.

Ruby shook her head and spoke quietly. 'Get them then. I'm not sure why they're not down here already,' and then she looked pointedly at Jerome. The man dashed off up the ramp. 'Oh, I have an idea for while we wait for that,' she said perking up. 'Let's play "Guess the City"! I read out a list of cities we're going to target next with the detons after we've finished in Lisbon and you have to guess which one I've chosen.' She turned to Lessey, her eyes sparkling with the genuine excitement she imagined young children must get from time to time.

It was a strange way to behave. Everything she did was strange. Children could not do the things she did or say the things that she said, could they? For the first time, Lessey maintained eye contact and Ruby responded by raising her eyebrows and widening her eyes.

At which point, the penny finally dropped. 'Lee?' she whispered. 'Is that really you?'

Ruby spread her arms out wide and grinned a grin that was all the more frightening because of how young its face's owner was. 'Oh, yes, President Lessey. I'm back!'

Ruby

<*Satisfied with your performance, Klavon?*>
    Oh, yes. Satisfied... for now. I enjoyed winding her up.
    <*She wasn't that bothered about the flyers.*>

No. I have to say, Arrix, that she is an extraordinary woman. She only really cares about power. I like her. She might be worth keeping.

<I agree. What about her major?>

Not bothered.

<He's an extra pair of hands as long as he does what he's told. He seems loyal to her.>

Maybe.

<Odette has done well isolating where the quarton is. I told you it was in there.>

We need to extract it from the metal? We can't leave it where it is?

<It's small. If we are going to use it to get Fen back, it stands a better chance if it's out so that it is pure. We mustn't touch it – your habit of destroying quartons when you do will not be helpful.>

Won't Pella need a quarton wherever he is to make the link work?

<Possibly. But I think the coding will find a way to reunite the four of us. Connected to dark energy through the MASH, the quarton will shine like a beacon. She is coming, Klavon, and there is nothing that will stop her because the coding wants it. I have underestimated her in the past; we mustn't this time. She is strong competition so we will have to be ready.>

And the MASH will destroy her?

<You know how Chuck turned that thing on me and my warriors.>

You survived.

<Its range was too wide. She won't be able to survive if we do this properly.>

Good. I'm looking forward to it... I'm hungry.

<Hungry for power, for blood, for success?>

No, I'm hungry for food.

<There are supplies in the flyer, but can you not resist? We have things to attend to.>

And if this body fails, what then?

<If this body fails, I find another one.>

I find another one? That's not good teamwork, a bit of a giveaway as to your intentions.

<Yes, I suppose it could be seen like that.>

Fen

The summit turned out to be exactly that, much to Fen's relief. The mountains with the steps were clear to see and not as far away as she had feared. There was a steep descent onto a plain while the river meandered a long way to the right, and then was lost behind forest. She could just make out a gap to aim for at the base of the mountains which should, she hoped, lead her to the bridge.

If she remembered correctly, the city – the powerbase from which Arrix controlled the planet – was on the other side of the mountains. She could not recall spending much time in it, though she did remember one thing: the bridge was quite a journey from there, on foot anyway. In her head, the stepped mountains had been her goal, but it could well be that they were just a checkpoint along the way. It was a blow, made worse by fatigue and, having stopped, she realised she was very cold. The wind was not that strong, yet had a bite to it – a stark reminder of how ill-equipped she was for this sort of journey. Her trousers were quite thick, but the two layers she wore on her top half were nowhere near enough protection. She needed to get out of the wind and down to a lower altitude as quickly as possible, otherwise she was going to freeze.

Unfortunately, she lost her footing on the downward slope and found herself on her backside skidding feet first on top of scree. The stones kicked up around her as she frantically tried to dig her feet in to slow down, but momentum built as the slope steepened and she was soon careening out of control. She put her hands out either side but the skin was ripped off them in an instant. Even lying down onto her back and thrusting her elbows out made no difference. Both containers were lost as the straps broke and she continued to slide, twisting and turning in the vain hope that she could get a grip and her progress would be slowed. With some adjustment of her body, she was able to steer a rough course between the bigger rocks and at one stage she came perilously close to flying over the edge with a sharp drop before she turned back inwards. But she could not miss one large boulder and took the brunt of the collision with her left thigh. She was going at such a speed now that if she dug her feet or any other part of her body into the loose rocks she would just end up flipping over and tumbling the rest of the way. Her back and backside were being scratched and pummelled raw to the extent that there would not be much of her body left at this rate. Her plight worsened as she thundered towards a line of trees. Ignoring the pain, she thrust out

212

both arms to the side and repeatedly kicked down into the stones with her heals. A tuft of grass flashed by, too quickly for her to grab, then another and another. The fourth one she just about managed to latch onto with her left hand, nearly popping her shoulder joint out as the bulk of her body continued the downward fall. Somehow, she managed to cling on.

She lay there for a moment, panting and with her arm stretched above her head, not daring to let go. Eventually, she rolled over onto her front and carefully eased her knees up so she had better purchase. There was no way she would be able to stand, but she was only a few metres from the trees. If needs be, she could let herself go and would not be badly hurt if she did hit a tree from that distance.

So engrossed was she in preparing herself for the possibility of more pain, she did not hear the sound of the flyer approaching. It was only when it hovered slightly behind and to her left, did she realise she had company. And it was only when Taron's tall figure appeared at the side door and dropped a pole with a rope attached into the ground, did she realise she was being rescued.

She must have passed out because she was not aware of being taken into the flyer or of the subsequent treatment that was applied to her back, legs and arms which had been ripped to shreds. She woke up on the floor, half on her front and half on her side, to be met by Pella sitting across from her. He had a tray on his lap covered with bloodied swabs and was examining a box in his hand. He looked up when she grunted.

'We had to do it the traditional way, at least by Garialian standards,' he said matter-of-factly. 'No medi-pod on board, but Taron found the equivalent of a good old-fashioned first aid kit. Remember those from Earth? I'm looking for clues as to exactly what it is I've put on you. It's got some symbols on which Taron said probably meant something to anyone with medical training, though I can't understand it. No need to read anything, if you remember from your Rana days – everything was fed directly into your brain. Useful emergency backup this, though. Being hauled from the skies by a river monster must count as an emergency, but it didn't help the poor sods. Sorry, I'm rambling.'

So they were in the flyer Taron talked about that had been downed by the Laric. Incredible!

'What do you think this squiggle means?' Pella held up the box and pointed to one of the symbols. She squeaked something that was supposed to say she had no idea. 'Sorry, shouldn't ask the patient difficult questions. Shall I stop talking?'

'No... Thank you, Pella.'

'For what?'

'For being you.'

He smiled. It was a smile the person called Mark might have done, but as far as Fen was concerned, it made no difference whose body he was in. He was her brother and it did not matter who or what he looked like. He had come back for her.

She was keen to see Taron, if she could move. Her right arm was directly out in front and she had been held into the sideways position by a combination of Pella's booted foot which was against her thighs and something else against her chest she could not

214

identify because it was wrapped in Pella's top. Pella had followed her gaze.

'Apologies for the crude props. We had to do this while the injuries over your back heal. Taron thinks that it won't take long, if the stuff in the bottle is what he thinks it might be. He says he remembers you – well not you, exactly, the previous you before Rana – giving him something similar when he was young after a fall. It was a deep cut and it healed up in no time.' He put the box and tray to one side and leant towards her. 'How are you feeling?'

She hurt all over. 'Pretty awful.' She shifted her bottom leg and yelped as she felt a jabbing pain.

'Try not to move until the pain relief kicks in. You'll be as good as new... if this stuff works.' He opened the box and lifted out an orange bottle. 'See? I have no clue what it is.'

Fen tilted her head back. Taron was standing at the front. She had noticed mild gusts of warm wind coming from there and realised now that there was no covering. It was completely open from top to bottom.

'Taron reckons the Laric pulled this whole thing down, bit off the front and then helped itself to the warriors inside. The one that survived must have got out the other end. I'm amazed this thing is still flying. He's taking it very slow, mind.'

'Taron – is he alright?'

'He says he is, but I'm not so sure. That existing wound has opened up and he's got two more nasty injuries; one on his left lower leg and he can hardly move his arm. He won't let me look at them. Wouldn't even let me put on any of the magic potion. Just as well in some ways as there was only just enough to cover your injuries. I've had to leave some of your minor scratches to heal on their own.'

Fen started to protest. 'Don't waste your breath. I tried to save him some, but he insisted you needed it more. I didn't want to argue with a warrior.'

It hurt to speak, yet she could already feel some relief to the pain at the top of the back. It was working its way down. 'How did he...?'

'Survive? God knows, but he did. He reckons the Laric is dead. Got it in the eye with those bits of wood, probably pierced its brain. We walked all the way along the river worrying about that thing attacking again and we needn't have bothered! So inconsiderate of him not to find us straight away and tell us.' He smiled again to show he was joking. 'He nearly drowned in the process though. Washed up just where the river diverted away from the Brack. If we hadn't gone off up the hill there, we would have found him.'

'The flyer?' The pain was definitely easing. It was like a warm glow melting through her body. Whatever was in the bottle was powerful.

'On the opposite bank. They had never recovered it. Too busy rebuilding the bridge, I guess. He swum over and got it going. When I left you, I headed back down the way we had come and ...'

She interrupted. 'I'm so sorry, Pella. Really I am. But I had to tell you.'

'I was mad – I have to admit.'

'That person that killed you at the Brack was not me. Well, it was, but it wasn't the me that I am now.'

'I know. Anyway, I was shattered so I stopped. Fell asleep, of course. When I woke up, I made my way back up to the clearing but you'd gone. Then this thing comes floating up with Taron inside and we came looking for you. You weren't hard to find. You did what Taron had suggested and headed for the steps.'

Fen shifted her thigh, encouraging Pella to move his boot. 'Help me up, Pella, please.'

'Are you sure?'

'Yes. I feel okay. I need to speak to Taron.' She was aware she had some unfinished business with Pella, but that could wait for a moment. She had to get to Taron and tell him how she felt about what he had done. With Pella's help, she got to her feet and limped towards the front. It looked like the Laric had helped itself to more than just the warriors because the craft was a shell, save for the odd fitted compartment and some straps dangling down. Steadying herself on the curved wall with her hand, she felt a slight pang on the palm and she glanced down at it. She knew both hands had taken a beating on the slope yet all that she could see was a few scratches. If the rest of her was in a similar state, she would certainly be able to cope with that.

As she got near to Taron, he heard her and turned so that he was side on to her. Pella had not mentioned his face. The original scar had been added to substantially and he was barely recognisable, a mass of open wounds with green pus on the edges which looked like they were in desperate need of attention. His lower legs had been strapped back up, but she could tell he was uncomfortable by the way he held himself. He tried to right his body, maybe conscious he was being checked over. The tunic he wore was in

217

tatters, tied in a crude knot so as to cover part of his lower body. She could see what Pella meant about the existing wound on his side. It gaped like a fissure on a volcano and there were fresh cuts all over his torso. As Pella had explained, his arm hung uselessly by the side.

'You are more well,' he said simply, his eyes flicking back and forth to the front. In his stronger hand, he held a small stick which he adjusted slightly in response to the flyer's movements.

'I'm fine. Taron...but you... you're badly hurt.'

'I am alive.'

She nodded gratefully. 'How, I don't know. You came back for me. I... I... don't know how to thank you.'

'Thanking me has no meaning.'

She smiled a half smile. 'It does mean something. What you've done means a lot to me. But look at you. We need to get you help before you...'

'No need. I can survive like this. I am a warrior.'

She nodded. He had proved that beyond all doubt. 'Pella has explained what you did.'

'There is more to do. We are not finished. Come forward, with care.'

If the flyer had ever had any seats, they certainly were not there now. Very conscious they were in a craft with a yawning hole, Fen stayed on the opposite side of where Taron stood, and felt her way closer, caressing the wall for support. As she eased forward, she could see they were following the river to her right, not that high and were actually travelling quite slowly. The mountains with the steps were no longer in view. She scanned the landscape for something familiar. 'Where are we?'

'See?' He pointed to her left. 'That is Garla.'

The city – or, rather, what was left of it – stood to their left. As Taron gently brought the flyer to a stop and turned it so they were fully facing it, Fen felt a twinge in her stomach; it was not unlike the London she had scavenged in. The buildings that remained may originally have been Garalian in shape and design, but thousands of years of decay gave them a similar feel to the ravaged ones of London, struck by missiles in the Power Wars. In the distance, tall thin structures were dotted around, too far away to make out in detail, except for their jagged edges and spikes. In the foreground, stood a pyramid shaped building which might once have been similar to other buildings which had since lost their tops or sides. Remains of giant tubes lay on the ground or propped precariously against other buildings and there were as many craters as there were mounds of collapsed structures. Fen felt the flyer shake a little as Taron took them slightly higher. From there she could just make out a network of pathways which might have once been part of a grid system for moving around the city at ground level. There was one incredibly long building, pockmarked with holes which caught her eye.

'Arrix's original residence,' Taron explained.

Mention of his name again made the connection to her past in London all the stronger. The sight of Arrix – Marston as he was in that incarnation – standing at the end of the Friendship Bridge on the Thames, revelling in her pain and ready to claim victory – flashed before her. And then Klavon – reincarnated as Bill, the

219

Eastsider's leader – snatching that victory away from him at the last moment. Yet Arrix kept coming back – again and again. She could sense his presence now – not here, not on Garial, but he was close. Just like the quarton block she had found in London, she was drawn to him. If she wanted to get to Martha, she would have to go through him first... and possibly through Klavon too. The fact that Taron was showing them Garla suggested it might be crucial in bringing her a step closer to that confrontation.

Pella had joined them. 'Does anyone live in the city now?' he asked.

Taron stared outwards. 'The planet has grown again and plants and animals have done well, but no life form dominates since the Garalian population died out. The warriors struggled to find the resources Arrix wanted to rebuild the bridge. We had to search far and wide – not in Garla. There is little left here, as you can see.'

'Why have we stopped here, Taron?' Fen asked.

He turned back to look at her. His battered face was even harder to read, but his eyes grew as he spoke. 'I don't think I have much time left.' Before she could say anything, he made a sound – something in Garalian. 'You have them still?' He paused. 'I cannot find the word in English for them. Discs, maybe?'

'Halos!' Pella said suddenly. 'I've been wracking my brains trying to think of what we called them. Halos.'

Fen must have looked baffled because Pella immediately went to the back of the flyer and returned with the top he had used to help keep Fen off her back. He undid the zip to one of the pockets and pulled out one of the rings Taron had dropped to the floor at the complex.

Fen put her hand to her mouth. There had been so much going on, she had completely forgotten about the battery rings. Frantically, she patted down her clothes and quickly realised the pockets, and indeed much of her leggings at the back, had gone. She felt for her front pocket and breathed a sigh of relief. The halo had survived a rollercoaster ride down a river and a death defying slide down a mountain, but it was there. Somewhat embarrassed, she held it up. 'I knew I'd kept it safe!' she joked.

'Good,' said Taron and with that he turned about and navigated the flyer down towards Arrix's residence.

'He doesn't give much away, does he?' Fen whispered to Pella. She moved slightly away from the front as Taron picked up speed.

'Did you ever come here when you were Pella?' she asked. 'Garalian Pella, I mean.'

'I must have at some point. We probably did as young children. This was the centre of Garial, but all my work was done back at the science complex when I worked for Arrix.'

'I don't remember it as a kid, but I do remember avoiding it as an adult.'

'Not a good place for rebels to hang out, I guess.'

'No. And when we planned our route to the Garial Bridge, we would certainly have stayed well clear. I'm sure the bridge wasn't far from here though.'

Now and again, she leant forward to look down at the city. It was even more decrepit closer up. She could not get that impression out of her head that this was London and she found herself experiencing the dread she felt on an almost daily basis there, brought on by being scared, desperately hungry or cold – often all three.

As they approached, the damage caused by age became even clearer to see. Arrix's residence was once huge – Fen estimated a couple of kilometres long, possibly – but what had appeared to be intact flat roofs from a distance had collapsed down in large segments at the nearer end. It looked like, originally, it might have been a confusing layout; zigzags, curves and broken spheres built on different levels of ground, mixed up with more conventional rectangular sections.

The holes she had seen from afar were not signs of damage after all. Faded brown, pink and yellow pathways, like snail shells, spiralled down underground, presumably to more levels below. In its pomp, the building must have dominated the city, an imposing place, she thought, from which Arrix could control those around him.

Taron brought them down onto a low roof, right next to an impressive silver dome with large struts that curved up to meet at the crown. At the very top was a statue, a figure wearing a purple gown that was shaped to billow out behind. Taron signalled for them to follow him out through the front of the flyer which involved a low jump down. There was a loud clang as Taron landed, his good hand immediately reaching across to the wound on the opposite side. Pella and then Fen followed him down. Taron was struggling, that much was clear, yet he waved away Fen's offer for help and set off towards a metal balcony that hugged the side of the dome.

As they set off after him, Pella pointed up towards the statue and muttered, 'Arrix?'

'Guess so. Watching over his minions, no doubt.'

She felt fine now, no pain whatsoever. There was little wind blowing, but she could feel warm air on her skin at the back and wondered whether she was fully decent on not. It felt foolish to worry, yet she could not resist another quick pat around the leggings in particular. Pella caught her up and raised an eyebrow.

'Just checking the halo is still there,' she lied.

He smiled. 'Bit draughty, is it?'

'What? Oh, no, I mean yes... a little.'

He dropped his pace a touch and then caught back up. 'A few holes but you'll survive.'

She threw him a stern look and he flinched back. 'Whoa! Don't give me the big sister stare. I'm only trying to help you preserve your dignity.'

She tutted and shook her head. 'Maybe dignity is the only thing I have left to preserve.'

'That's not true and you know it. You've got me, for a start.'

'After all I did to you?'

He clasped her elbow and pulled her gently to a stop. 'Whatever you did back then does not make you who you are now. You could not help it and you soon realised that, tried to change. You can't let actions you did thousands and thousands of years ago define you. This,' he moved his hand up and down towards her, 'is who you are. You are Fen, just like I am Pella. Two parents who are so desperate to get back to their children that they would do anything, including travelling across the galaxy, to get to them.'

223

'And kill anyone who gets in the way.' The words just came out, the anger surprising even her.

'Yes,' Pella said solemnly. 'That's all part of it. I kind of understand that now.' He looked up at the statue. 'We have to bring Arrix down. You and I... together. Permanently this time.'

She followed his gaze upwards. 'I want payback for all he has done. Payback for all the hurt – payback for Sam, for Martha, for Ruby, for you and me....'

'I get that, and I'm with you all the way. '

'I'm so... so...' As his words sank in, her voice trailed off and with it, the anger, to be replaced by huge relief that she was not on her own. She jumped forward, flinging her arms around his neck. She felt his arms around her waist and then he pulled away.

'Sorry – your scratches! I didn't mean to squeeze so hard.'

She laughed. 'It's fine. Come on – we've lost Taron somewhere round this dome. He must be way ahead. We've got some catching up to do.' She set off at a jog and together they followed the curve round.

It straightened out slightly before the balcony dipped down a slope towards a large vertical cylinder. At the bottom of the slope, cut into the dome, was a large arched door and, just inside, lying across the threshold, was the warrior.

From the look of him, there were unlikely to be any more miraculous escapes or recoveries.

Mackenzie

From the other side of the MASH, Mackenzie watched through the windows as Don and Shaw were made to sit on the floor at the bottom of the slope. They, with Lessey, had their backs to him which meant he could barely pick up snippets of the conversation, but he was pretty sure that Lessey would be trying to strike some sort of deal with Ruby. She was clever enough to realise that, since she was still alive it would be for a reason. Mackenzie had never trusted her. She had been a victim of the original attacks, yet would not hesitate to change sides if she could see an opportunity to profit. Whether she was still blind to Ruby's origins and motives, he did not know. Even if she was, it probably would not make a great deal of difference.

Odette seemed convinced by his lie as to where the quarton was because she left him to go to speak to Ruby. With Don as his only reliable remaining ally, Mackenzie now had to find a way to communicate a new plan which was, fortunately, forming in his head. The basis of it was crude and depended on a lot of things he had no control over. But his father had taught the young Mackenzie that he could only affect what he could affect; everything else was outside of his influence so he should not worry about it. This idea had encouraged him to do a lot of brainless things in his life and it seemed he was about to try another one.

The plan had two main parts: while Ruby and the others were distracted melting down the metal plate to find the quarton, he would steal the MASH with Don, drive it out of the department store's loading bay and then turn it on Ruby and the others. There were three problems he could see with this part of the plan. The first was that Lessey and Shaw would be collateral damage. Unfortunate, but he could live with that. The second was that he would have to act extraordinarily quickly to avoid Ruby taking more lives with the detons. And the third was that getting away might be an issue because he was tied up and had a gun pointed at him most of the time.

The second part was more straightforward in the medium term: find the quarton and wait for Fen to come back. Again there were problems with this, and it was not just the difficulty that it was very much dependent on the first part working. He did not know where the quarton was, if indeed it was there at all, and it might take him an age to dismantle the MASH to find it. Still, he would have some time on his side if Ruby's immediate threat had been snuffed out. Relying on Fen coming back was a big risk – who was he trying to kid? – a huge risk, but if she did return, he would have cleared a safe passage. He was convinced that if he used the MASH on Ruby directly, she – Arrix – was very unlikely to ever come back.

But there was another issue which Mackenzie had not anticipated. There was no way he could have unless he knew much more about how the coding operated. It was a significant problem and it was this: the tiny piece of quarton was indeed exactly where Mackenzie said it was – in the front plate, under the vehicle, driver's side – secreted into the metal sheet by Chuck when it was melted down and before it was shaped by Mackenzie to be fitted. Searching for something that is actually there is invariably a lot quicker than searching for something that is not.

Mackenzie had less than fifteen minutes before the quarton piece would be found.

That was not going to be nearly enough time.

Klavon

Klavon would never forget and he could never forgive. The hate he had for Arrix was always there, part of who he was now and who he had been for thousands of years. The images of his home destroyed and seeing his family murdered, had changed him and changed his future, setting him on a wild and vengeful course forever. Every day, he relived the last moments on the Garial Bridge, his father's data droplet in his hand, the proof that Arrix intended to use Garial and its people as a stepping stone along the way to eternal life. That should have been it – to watch Arrix suffer in those last moments while his dreams were shattered. The ultimate revenge.

But it had gone on and on for millennia, and still he could not be rid of Arrix. No matter how many times he was knocked down, he just kept getting back up, the last time, most annoyingly, into the same body as Klavon.

When they had first been joined together, it had felt good. Two strong personalities working for complete power over and domination of those around them so they could have eternal life. They both wanted the same and they had been put together to achieve that aim. They had much in common: equally ruthless, equally ambitious, highly intelligent and very determined. However, Arrix was always there – watching, listening, criticising.

Klavon had been the first to take over Ruby's body so he had the control over her functions such as talking, moving and eating. He had tried, in the past, to enforce his choices on Arrix when they had disagreed on action. Yet, somehow, they always tended to do what Arrix wanted. Klavon's only real input was how they went about doing it. It had been enough to carry on the role as the 'scary little girl' while they working towards the same end, but now they were close to their goal and it was time to think about how he was going to get rid of his unwanted partner.

Arrix was placing a lot of faith in the MASH destroying Fen when she returned. Klavon had no doubt that it would do that, but he wanted it to do much more. He just needed to get out of this shell and into another one, without Arrix. He had his eye on a body that was much more in keeping with the large – very large – profile he liked to maintain. It was a bold, dangerous – to the point of suicidal – move, and one that had to be well timed.

Just a couple more issues to finalise, then he would be ready. And there was nothing that Arrix would be able to do about it.

Lessey

'People of the world...'

'It's a corny start, President,' said Ruby, 'but I like it.'

'You wrote it!'

'Exactly.'

Lessey's confidence was growing as she gradually realised how straightforward it was going to be to take over this operation. There were five or six hostiles in the bay, at most. If she played this right she might even be able to con Mackenzie and Berretti into balancing up the odds a little and make the job even easier. What was more, she had everything she needed right here in this room: the MASH, people with knowledge on how to use it and valuable data about the dark energy sources. Even the scare tactic she was putting out to world leaders was going to help her get what she wanted.

She accepted something strange was going on here with this girl, but, at the end of the day, she was still just a girl. A possessed girl, maybe, but still a girl. Lessey had rebelled against the teachings of the church and actually had an open mind about life after death. Her brain – not her eyes – told her what was real or not. Aliens were not real; if she went along with Don and Mackenzie that they were, this would be an impossible situation because there was no way she could beat a hoard of alien ships. But she could beat countries and alliances and she could beat – or at least, ignore – a ghost. Particularly one occupying the body of a girl that was not that many years out of nappies.

'People of the world,' she continued, 'this is President Lessey. Contrary to my last statement about having no involvement in the deton attacks, you will have realised by now, through the attacks on Lisbon, that it was a false statement. I am taking full responsibility for the attacks. They will continue at thirty minute intervals in cities of my choice, unless you show me you have taken positive action on the following: all short range missiles that you hold – as declared to the Southern Alliance – will be stood down with a view to being destroyed. I will be sending representatives from my cabinet and military to the six major nations initially to confirm this is in process. This is not up for negotiation. You have twenty-four hours to comply.

I am now handing over to Colonel Berretti of the Southern Alliance. Sending his verification codes now. Colonel Berretti.'

'Sadly,' said Don, 'I can confirm that President Lessey is behind the deton attacks. I am with her now and she has provided proof to me that she has the capability for more attacks. My recommendation is that you follow her instructions. I will speak to my own superiors about the support we can give to those six nations in the process she has outlined, and to other nations who will be affected by President Lessey's actions. I say this with a heavy heart.'

'Great!' said Ruby. 'That'll do, for now. I have more speeches planned, but in the meantime we have some preparations to carry out.'

This really was working out very nicely indeed. Ruby had foolishly allowed her to be in contact with Barrow to arrange her people to do the verification of the missiles being decommissioned. She had even let her use her own bracelet for contact which allowed her to double swipe to close the call, a signal for Barrow that she needed backup, and, of course, to reveal her location. She trusted Barrow to act sensibly – he was the head of her military, after all. She would expect him to involve the English in the operation to rescue her as they would have local knowledge of the layout of the building. Ruby's plans to disrupt other countries tied in well with her own. Lessey was not after complete world domination – not yet – but they would have to sit up and take notice of her after what they thought she had done.

'Right, Odette,' said Ruby. 'I see that they've started to melt down that panel you think holds the quarton.'

'Yes. We will soon know if it is in there.'

'It had better be. Have you found out how the MASH works yet?'

'Nearly. Give me another five minutes with Mackenzie.'

'Be quick. I have plans for him.'

Odette returned to the MASH leaving Lessey, Don and Shaw with Ruby and Jerome.

'Now...' began Ruby.

'What do you mean, you have plans for Mackenzie?' Don suddenly piped up. 'What more do you want from him, from any of us? This is madness. You're killing innocent people. Do you care at all? This can't be what you really want.'

Colonel,' said Ruby, 'I suggest you be still and do what you're told. At the moment, your cooperation is stopping us using the detons on the next city on the list where more people will be killed, innocent or otherwise. You think you might have an idea of what I want from your involvement last time, but you don't really. You can't possibly begin to understand me. No one can – I'm a complicated girl.'

'And you, Lessey.' Don started to get up, but a wave of Jerome's gun forced him back down. He spat out the words. 'You should be ashamed of yourself.'

Lessey ignored him, instead addressed Ruby. 'Since we have a sort of understanding, will you let my major go? If you give him his bracelet back, between us we could liaise with our people to make sure they know what to say to the various governments when they supervise the missile decommissioning. I'd like to make sure, for all our sakes, that it's done properly.'

'Very thoughtful, President Lessey'. There was that sarcasm again – definitely something about the Lee in her. She's just a girl, just a girl – she had to keep telling herself that. 'I think I can trust you both not to pull a fast one on me. Jerome, make sure Major Shaw has his bracelet returned. You won't mind, President, if Jerome listens in?'

'No, not all.' It was not ideal but was as much as she could expect. They would be able to get some messages to the right people in the way she wanted.

'Good. Well, to work then. You make your calls, Odette is dealing with Mackenzie and I'll... well, I'll go off and enjoy myself while it all happens around me.'

Lessey waited until Ruby had finished having a quiet word with Jerome and was out of earshot before she spoke to the Frenchman.

'Jerome, isn't it? Why don't you go and find Major Shaw's bracelet while I start to make some calls?'

Jerome looked directly at her. 'And let you send more secret messages to your general? No chance.' He winked, pulled out his gun and fired two shots, one for each of Shaw's arms.

Ruby

<Klavon. Was that entirely necessary to tell Jerome to do that? I thought we were going to use both Lessey and her major. And since when did you start making such decisions on your own?

Klavon... Klavon? Are you there?>

Part 5

Fen

'He's dead, isn't he?' She looked up at Pella who responded with a drop of the eyes. 'He said he didn't have long. I had hoped he was wrong, but it seems he wasn't.'

They had no choice other than to leave Taron where he had fallen. Fen straightened out his legs and insisted they turned him over onto his back and place his arms across his chest. There was no religious significance to the action, it just felt right; she could not explain why. She had barely known him – in this life, anyway – yet she was distraught. The positive feelings connected to the visits to the waterfall that they had enjoyed together as mother and child in that previous life, she deliberately pushed back. She shed a tear but that was all. Any more than that and she would have collapsed in an emotional heap. The connection was deep and the loss greater for it. Taron had done so much for them in such a short space of time.

He was originally supposed to be their executioner; he turned out to be their saviour by getting them safely to the very brink of the bridge. But he had stopped in the city – no explanation, no clues as to what was here at Arrix's powerbase that was so important. Why had he not taken them directly to where the bridge had been originally? There had to be a reason.

There was only one way to find out and that was by following the path he had set them on, through the arched doorway, and hope that whatever it was he was taking them to be obvious and easy to find. As a scavenger, she was expert at finding things. On this occasion, it would have helped to know what she was looking for.

Everything suggested that Taron was leading them to the top of the dome. They had started quite high by landing on a roof and had continued going up further along the balcony, so Fen was not surprised that the narrow corridor they found themselves in continued the upward trend. They were soon tackling an incline which, judging by the sloped walls on one side, seemed to be following the inside of the dome. Luminous crystals embedded in the walls twinkled seductively and with the occasional opening with views out onto the city gave light enough to plot their way. Fen detected a slight warming sensation around her lower back around the quarton fragment, a feeling that intensified the higher they got. Maybe that was the reason Taron brought them here – this could be a place where the connection between quartons was strong.

Was this the reason the dome had been built? Surely it was not another gateway like the bridge? Its design and shape were too intricate. More likely it was built to house Arrix's statue on the top of it, a shrine to his ego. It had certainly been built to last, although that that too was inconsistent since Arrix's plans, with no concern for its future, had always been to abandon Garial.

She began to feel more anxious as the light darkened and the air became mustier. Just as she was beginning to wonder if they would ever reach the top, a door opened up to their right, presenting them with a wide high stepped staircase, built for the long legs of a Garalian.

'This way, I reckon,' she remarked with an ironic smile as she grabbed a handily placed handrail and hauled herself up the first step. It was a real effort and she lost count of the steps, but, eventually, after several ninety degree turns, she could see a bright light which she hoped would signal the end.

The stairs opened up onto a large room which had to be the inside of the very top of the dome. Gold coloured walls, made brighter by the daylight that seeped through, shaped up to form the inside of the crown many metres above their heads. The floor was a deep blue which caught the light, shimmering with more subtle shades as Fen moved around. She ran her hand along the inside wall. It felt bumpy to the touch, cold too. It was a simple, beautiful room, with absolutely nothing in it.

'Well, that was a waste of time,' Pella commented.

'Perhaps we missed something?'

'Don't think so. I was looking out all the way up and there was nothing obvious.'

'Me too. The quarton has been tingling away inside me, but I can't see anything here it would connect to.'

'That has to be significant though, the fact you felt different.'

She walked right round the edge, all the while scanning up and down, hoping to find something, anything, that would give them a reason to be there. On a whim, she walked to the dead centre of the room and stood directly under the apex. She tilted her head right back and fixed her eyes on the point where she supposed Arrix's statue would be on the top.

Looking up, saved her life. She spotted the cracks developing directly above before the apex opened up with a tremendous bang and the statue came crashing through. She shouted a warning to Pella and ran back, flattening herself against the wall. The statue landed with a bone jarring thud upright on its plinth, wobbling from side to side and in danger of tipping one way or another.

Through the dust, she shouted, 'It's going to fall over!' There was no response so she called out again and again, all the while tensing her body, ready to dart one way or the other. The dust stuck to the back of her throat and her cries became a series of useless splutters.

She was desperate to locate Pella and to get out of there. When she was sure the statue was reasonably stable, she moved round the edge of the room in search of him. He was on the other side, pinned to the wall, his hands splayed out, and his face covered in brown and yellow grime. The whites of his eyes stood out, staring up at the statue.

'We've got to go,' she said, tugging his arm. She had no idea what state the stairs would be in, but they had to try. He did not move. 'Come on, Pella. Pella, are you hurt? Talk to me!'

A menacing creak from the floor to their right was followed by more scraping and grinding noises suggesting it was in danger of continuing its downward journey.

That they had met Taron at the complex in similar circumstances when he had come crashing through the ceiling did not occur to her until she followed Pella's gaze up. Below Arrix's expressionless face was his breastplate which was covered with brightly coloured rings of different sizes. Covered, save for two very obvious gaps next to each other towards the base of the plate.

Pella raised a finger. 'Halos.'

This was why Taron had brought them here. Taron had dropped the two halos she and Pella were looking after shortly after his dramatic arrival and knew they needed more to give them a chance of getting back to Earth. She forgot about the immediate danger for the moment as questions fizzed into her brain. Why were the halos on Arrix and was it him who had arranged to hide them in plain sight, as it were? How did Taron know about them and why the secrecy? What exactly were Taron's motivations for helping them and could he really be trusted if there was this strong link to Arrix? In the absence of any other strong option, she decided she had to trust him, at least for now. They had to take what halos they could and get out of there as quickly as they could.

'I'll climb up,' she said.

Pella was suddenly alert. 'No! I don't think they're all halos. I'll know which are which when I get up there.'

'How?'

'By their size. They'll be uniform.'

'In which case, I can do that. This scavenger body was made for climbing.' She was off before he could argue 'No disrespect, Pella,' she said over her shoulder, 'but yours wasn't.'

The statue had to be at least five or six times taller than her and would be incredibly heavy so she was not worried that her weight would make much difference to its stability. If it was going to go down, it would do it with no help from her. She took a few seconds to work out a route up. A couple of large pieces of rubble would give her a head start to take her to the top part of his extended legs. From there she spotted potential handholds on the joints of his upper legs and another one at the base of his cloak. After that, she would have to see.

She pulled out the halo from her pocket to remind herself of its size. She had her eyes on some just above the ones that had been in the gaps.

'Wait!' said Pella. 'They may not come off easily.'

'I'll manage,' she said confidently as she started to climb.

Taron had got them this far. It was her job now to make sure his sacrifice was not in vain.

Mackenzie

Mackenzie did not see Jerome fire the shots, but he, like everyone else, heard them along with the screams which echoed around the bay. Ignoring his guards, he ran round the front of the MASH and towards the base of the slope. He was aware of the guards following, but he did not care; his main concern was for Don.

The scene that met him was not pleasant.

Shaw was half on his side, still propped against the small wall that he and Don had been sitting against. His arms were crossed, his hands pressed against the wounds further up, and his army issue tunic was already covered in blood down to both wrists. He had his eyes shut tight and his face was white as, through gritted teeth, he attempted to stifle the screams. The noise that came out instead reminded Mackenzie of a dying fox he had accidentally run over once. That one, he had had to put out of its misery. Hopefully, something could be done for Shaw, but with his hands still bound, Mackenzie could do nothing practical to help. Fortunately, Don was onto it. He had already pulled off his jumper and started to rip his shirt apart to provide bandaging. Jerome was doing nothing to stop Don, but his face was set in an amused half grin. Lessey was frozen to the spot, her face aghast.

Mackenzie stood over Don and Shaw, feeling as useless as Lessey looked, then he twisted round and started towards Jerome. 'Why?' he shouted. 'Just tell me why?'

The guards grabbed hold of him by his shoulders and wrists and held him back.

The Frenchman snorted. 'Orders.'

Mackenzie looked around for Ruby who had settled herself on a bench on the other side of the bay, apparently now engrossed with something on the floor. He shook his powerful shoulders and nearly escaped the guards' grip.

Jerome twitched his gun and Mackenzie stopped. 'You're a monster,' he growled, then shouted across, 'all of you are monsters!'

Don had managed to shred two rough strips, one of which he placed around Shaw's arm where there was the most blood, tying it off tightly. The action drew a whimper from Shaw.

'I need to take a proper look,' Don said, starting on the other arm. 'These won't work long,' he said turning his head. 'For the love of God, get me some proper bandages and something to kill the pain. Then he needs a doctor.'

Jerome shrugged. 'Non. Not possible.'

'He could bleed to death!'

'Come on, man!' Mackenzie pleaded. 'This isn't necessary.'

'Take him,' Jerome said to the guards and Mackenzie was whisked round and marched back to the MASH. He took a final look over his shoulder to see Shaw unconscious now, slumped on the ground with his head on Don's jumper, and friend preparing more strips to soak up the blood.

Odette was waiting for them. She spoke to the guards. 'Put him on that seat in the back, then I want you to get that plate off. Ruby wants to watch when you use the heat torches to melt it down.' She looked across pointedly at Mackenzie who, with a gun at his back, was being encouraged into the MASH. 'We all want to see the quarton appear.'

She joined Mackenzie inside the MASH on the front seat as he was thrust onto the seat behind. 'He's fine,' she told the guards. 'I have my gun. Get the plate off.' She took her gun out of the holster as they left. 'I have more questions, Mackenzie.'

'Odette...' he began, but she shook her head.

'Non. I can do this without your help, but it will be quicker if you cooperate and then you and your friend may not die.'

'You've seen what Jerome and Ruby are capable of,' he added hurriedly. 'You're making a big mistake.'

'I know already what they are capable of. Are you going to answer my questions or not?'

He looked at her, but her face gave nothing away. He paused and then said, 'What do you want to know?'

It did not take long for the plate to come off by which time Mackenzie had filled in some of the gaps in Odette's knowledge. She had demanded a quick run-through of the main component parts at the back. Her brain was quick and, through the follow-up questions she fired at him, she continued to understand far more than she had a right to in such a short space of time. By the end, she had as good a working knowledge of how to use it as he did. His hopes that she would be willing to renege on actually following Ruby's plans were fading fast.

Mackenzie heard voices approaching and he looked out of the side window. One of the voices belonged to Don who was being accompanied over.

'Major Shaw is already unconscious,' Don said. 'He might die unless I can stop the blood flow.'

'That's not what I asked you,' said Ruby. 'Have you made the announcement to the nations as we agreed?'

'Yes, but...'

'And you, President?' she said without turning round to Lessey who was a few paces behind with Jerome.

'Yes.'

They all drew to a stop. 'With no tricks?'

It was Jerome who answered. 'No tricks. They both said everything you wanted them to say.'

'Good.' Ruby walked round out of sight for a moment and then Mackenzie saw a small hand tap on the front windscreen. 'Shall we get this quarton, then, if you've got all you need, Odette?'

Odette gave a thumbs up and shuffled back on her seat, allowing Mackenzie, rather awkwardly, to pass through and out the passenger door. He was definitely not built to get in and out of vehicles with small doors, yet here he was being asked to do so again and again. Having his hands tied did not help matters, and he nearly lost his balance as he stepped down into the space next to the MASH where the steel plate lay on the ground. Everyone except Shaw and one guard were crowded around. He managed to catch Don's eye. He looked mentally battered, yet Mackenzie saw enough there to know that, should they have the chance to make a move, he would be ready. Despite the desperate situation, it gave him some solace.

As two of the other guards set to work with the heat torches, Mackenzie thought of Chuck and the original message he had recorded with Lee. Chuck had said that he hoped no one would have to listen to the message as it would have meant he would have failed. Mackenzie could not accept that his friend had. Chuck had given his life to stop Arrix. He had destroyed a whole army and prevented the invasion. Yet with only the resources available to a little girl, Arrix had found another way. Mackenzie really should have been good enough to stop him, but he had been unable to. It was Mackenzie who had failed.

Apart from the crackle from the white hot flame, there was silence. Even Lessey seemed entranced as the two men worked their way over the plate towards the middle section, examining each section carefully before it was given a chance to solidify again. Just before they reached the middle, a glowing bright green light appeared which, as the steel melted around it, became more vibrant. It was a dominant presence, even in the massive space of the loading bays.

'That's not supposed to happen,' muttered Mackenzie to himself. He could only assume Chuck had made the plate up himself. They did not have many secrets between them, but this was one Chuck had kept.

Ruby's eyes were glinting and she had a manic grin on her face. 'Careful now,' she said to no one in particular. 'Don't be fooled by how much it's shining. It's tiny. Use the tongs to get it out of that section, keep the heat on it and take off the surrounding metal bit by bit.'

Jerome picked up a brick and set it down on the floor nearby, onto which the melting metal with the quarton inside was carefully placed. Wearing thick gloves, Jerome worked on the metal using smaller tools to cut and scrape away the excess metal before the steel set again. Very soon, the quarton was clean and cooled sufficiently to be picked up with a pair of tweezers. Jerome offered it to Ruby who put up one hand to decline it.

'Put it in something and give it to Odette to look after for now. I'd better not touch it... just in case.'

That comment seemed to pass the group by, but Mackenzie understood the reference to the quarton's possible destruction and that of the four Garalians connected to it, if Klavon had touched it. Perhaps it might not be a bad thing if he did. Even if Fen could not return as a result, at least the world might be rid of the horror show that was Ruby. For now, at least.

For a moment, Ruby seemed mesmerised as Odette held out a small metal box in her palm and Jerome placed the still glowing quarton inside. She quickly snapped out of it.

'Right, on your toes now, people. I want one of you to keep an eye on the prisoners, the others, Jerome, I want posted around and on high alert. Odette, I'm with you inside the MASH.' She clapped her hands with glee. 'We've got visitors coming soon and I want to make sure they have the warmest of welcomes.'

She looked across at Mackenzie. Arrix had studied him with his alien features just before Mackenzie had fired the MASH. On that occasion, Mackenzie had felt terror and evil, all in one go, but this was not the sum of the feelings he got now. Ruby's was a look that had something with another layer to it, something with more mischief and callousness behind it.

It was a look that Lee had given him and Chuck when they had first met in Paris.

It was a look that suggested Klavon was in control.

Fen

The climb up Arrix's statue involved one or two heart in the mouth moments and a period of self-doubt as she reached the point where she could touch the rings on his breastplate. None of them looked the same as the halo she had in her pocket and none of the ones around the gap where she thought hers and Pella's had been taken from came off. Close up, it was hard to compare exactly, but there were definitely ones which looked much bigger and one or two considerably smaller which she decided to ignore. There were dozens more which could be halos.

She managed to get herself in a position where her feet had decent foothold enough so that she could hang on with one hand and get the halo out of her pocket again. As logically as she could, she went along as many of the bottom row as she could reach, holding up the halo to each ring. If it was within a few millimetres, she put the halo back in her pocket and tried to pull it off. She began to despair when none came off. However, she had more success on the next row, the first one she tried coming loose with a sharp tug. She was tempted to hold her arms out in triumph but thought better of it when she looked below at Pella's concerned face.

'Be as quick as you can,' he called up. 'Drop them when you have them. I'll catch them.'

She did as he suggested, working along the next two rows and then looked for a further way up. She quickly discovered that there was a reason she had not been able to see a route up beyond a certain point – it was because there was not one. This was definitely as far up as she could go. She had collected ten halos in total and had to assume that would be sufficient to get them home. How, she did not know, but she could worry about that when she had got back down.

Her fingers were very sore where she had been gripping jagged edges and her arms and legs were screaming at her that they had had enough, so she called out below: 'Coming down... that's all I can reach.'

Without being able to see the hand and footholds as easily, it proved to be trickier than climbing up. 'A little bit of a steer would be appreciated!' she added, waving her foot around hopefully before finding a secure point.

With a final backwards jump, she made it to the bottom where she brushed off some of the muck and dirt from her top and hands. 'Phew!' she said turning round. It was at that point she realised why there had been nothing in the way of encouragement or guidance for the last few minutes. There was no sign of Pella.

With a feeling of dread building in her stomach, Fen quickly skirted round the statue. She called out to him, but he definitely was not in the dome.

A loud creak from around the base told her it was time to get out. The entrance to the stairway was partially blocked by a broken section from one of the outside struts, but there was just enough space to climb over and onto the stairs. She continued to shout as she clambered down the stairs, trying not to contemplate the possibility that he had double-crossed her. She preferred to tell herself that he was going to jump out from around one of the bends and surprise her with a poorly judged joke. She would even forgive him if he did that as she approached the doorway at bottom of the stairs and there was still no sign of him. If he was still moving away, he could only have about five minutes on her. She would fancy her chances of beating him in a foot race if it came to it so she set off back down the corridor they had come up at a sprint, saving her voice for a few choice words she had planned for him when she caught him.

It was when she reached the bottom that it hit home that the unthinkable had, in fact, happened. With the entrance to the dome they had used in sight, she slowed right down as it became very obvious that not only was there no Pella, there was also no Taron.

They had left him inside, right by the door. Both had accepted – both – that he was dead. It was hard to remember but had Pella been keen to give his opinion? Not really. Regardless, it did not change the conclusion she came to – she had been tricked.

Taron's injuries were genuine, of that there was no doubt, so maybe he and Pella had decided that, since they were too weak to get to the halos, Fen should be the one to get them and then they would make off with them... together. But why? What would they gain by leaving her out? So much had happened since she arrived that it was too much to think it was all a ruse to get hold of more halos, yet maybe it was. They would have had time to make plans before they had picked her up in the flyer on the mountain. As mental and physical exhaustion began to take over, she could think of no other plausible explanation.

Putting her hand to her forehead, she leant against the wall and slid down onto her haunches. People she had strong connections to, people she trusted, had conspired to deceive her. With Sam dead, without Chuck and Mackenzie and the likes of Don Berretti, no one had come as close to understanding her as Pella and Taron had. To Pella especially, she had opened the door to her heart and it seemed he had walked right through it. She was alone, trillions of miles from where she wanted to be, and she had no clue what she should do next.

Crying was not going to help in the slightest. But she decided she was going to do it anyway.

Lessey

Lessey had not particularly enjoyed speaking to the leaders. Frankly, she was not in the mood to go along with this objectionable little brat much longer and was beginning to wonder whether it was worth all the effort. In addition, her main man had been shot. As hopeless as Shaw could be sometimes, he was all she had for the moment, but he would not be much help now with holes in both arms. Used to seeing the odd act of violence growing up in a rough part of Dublin, the sight of blood had not bothered her. The casual way in which Jerome shot her major, had. As had the fact that they had been on to her plan to leave a clue as to her whereabouts. Were they psychic or something? The theory that Ruby was some kind of spectre was gaining credibility.

It was fortunate they had given Lessey a script to follow as she was still recovering from the shock, though she had been with it enough to appreciate from the leaders' livid reactions that she was now fully committed to this course of action. Since they well and truly blamed her now for the deton attacks, it placed all of her eggs firmly into one basket. She needed to find a way to dump the girl quickly, use the turmoil created, along with the resources Ruby had, and strike so much fear around the world that everyone would go along with whatever Lessey demanded.

She did wonder what all the fuss was about now, everyone crowded around a bit of metal while a couple of Frenchmen played with blow torches. But her ears pricked up at the mention of the word, 'Quarton' and something else about tempting Fen back. She was aware of some sort of connection between Ruby and that alien-woman, as she had called Fen. It appeared that this quarton thing was inside a sheet of metal. Now that could be interesting.

She watched and waited – though it was a big disappointment when it was finally revealed. It looked pretty enough with the shiny green light, but there was barely anything to it. It seemed unlikely to be the secret to the massive energy resource that she had been hoping for. It was so small that they put it into a tiny box. Now what was going to happen?

Whatever it was, they were not paying a lot attention to her just at that moment, so Lessey edged slowly towards Odette. As the guards moved to the positions that Ruby had instructed them to, Lessey grabbed the youngster's gun from her holster and shoved it hard into her back. With the other hand, she tapped Odette's wrist.

'I'll take the box,' she hissed, smiling as Odette opened her hand and dropped it into hers.

Ruby had spotted her now. Lessey waved the box in the air. 'A lovely gift, thank you,' she said. 'You must have known I'm from the Emerald Isle. Us Irish love our green jewellery.'

'I wouldn't, President Lessey,' Ruby warned.

'Oh, I would. You're not playing by the rules so nor will I. You obviously need this little one here. If you want to keep her and this,' she flicked her head towards the box, 'then I suggest you start playing ball.

Stay exactly where you are,' she shouted. Then, using Odette as a shield, she steered her towards the passenger's door and up into the MASH, signalling for her to move to the driver's position as she followed her up.

Settling into the passenger seat, she noted that no one had moved. She was not home and dry, by any means, but she was rather pleased with the way it was turning out. She could yet make something rather spectacular out of this situation.

'Now,' she said to Odette. 'You know how this thing works, don't you? Show me the button that blows everything up.'

Fen

Fen was losing track of time. With thick clouds coming and going and neither sun setting fully, there was no easy way to judge what part of the day it was. She was not convinced it mattered that much. Somehow, she talked herself into standing upright and walked out of the dome, back the way they had come from the flyer. She was not expecting it to still be there and she was right – further proof that Taron was alive and active. Perhaps she should be pleased that he was not dead? She did not feel that pleased, nor did she feel anger. Whatever their motives were for abandoning her, maybe they were better than hers which, she had to face it, had been driven in part by hatred and revenge towards Arrix. She tried to draw on those emotions now to see if it could spur her into action, but she could not feel it in the same way.

She wandered aimlessly around the rooftop, hoping something would pop into her brain and tell her what to do. After a short while, something did, driven by some basic needs – she was thirsty, had hunger pangs and needed to relieve herself. She quickly attended to the easiest of the three needs and then turned her attention to the more challenging goals of finding food and water.

She wondered, briefly, whether the coding was going to intervene in some positive fashion on this or make her life hell for a while longer. To a large extent, that was out of her control. What she could influence was what she did – doing something was much more preferable to sitting around waiting for solutions to fall into her lap.

There was nothing on the roof so she would need to get to ground level. That would be an achievement in itself. It offered no exit points other than the way back to the dome. On the opposite side was a collapsed building, too far down and too risky to jump onto. One of the other sides overlooked scrubland and had an even bigger drop, thirty or forty metres to the ground. The side in the direction of the city looked more promising. A dilapidated sloped roof ran off it and led to a mangled tube which zigzagged its way down the outside of the building. In London, she had seen examples of similar tubes. She was no architect, but she had always assumed they were ventilation pipes, although this one's large size suggested it might have some other function.

The tube was well worn, enclosed in some places, open at the top in others, barely attached to the building in most. If she could get onto it, she might be able to work her way down the outside and drop down inside where there was a gap. With luck, it might take her all the way down to the bottom.

'There's only one way to find out, Fen,' she muttered under her breath and headed for a point on the sloped roof which looked vaguely stable.

The first part went well. She managed to shuffle down the roof on her backside, get onto the tube and crawl for quite a distance on top before she was faced with a large hole. As she sat on the edge contemplating the drop, she could see that the tube, opaque from the outside, would have been transparent from the inside if it was not for the filth that had built up. She landed with a squelch into thick, black, sticky gunge. It helped break her fall, but she could not stop overbalancing backwards into the foul-smelling mess.

With some effort, she stood up, her arms, legs and back covered, only to slip straight back down again after a couple of steps. The stench was overwhelming, catching at the back of her throat as she struggled to her feet again then coughed, spluttered and squelched her way through the tunnel, doing her best to avoid the dripping globules that splattered from above. The insides seemed to move with her. If she had been swallowed whole by the Laric, this is what she imagined it would have felt like.

With some relief, she came to a section with a large opening at the side. Gratefully, she gulped mouthfuls of fresh air and steeled herself for what looked like about the same amount of hell to negotiate again to the bottom. It was at that point she realised that the feeling she had just noticed of her left leg sinking further down into the gunge was not correct. When she looked down, it was quite the reverse – the gunge was actively sliding up it.

She pulled her leg up but, as she did so, the same thing happened to her right leg and immediately again to her left when she placed it down again. Every time she took a step forward, she felt her feet being sucked down followed by the inevitable movement up the leg. Before, the suction had been almost passive. Now there seemed to be a deliberate attempt to capture each leg and hold on. As she moved forward, each movement became harder. Very soon a herculean effort was required just to take one step. The smell had, impossibly, got even stronger, made worse by the fact she was panting hard.

Breathless, she was forced to stop, at which point there was a sudden tightening around her feet and ankles. She could not move her legs at all now, and she watched in horror as the black muck began to rise again. It was soon above her knees. When it reached the top of her legs, tiny root like jet-black threads emerged from the mud. Some wrapped around her thighs whilst others continued to snake up towards her waist. More and more threads appeared around her now, coiling directly upwards and latching on to different parts of her body. She flailed her arms as she felt contact with her hands and wrists. The threads responded to her movement, lengthening, twisting and multiplying, coming at her from all sides and joining to form a macabre dome over her head. Her wrists were firmly gripped now, her arms pulled out and back, splayed at an angle she would never have thought possible. She twisted her head away as a thread touched her nostril, only to be met by another one from the other side which started to wrap itself around her forehead. Her chest tightened as more wound themselves around and around her waist and torso. She lost all feeling from the neck down until soon, as her entire head was enveloped, the only sense left to her was that excruciating smell which found its way through tiny gaps in her nostrils.

She was a fly in a web, helpless, with her life being squeezed out, little by little. There could be no way to survive this, surely? No rising from the dead, no body swapping, no reincarnation, no way back. Maybe this was the only way to be free of the coding: by having the very existence crushed out of her, her body turned to mush and her life force lost forever in a river of mud and slime. Through it all, she snorted an ironic laugh – at least she would not have to meet Arrix again.

Neither, though, would she get to see Martha.

That hurt. To have gone through all she had, only to be thwarted because she had chosen the wrong route was, frankly, maddening. If she was going to die, she decided, she was going to go down fighting.

Mackenzie

When Lessey put the gun to Odette's head, that was the split second Mackenzie and Don might have been able to do something. But it was so unexpected, the moment came and went. And with Jerome and all the other guards with their weapons drawn, it was impossible to take advantage of the situation. That was not to say that another opportunity would not arise, and Mackenzie could see from Don's quick raise of the eyebrows that he thought so too.

Lessey was now in the MASH with a gun, in exactly the situation Mackenzie wanted to be. She would have her own reasons for doing what she had just done – he did not think for one minute that she was doing this as part of any kind act – but at least it had unnerved Ruby and bought some time.

By the looks of things, it had done considerably more than unnerve her.

From the way Ruby's face contorted – into shapes that no young girl should possibly be able to produce –there seemed to be a fight for control from within. Her eyes, wide and staring, flicked from side to side and up and down. The cheeks, alternating between crimson and pale white, puffed in and out, her mouth opening, as if to speak or scream, between breaths. Her fists clenched into tight balls, then exploded open before clenching up again. Her whole body jerked back and forth, left and right, every action having an opposite reaction, as a battle raged between Arrix and Klavon.

The guards watched on totally bemused. Prompted by one, Jerome walked over and gently touched her shoulder, but his gesture was rejected with a wild swing of the arm followed by a look of pure fury which forced him to retreat several paces. It was a war for which Mackenzie wanted no victor, but the fact that the others were concerned was a good sign. Ruby, in whatever form, needed the support and help of others. Maybe – just maybe – the tide was turning against her.

He checked to see how Odette was dealing with it from the MASH. Lessey was on the other side of her, looking over her shoulder and as intrigued as everyone else. Odette, too, was watching closely, but stared directly at Mackenzie for a moment.

'See?' he mouthed.

Her face gave away nothing. It seemed Mackenzie might have to rely on his own resources if he was going to sort out this mess.

Ruby shuddered then froze, before her face relaxed into a neutral expression, like a china doll. Whatever had been going on inside had been resolved. Very deliberately, she moved her head around, as if reminding herself where she was. Her brow furrowed and then she nodded before beckoning Jerome over to her with one finger.

Jerome took a few tentative steps before stopping. 'Give me your gun,' Ruby said, her voice ominously quiet.

Jerome hesitated. 'Why?'

Her tone did not change as she repeated the instruction: 'Give me your gun.'

There was silence, broken only by a whimper from Shaw in the background. Jerome looked around for support from the other guards, but they seemed unwilling. Reluctantly, Jerome put the nozzle of his gun in the palm of his hand and held it out to Ruby.

There was never going to be a better chance than now. If Mackenzie could take out Jerome, Don would back him up. As Ruby grabbed the handle of the gun, Mackenzie rushed at Jerome. Mackenzie had many attributes which allowed him to come out on top in most combat situations, but stealth was not one of them. Both Ruby and Jerome heard and saw him coming. Jerome, realising he was the main target, made a frantic attempt to take back the weapon. The gun went off just as Mackenzie's right shoulder rammed into his side. Both men ended up in a heap with Mackenzie on top and the gun spinning off to one side.

Mackenzie had fallen onto his injured shoulder, and he knew it. But Jerome had come off considerably worse. As Mackenzie rolled off him, he could see the large hole in his chest. He was quite clearly dead. Out of the corner of his eye, he had seen Don respond to his attack on Jerome by lashing out at one of the guards, but another had him covered with a gun now. He stood nearby with his hands raised, looking ruefully back at Mackenzie. Cursing the bonds that held his hands together, Mackenzie floundered around in an attempt to get up. He stopped when he saw Ruby standing over him holding the gun.

'You won't be needing that body anymore, big man,' she said.

It was the last thing Mackenzie ever heard.

Lessey

It all happened so quickly. 'What the feck...?' was all Lessey could manage as first Jerome was taken down and then Mackenzie was shot.

With the guards seemingly rooted to the spot, Don rushed over to Mackenzie. As he did so, Ruby collapsed to the floor too, forming a macabre triangle of bodies with Mackenzie's and Jerome's.

Odette turned towards Lessey, her face ashen, her hand over her mouth. The reaction summed up the last mad thirty seconds very well and Lessey nearly did the same back, before she was hit by a sudden moment of decisiveness.

'Right,' she said. 'That's all fine. Let's go!'

She was met with a blank stare.

'Get yer hand off yer gob and let's get the feck out of here. Come on – drive!'

'I... I don't know if it will start.'

'Well, now's the time to find out.' Lessey lifted the gun and placed it between Odette's eyes. 'Isn't it?'

The girl nodded. She leant down between them and pressed a button. To the left of the wheel a virtual mini dashboard sprang up and there was a low whine as the engine fired up.

'Good girl!' Lessey said. 'Now, get us out of here.'

Odette grabbed the wheel and accelerated away. Lessey expected gunshots to be ringing in her ears as they roared through the bay, past Shaw and up the slope, but there was nothing. She barely gave her major a second glance. Halfway up, she checked in the passenger mirror. There had been some movement in the bay: Don was still attending to Mackenzie and the guards were now split between Ruby and Jerome.

Lessey could hardly believe her luck and she chuckled as she sat back in her seat. She immediately sat forward again after they took the last bend and the closed door loomed in front of them. Odette screeched to a halt.

'Tell whoever's on the other side to open it,' Lessey said.

Odette spoke into her bracelet and the door scraped open. When there was enough space, Lessey shouted, 'Go!' and they were through it before the pilot, who had been left there on lookout, could react.

A quick check in the mirror again and Lessey was satisfied she had got away scot-free.

'Right,' she said to Odette as they headed away from the store. 'Give me your bracelet. I've got one or two calls to make.'

Klavon

Their partnership was always doomed, yet it had got them this far, almost to the point where they only had to settle who was going to have absolute control over the coding. As far as Klavon was concerned, it was going to be his to manipulate as he saw fit.

It already was. It had evolved, its powers strengthened and diversified and so had he. He had managed to silence Arrix and now he was ready to leave this girl's body. He wanted something better – a body that was befitting someone of his stature, big and

258

strong, closer in form to the Klavon that had destroyed the Garial Bridge.

He had not meant to shoot Jerome along the way. The man had been loyal and was useful, but accidents happen and the gun had gone off. No matter; he had what he wanted and Mackenzie's dead body was his now. He would reclaim the MASH and make sure he was the last one left.

Arrix had always said that Klavon was impulsive, and that planning and paying attention to detail were not skills he possessed. Arrix was absolutely right. If he had not been, Klavon might have been much more careful with the gun and ensured there was not another body available for Arrix to jump into.

Fen

Fighting back meant deliberately removing the block her consciousness had put in place to help her cope with her current dire situation. Being more aware was not a pleasant state to move to as it involved some considerable discomfort.

She was being squeezed to death. Her breathing, which had become more and more shallow, became a battle now as she struggled to stay alive. Tendrils had already worked their way up her nostrils and she could feel them snaking down the back of her throat. She gagged which came at a cost. Her mouth opened and immediately more tendrils forced their way in. Frantically, she tried to spit them out, but still they came. Each breath in brought a renewed attack through her nose and mouth and it became an impossible task to breathe and keep them out. Frantic now, she bit down. Her teeth sliced through the tendrils as easily as a knife through butter. She felt a slight twitch, a reaction possibly, before the tendrils began their relentless pursuit down her throat. She bit down hard, again and again. On each bite, she spat out a mouthful of slime. By biting, snorting and spitting, she found she could get into a breathing rhythm, of sorts, and slow the progress. She was alive – just – but how long she could keep this up, she had no idea.

Then, gradually, the tendrils snaking through her nostrils began to retreat and there was less probing around her mouth. From somewhere, she found the strength to move a finger and a thumb, located a tendril and squeezed it tight. It popped surprisingly easily and she detected a slight loosening of the creature's grip.

She was hurting it.

She found another thicker strand, did the same again and her whole hand became free. With it, she grabbed a chunk and squeezed as hard as she could. There was a satisfying squish as she broke through which resulted in a further slackening. Tendrils dropped from around her head and neck and she was able to move her legs and arms. She could not get rid of the thing quick enough now. She stamped, clawed and crushed until she felt the last piece slip away from her ankle. There was a loud slurping noise and much of the mud around her feet started to flow upwards. Desperate to get away from the vile smell and that feeling of violation from within, she headed down as quickly as she could, slipping and sliding, not caring much how she got to the bottom or whether there were more traps or even holes she might fall through on the way. Nothing was going to stop her now. She burst through the opening at the end, stumbling and somersaulting her way to safety and fresher air.

She ended up, almost comically, sitting on her backside, her legs stretched out in front. With a quick glance behind, she got to her feet and ran.

Breathlessness slowed her down and brought her to an eventual halt. With her hands on her knees, she took in great gulps of air, retching as gut churning aromas assaulted her nose and the back of her throat. From somewhere, she had found the will to survive. She might live to regret that decision if she had to live with this stench over her for much longer.

After a while, her breathing returned to normal and she drew herself up to take in the surroundings around her. She had run in a straight line away from the dome, a good couple of kilometres at least. She was on a road of sorts, covered in potholes and debris and flanked either side by a mixture of open spaces and decrepit buildings. Looking back along the route she had run, it was a miracle she had got this far without falling and causing further injury.

Some of the grime had begun to dry already so she brushed and shook off what she could. It did little to reduce the smell, but she felt a little better for having done it. Her desperation for water was now driven by both thirst and the need to get the slime out of her system. It would not be an easy task in a city uninhabited for thousands of years, although they had found water at the complex which gave her some cause for optimism. The fact that cities were normally built in places where natural resources were available had to be a positive sign. Perhaps the river they had travelled on might have a branch coming off it in this direction. There was no way she was going to retrace her steps to see if she had missed anything, so she plumped for continuing along her current route. As she walked, her mood took another dive. Being on the verge of death yet escaping it so many times was not a recipe for happiness and fulfilment. Her life as Fen – more than any other of her previous lives – was full of such contrasts. She questioned whether it would really make a difference to Martha if she lived or died. Was it even worth the effort of looking for water now when there was bound to be something else afterwards that pushed her to her limits again, shunted her back towards death and all the mental and physical torment that entailed?

She was so preoccupied by these thoughts that she nearly missed something that had been staring her in the face since she had been on the roof by the dome. It had been getting increasingly dark since she had come out of the dome and the light had faded considerably more in the last few minutes. Yes, the planet's light was affected by the movement of its suns, but it was also affected by the clouds. Those clouds had been bubbling away above her head to the point that they were more than ready to dump the heavy amounts of water inside of them. She looked up just as the first few splatters of rain started to fall around her.

She stood there with her mouth open and savoured every tiny drop until, eventually, the rain became torrential and she was soon taking in enough to quench her thirst. After that, she spread out her arms and let the water wash away the filth. It was not the sort of rain anyone would usually stay out in at all. To Fen, it felt like heaven. Even after the dirt had gone, she stayed put, eyes closed, mouth open now and again and her arms by her sides as the water continued to cleanse her inside and out.

Once more, something had happened to turn things around for her. Although chilly, she felt fresh and new, ready to face whatever challenge the coding threw at her next.

What it threw at her next was not all what she was expecting. When she opened her eyes, she was back in the room she had shared with Lee in the department store in London.

Arrix

Of course, it was far from over.

Klavon might think he had the means to win but he did not. Arrix was well aware that the coding was evolving. Of all of them, he had lived with it the longest, understood it the best, used it the most. Evolution was part of its makeup which was why Arrix craved it so much. If it did not evolve, it would not meet his needs. It was still evolving now and was meeting his needs very nicely.

Building the Garial Bridge had been the start of the real evolution. Up until that point, Arrix had been living over and over in new incarnations, always the soul that made Arrix who he was, but never quite the being he wanted to be. The reincarnation called Arrix – a leader, capable of doing whatever he chose – was who he really wanted to be, and the building of the bridge had been the first stage on a quest to stay that way.

However, his will to span the galaxy in search of new quartzite to make new quartons was only part of the grand plan. The quartons were always going to be a temporary measure, a link between him and the coding, there as long as he needed them. There until he found something more manageable, less clumsy, with less effort required. It had gone wrong when the bridge was destroyed by Klavon and it had taken thousands of years to get back on track. But Arrix was patient. He had let the coding adapt to its environment and had adapted with it.

That was evolution.

Arrix no longer needed a bridge full of quartons to help him move from place to place and to live on and on. Small amounts – like the slither he left on Garial in a duplicate body, like the fragment inside of Fen and like the tiny piece Chuck had left in the MASH – were all that were needed, and not for much longer either. He did not need his warriors. He had survived without them and was close to conquering the Earth again. It had taken a year sharing a girl's body with Klavon to make him understand that fully, during which time they had built a new army with everything it needed. And he would do it again, in any circumstances, because he was the coding's keeper and they were the perfect combination. Adapt and evolve – both of them, together.

So when Klavon decided he had had enough of their partnership, Arrix had stayed quiet and let the coding do the rest. The oaf had seen what he wanted – Mackenzie's body – and grabbed the first opportunity the coding had given him to get out of Ruby's. The coding could facilitate a body transfer at will now and Arrix had seen that one coming a long time ago. Arrix had gone along with Klavon's blind and stupid urges, knowing another body would be available. Jerome's was perfectly acceptable; strong, capable, a familiar face to his followers and was well respected.

As for Lessey grabbing control of the MASH, what could she do with it? Nothing without Odette's cooperation and Odette was loyal to the cause. She would be even more loyal when she realised who Jerome was now.

His followers were crowded around his new body right now. There seemed no better time to surprise them. He opened one eye and smiled Jerome's smile.

'Bonjour! Did you miss me?'

Klavon

Klavon, in Mackenzie's body, had been rolled onto his side by Don in an attempt to revive him. From there he had a fairly good view of proceedings. The MASH had gone, which was a slight concern, but he would soon get it back. Don was being watched by one of the guards. Klavon's old body – Ruby – was lifeless at his feet. And Jerome... well, maybe he had survived the accidental shot as there was some movement in his legs. He was a valuable asset so he hoped that was the case.

Now would be a good time for him to reveal himself and take control of the situation. Yet, he could sense something was wrong.

A few moments later when he heard Jerome speak, Klavon realised exactly what it was.

Fen

Her first thought was for Martha. If this really was her old room, it meant that she was back on Earth and an awful lot closer to her daughter. She needed to believe it first though. Then she could dare to hope.

The room was as she remembered it to be. There was the door to the cupboard where she and Lee had stored their sleeping bags, still hanging by one hinge in the corner. The remains of the rubber mattress she had used was on the floor opposite where Lee used to sleep. Behind it, at the end, was the secret hole in the skirting where Fen had hidden the quarton, its temporary covering disturbed when Lee had been bribed by Arrix into betraying her friend. The room even had the same musty damp smell that she had woken up to every day, before dragging herself from her bed to face another tortuous day scavenging for scraps. It was like going back in time, as if nothing had changed. She half-expected to hear Sal's gruff voice through the door behind, shouting out her name, ordering her to him. She shivered at the thought.

She wandered over to the cupboard and ran her fingers over the wood of the door. It creaked as she moved it, threatening to fall off the hinge. Next to it was the cracked mirror she had never used. She looked into it for possibly the first time and barely recognised the face that stared back at her.

Underneath what used to be tight black curls that now lay splattered across her head were the deep brown eyes that Sam always said he loved. They were bordered above by eyebrows streaked with yellow and brown slime, and below by bags, puffed and heavy with fatigue. Scars crisscrossed her cheeks, competing for space with white blotches she did not know how or when she had got. Her lips were very pale; two thin white lines above a chin with purple bruises either side of a dimple. It was a face that had met death many times and come through the other end – and even in the dull light of the room, it showed.

Yet, it was also a face that, miraculously, was home. She watched her brows furrow slightly as she took in the implications of that. Home. Home was where Martha was, home was safe. Home was where the chance for happiness lay.

But she was not fully home, not yet. To get there, she would have to get through Arrix first.

There was a short burst of heat in her back and she knew the piece of quarton had made contact with a piece somewhere nearby. It was very close, moving away, but not far. The heat faded and she turned away from the mirror. She stood there looking at the door. After a few moments, she was not at all surprised to hear a polite knock.

'Come in,' she said.

Nor was she surprised to see the slightly bashful looking face of Pella appear through the gap. 'Are you ready for this?' he said.

She spread out her hands. 'Do I look ready?'

'No... I mean, yes... erm... not yet, maybe?'

She scowled at him. 'Let me do something with my hair while you tell me where the hell you've been and how I got here.'

'So you're not actually going to do anything with your hair, then?' Pella said as she brushed past him.

'It's called sarcasm, Pella. You've got some explaining to do, but first tell me if you know where Arrix is.'

'There's a group of armed people in the loading bay. Taron is pretty sure Arrix is amongst them, though hard to pinpoint.'

'Taron? So he's alive.' They were already at the stairwell. Without thinking, she had led them straight there, taking a left out of her room followed by a couple of right turns. The familiarity of the place was so weird on the one hand yet also oddly comforting.

'Where is he? Is he alright?'

Pella's eyes dropped. 'Not really. He's alive but only just. We both arrived two floors down. I came up to look for you and he went for Arrix. He made it back up to the floor below to tell me where he was and then collapsed.'

Fen was already on her way down. She found Taron near the stairs, half propped up against a wall, leaning across a stack of mannequins. She crouched down and when she said his name, he opened his eyes.

'You're making a habit of this,' she said gently, trying to smile reassuringly. 'Falling over, I mean.' She nodded at the mannequins. 'Friends of yours?'

Taron grunted and his mouth twitched, as close to a laugh as she was ever going to get, she guessed. She put her hand to his face and stroked his cheek. 'What can we do?' she asked.

His voice was barely audible. 'Nothing... this time.'

'Honestly?' As she said it, she knew it was true.

A mixture between a rattle and a moan came from somewhere deep inside him. 'Listen carefully.' He reached for her arm to pull her in. 'You sent me.'

'I sent you? What do you mean?'

'I understood.'

He stuttered and closed his eyes before lapsing into a sequence of wracking coughs. Fen looked helplessly up at Pella. He shook his head and said simply: 'Wait. He wants to tell you himself.'

A dribble of blood appeared from the corner of Taron's mouth which Fen wiped away with the sleeve of her top. The warrior was barely hanging on.

'I ignored you.' He had to be talking about her previous life. 'I was angry.'

'Yes, I understand.' That image of her in a previous incarnation shooting at the young Arrix and hitting Taron, her son leaving... Of course he was angry. She had never had a chance to explain, though she knew she had tried.

'I followed Arrix and became a warrior.' More painful coughs – it was breaking her heart to watch. 'But then I... I... believed.'

He went silent and she thought he had gone. She turned to Pella. 'Believed what?'

Before Pella could say anything, Taron spoke again. She put her ear right to his mouth. 'Believed you.' Then his lips froze and his chest came to a stop. Fen pulled back a little and put both hands on his cheeks. The black part of his eyes had been wide, but, as she looked at him, they contracted and faded away to almost nothing.

She had said goodbye to him at the dome not that long ago – to have to do it again was all the more painful, especially here when she was so close to... well, close to whatever her destiny would bring. She was powerless to help him now, but she could still help Martha.

She kissed her two fingers and placed them on Taron's mouth, then stood up. It surprised her how strong she felt suddenly. That strength had come from Taron. However, there were still massive gaps in her understanding and she needed them to be filled in, otherwise what she had to do next would make no sense.

'Right, Pella,' she said. 'I do hope you can tell me more. Talk.'

Lessey

'Where are we going?' said Odette.

They had barely driven a few hundred metres away before Lessey told Odette to circle round while she worked out what to do next. Lessey had got out of a very sticky situation by the skin of her teeth, and there was still a lot of work to do if she were to achieve her aims. She needed to stay close to the store and she needed backup, quickly. She tried to get through to Barrow and failed, presumably still blocked by whatever method the girl had used earlier. No matter – she knew the English would have eyes on them. It would not be hard to ignore a truck with a gun on top driving around the place.

It did not take long. An English flyer appeared from the direction of the river and hovered beside them. The pilot signalled for them to stop and landed just behind the MASH. Armed, he and a soldier got out and positioned themselves either side to the rear.

One of them barked an order: 'Come out, slowly with your hands raised.'

'Don't move,' she instructed Odette. She opened her door slightly and shouted out, 'I'm President Lessey. I need your help.'

'Prove who you are,' one of the soldiers called back.

'What?'

'Prove who you are.'

Lessey mumbled to herself before yelling, 'I'm the feckin' President! Get your feckin' backsides over here... now!' She glanced across at Odette and added, 'That should do it.'

Somewhat cautiously, the two soldiers appeared next to Lessey's door which she had opened fully. 'Satisfied now you're up close?' she said. 'Is this stunning portrait proof enough?'

'Yes, President Lessey. Thank you.'

'Good. Patch me through to your P.M.'

The conversation with the P.M. was tricky, bearing in mind she had threatened to exterminate the world unless her demands were met, but Lessey was used to juggling carrots and sticks and she quickly convinced the PM to be on board with her new plan. Within five minutes, the only short-range ground missile the English owned was locked onto the department store and Barrow was on his way with two new flyers with air to ground missile capability.

She was so pleased with her work that she totally failed to notice the brief written exchange on Odette's bracelet between her and Jerome's new persona.

Arrix

Humans definitely had a gullible gene as part of their makeup, Arrix decided. Jerome had been fatally shot, yet here he was, back to life and the wound was healing nicely. These fools were happy to go along with this miracle. Still, whether they thought it was magic or aliens, it did not matter providing they were loyal to him. And they would be, of that he had no doubt. As tempting as it had been to take Mackenzie's body, being in Jerome's would give him the added authority he needed in these early stages. Jerome was well respected and would be even more so when they realised who was now inside of him.

Two of the guards helped him to his feet and they all stood back as he took a moment to steady himself. Then he looked each one in the eye and made sure they all understood exactly who it was they were dealing with. Satisfied he had them exactly where he wanted, he walked confidently round to Mackenzie, picking up Jerome's gun from next to Ruby's lifeless body.

'Klavon,' he said, 'how's the new body?'

The face was Mackenzie's yet he could see Klavon in the eyes. The slight green tinge that indicated the coding was active was a giveaway.

'You took a chance,' Klavon said. 'I'm awake. I was about to take over.'

'Yes, awake on the ground with your arms behind your back and a hole in your chest.'

'It's healing.'

'As is mine – more quickly, I would say. Make the most of it, Klavon, because you won't be around for much longer. Help him up.'

He turned to Don. 'Colonel Berretti, I definitely don't need you any longer.' He gesticulated to another guard. 'Take him to a quiet corner somewhere and dispose of him...' He glanced over at Shaw

272

who was still slumped at the bottom of the ramp. The moans and whimpers had died away now. '... along with the major.'

'Now, Klavon, let's get this sorted. She's here, isn't she?'

'Who?'

'You know who. I've felt it and you've felt it. Rana's here... and Pella too, I believe.' There was no answer. 'Come now, we all know which direction this is heading. Play along.'

'You think you've won, but the coding is telling me otherwise.'

'Of course it is. It does that. Listen, I'm stronger, Klavon, more cunning and much more worthy. You might think that having the body of a grizzly is going to help you. It won't. Your vanity is your weakness – one of them, anyway. What on Garial made you think I wasn't on to you with your pathetic plan to dump me? Even if I had stayed in the girl's body, I'd still be stronger.'

'Aren't you missing something?'

'The MASH?'

'It's gone.'

'Correct. Give me a second or two.'

Arrix looked at his bracelet and swiped through a couple of times to contact Odette. Satisfied she was on silent mode, they exchanged quick written messages. He finished with a verbal, 'Confirm understanding of exactly when, where and who,' and smiled when she replied. He had been explicit with what had happened and who she was dealing with now, not that she needed that. She was clever enough to have worked it out.

'There... done!'

'Whatever you do, Arrix, it won't work,' said Klavon. 'The coding is mine to own. Your time is up.'

'On the contrary, but don't take my word for it. Let's find out. We're going for a little walk up top. There we will meet Rana, Pella and your collective doom. Imagine what it's like to be split into a trillion pieces and dispersed around the universe and then multiply that by a trillion. You, my hairy friend, are about to experience exactly that.'

'Predictable. Are you, by any chance, going to use the MASH to do the same to me as we had planned for Rana and Pella?'

'Bravo. There will be no coming back from a concentrated hit of dark energy. The coding will have nowhere else to go other than to me. End of you. Eternal life for yours truly. Take over planet. Do what I like.'

They were distracted by a distant muffled yelp and brief clumping of footsteps on the stone floor. The source was the far corner of the bay where the guard had made Don drag Shaw to.

'Rana!' Arrix shouted, too late. The door shut and she was gone, as were Shaw and Don, leaving the guard spread-eagled on the ground by the door.

Fen

Pella did have a lot more to tell Fen but not a lot of time in which to tell it. He crammed as much information in as he could while they had made their way down to the loading bay.

Before picking up Fen on the mountain, he and Taron hatched a plan which resulted in Fen being duped – 'Although, I prefer the word, guided,' Pella had said – into thinking she had been

274

abandoned at the dome. They had a good reason to keep her out of the way.

'As you hoped, the bridge did return to where it was built. Taron had said at the complex that he thought the halos could help get us back, however, there was a risk that you might be killed if they were activated near you because of the quarton in your back. For it to work, you had to be close enough so that when we hooked up the halos to the bridge systems, they connected to you via your halo and generated the energy to send you back to Earth, but far enough away to do it safely. We were relying on some sort of connection between your piece of quarton and here to get you to the right place. Fortunately, it worked.'

'Why did you just leave me? Why didn't you just tell me that?'

'Because you might not have agreed to what we intended to do. There was a high chance that with so much energy from the halos, Taron and I would be blown up on the bridge.'

'You risked your lives – why? What about Ruby? You're as desperate to get back to her as I am to get to Martha.'

'Look, Fen...' There was an intensity that Fen had not felt or seen in this version of her brother. '... I want to be with Ruby, but I can't forgive what Arrix has done to us, to Garial and what he's likely to do to Earth. He needs to be taken down because, if not, there's no future for any of us, Ruby included. I'm not the one who can do it, though. You are. Your link with the coding is stronger. You've got more of a chance of beating him.'

'You're wrong. If I've learnt one thing through all the lives I've lived it's that we need good people around us. You're a good person, Pella. We may have lost Taron, but we'll do this, somehow, and we'll do it together.'

His face lightened a little. 'Just as well because, as it turned out, wherever you go, I seem to go. The coding at work, maybe?'

'No doubt.'

Fen still needed one more piece to the puzzle. 'How did Taron know where the halos were?'

'It was based on what you told him.'

'What I told him?'

'Don't forget, you and I came on the scene as Rana and Pella quite late on in Arrix's rise to power. When you were Taron's mother, there were plenty of other Garalians not happy with Arrix. A rebel group you knew of got access to halos which could be used as potential weapons. The authorities heard about it so the rebels hid them... in plain sight.'

'On Arrix's statue.' Someone had a sense of irony. 'Wouldn't their energy source be detected?'

'Apparently not. I've no idea how they were put up there, but you told Taron where to find them in a message you left him, by which time he was beginning to see the error of his ways regarding Arrix. You never gave up on him, Fen, just like you won't give up on Martha, on any of us, in fact. I can't forget what you tried to do for me when I was Forrest and I know that what you tried to do for Ruby was done with the best intentions.'

She was about to remark on how badly those things had turned out before Pella went on, 'Taron smuggled two halos to Earth when Arrix returned with the warriors, hoping to find a way to use them against him. They were the two he gave us. I've still got mine.

Have you got yours?' She nodded. 'Hang on to them. They might still be useful.'

Pella finished his story just as they arrived at the loading bay. The final piece to the puzzle? Not quite, but it was enough to be going along with.

When they opened the door and saw the guard about to shoot Don and Shaw, they jumped him and disappeared back inside with both men. Don quickly wedged the door shut with a metal pole under the handle. 'Just in case they follow.'

'I doubt he will,' said Fen. 'Arrix knows I'll eventually reveal myself,'

She was pleased to have spotted Mackenzie before they retreated, still alive although dangerously in the thick of things. She wondered out loud whether they should go straight back in for him until Don told her what had happened just ten minutes earlier. How he maintained his military poise as he spoke, she had no idea. She wanted to scream and shout. Instead, she said, 'Let's get somewhere where we feel a little more secure.'

Between them, they helped Shaw up the stairs. Fen, acting purely on instinct, led them to a room off a short corridor away from the stairwell. As soon as she opened the door, she recognised the room. It was the abandoned staffroom that she and Forrest had been locked in by Sal while he prepared for the attack on the Eastsiders. The wooden bed Forrest had lain on while she recovered from the injuries Sal inflicted on her was still there, as was the old blanket (now even more ragged after twelve years) that Fen had put over Forrest to keep her warm.

Once again, Fen was struck by the symmetry of how it was playing out: the Garial Bridge being destroyed and catapulting them to Earth; Fen landing in her old room; the loading bay, somewhere she had spent a lot of time in her scavenging days, the centre of action again; and now the fact they had ended up in the same room where she had begun to discover so much about herself and her connections to previous lives and people. It was no coincidence, that was for sure.

Shaw had already started to stir. By the time they lay him down, he was conscious, though still in pain. Pella set about checking the crude dressings Don had applied.

While he did that, Fen cut to the chase. 'What does Arrix look like now, Don?'

Don described the Frenchman, Jerome.

'I saw him,' she said. 'And you say Klavon is...'

'Is in Mackenzie's body, it seems.'

'It's just horrible,' said Fen, touching Don's arm. 'Mackenzie was a good man – a very good man. For him to be killed and then taken over like that... What about Chuck? Where's he?'

'He died at the Severn Bridge,' said Don.

Another devastating blow. The good people she had so relied upon kept dying. She was about to say for that reason she should carry on alone when Pella cut in. His suggestion made that idea very unlikely.

'All this makes it all the more important that we destroy Arrix. You'll help us, Colonel?'

'Of course.'

'And me,' said Shaw. 'I'm not letting them get away with this.'

'With all due respect, Major,' said Don. 'You have gunshot wounds in each arm. I suggest we leave you here for now and get help to you as soon as we can.'

Without using his arms, Shaw sat bolt upright, nudging Pella to one side. 'Well, there's nothing wrong with your stomach muscles, anyway,' Pella said.

'I won't get in your way,' said Shaw, 'and I think I can be of some help.'

'How?' asked Fen.

'They've got my bracelet, not my earpiece. The signal's bad just here, but higher up there should be nothing to stop me picking up official communications. You say she took the truck, Colonel Berretti?'

'Correct, with one of the young women. I don't know her name, but she seemed to know what was what. They reckoned she knew how to operate the MASH.'

'Can I check whose side Lessey is on?' said Fen.

'Her own,' said Shaw bitterly. 'I regret to say that it's taken me too long to realise that.' He had taken the opportunity to swing his legs round as Pella stood up. He looked up at the others standing around him and then honed in on Don. 'From one soldier to another: I'm with you. I'll do anything I can to help. If I get in the way, leave me.'

'He's stopped bleeding,' said Pella, 'although it won't take much for the wounds to open up again.'

'Then that's my risk, isn't it?' said Shaw. 'Check inside my ear. You'll see the receptor. Believe me, I can help.'

'I don't need to check your ear,' said Don. 'It's your call, Fen.'

'Come along if you want to. It's not going to be much fun, though.' Shaw nodded, grunting as they helped him to his feet.

'Where now?' asked Pella.

'Up,' said Fen. 'There's nothing in the loading bay to make them want to stay in there.'

Arrix

Dark clouds were forming in the south west and there was heaviness which suggested a storm was on its way. As Arrix stepped through the door at the top of the ramp and out into the dim late afternoon light, he smiled to himself; it was the perfect setting for a finale. He could feel the coding reacting, jumping around almost playfully in response to the natural phenomena, a slight buzz that fizzed and crackled over his new skin and made his hairs stand on end. He smiled. He and the coding were meant for each other, a perfect match from the day he had wrested sole control of it.

Yet it tested him still, setting him tasks to overcome so he could prove his worth. This was the latest and he was determined would be the last one. After that, the relationship would change. With no one left to challenge him, he would finally be its master. He ignored the small part in him which could have told him he thought he had been in a very similar situation before.

He concentrated on the many positives. The various alliances and countries had been scared by the detons. When they saw the power of the MASH, they would be petrified. He might even stay on this planet for a little while: bridge building to other worlds using quartons was not straightforward or as attractive as it once seemed.

As predicted, the two pilots of the flyers he had just summoned were prepared to take orders from Jerome. Hovering off the east coast, they were less than five minutes away and were ready to provide support if required. It was tiresome that he had to do these admin jobs, but Odette would soon be free to step up to the second in command role vacated by Jerome. Her loyalty would be rewarded for what she was about to do and he had made sure she knew it in that earlier communication.

'Well, we're here,' said Klavon. 'When is Odette going to start shooting?'

'As soon as Rana appears.'

'With Pella?'

'Correct, with Pella.'

'What happens if I break free from these cords around my wrists and pummel you into the ground? What will you do then?'

Arrix laughed. 'You like Mackenzie's body, don't you? The big, strong man – the perfect body type to swing and bash his way to victory. Angry, bitter, resentful – all ready to avenge the deaths of his family. You're still the old Klavon on Garial. All brawn – no brains.'

'I've beaten you to the quartons many times. And I'll beat you again.'

Arrix stepped up to Klavon and they stood facing each other less than two feet apart. The two men guarding Klavon tightened their grips on his arms.

Arrix sneered, 'Beat me again, Klavon? Really? How?'

'That would be telling.'

'You're weak, Klavon. Weak and hopeless... just like your father.'

He recoiled as a large globule of spittle smacked him in the eye. He wiped it away with his sleeve and then nodded at the guards. One of them responded by placing one hand on his fist and thumping his elbow violently upwards into a point just below Klavon's ribcage. As he bent double, the other man followed it up with a knee which crunched into his nose. Blood gushed onto the floor, but Klavon stayed on his feet and quickly drew himself up. The face that used to belong to Mackenzie was barely recognisable as such – the nose was a mangled mess with blood dripping through his beard. A large rip on his swollen top lip leaked blood into his mouth as he opened it to form a macabre broad grin. At least two teeth had been knocked out, one of which suddenly shot out at speed and hit Arrix on the chest.

Arrix looked down as it hit him. The patch of dried blood from the bullet wound inflicted on him – now fully healed – had provided a handy target. 'Classy!' He placed his heel on the tooth and ground it down into the dirt. 'But you won't need that where you're going.'

Fen

They went up a set of stairs that Fen knew were rarely used, even during her scavenging days. Shaw, insisting he was there to help and not be a burden, said he could manage on his own. He could move both hands to a certain extent, not enough to use the handrail but, after the first stumble, they guided him upwards. It was probably just as well as, like everything else in the former Westsiders' base, the handrail was falling apart. Fen could smell the decay. Everything on Earth, it seemed, was still in decline.

The exit out onto the surface that Fen had in mind had rarely been used by the Scavengers. Like the other exits, save for the doors in the main store entranceway, they were boarded up, partly for security and, in the early days, to limit their exposure to poor quality air. There was an added issue now that the very small amount of building above the surface that there used to be had been demolished. It included the section which had the exit door she had been planning to use. They had hit a dead end.

'This is as far as we can go,' Don said looking up the stairs at the pile of rubble blocking their way. 'What's down that way?'

He pointed to a corridor that led away from the landing they were standing on. There had barely been any light on the way up – just glimmers through cracks and holes from way above and the odd shaft of electrical light from the floors they had been on. The loading bay had been well lit as had her old room and other areas, but this floor was pitch black. Fen took a moment to get her bearings.

'We weren't allowed in this part of the building, but I did sneak out once or twice. Where we are now used to exit to the west.'

'In which case, we're on the opposite side of the store to we where came in,' said Don. 'That ramp was in the southeast corner.'

'So,' Fen continued, 'if this is the last floor before the surface, there would have been a door directly up those stairs and to the left. It had been nailed shut from the outside, but I used to... hang on, it's coming back... that's right, go along that corridor there and there's an air vent on the left which they unblocked when the air got better. The screws to the cover could be loosened by hand. There was another cover at the other end of the vent that was the same. It was a short crawl up and out to the surface a few metres from the door. I only used it a few times. Too risky. Sal's bullyboys used to patrol all over the store.'

'How far?' said Don.

'Not that far.'

'Let's go then,' said Pella. 'You lead, Fen.'

'Hang on!' said Shaw. 'I'm getting something through my earpiece.' He went to put his finger to his ear and then winced in pain. 'That won't work with that arm, or the other one,' he said. 'It's okay, I can just about hear.' They waited patiently as Shaw listened, his head tilted to one side in concentration. 'Okay, the MASH is located nearby and there's chatter that indicates there is some military back up around – French-Irish Alliance and English. Lessey appears to be in the MASH and in charge. You're right, Fen, about Arrix making his way to the top. There's a small group just emerged by that entrance.'

'At least we know where we stand,' said Don.

'The MASH is crucial,' said Fen. 'Whoever has control of that has control of everything.'

'And the French girl who was with Lessey knows how to use it,' said Don. 'Mackenzie was forced to go through it with her and by all accounts she was a smart cookie.'

'So Lessey is effectively in control,' said Pella.

'I doubt that,' said Fen. 'Arrix will find a way – he always does.' She had said it before... and thought it many times.

'Hang on!' Shaw interrupted. 'The English have got a missile ready to go on this place. There's potentially more on the way from the Alliance. I suggest we get out as quickly as possible.'

There was a whining sound from outside. 'Too late!' shouted Don just before a loud bang rocked the building and clumps of plaster fell around them. They stood still, tensed for the next one... but it did not come.

'A warning shot,' said Shaw.

'Okay,' said Fen. 'Follow me and stay close. It quickly doglegs to the left and then we'll be in the dark.'

'I'll take up the rear and help Major Shaw,' said Don.

'I'll go in front of the major,' said Pella.

Once total darkness hit, Fen felt her way along the wall with her hands. They kept up a reassuring chatter between them, checking on each other as they moved as quickly as they could manage. Fen was aware of the crunching of grit underfoot and the odd noise as an unseen stone or piece of metal was kicked. She was reminded of how annoying she found it when bits like these kept getting under her mattress every night in her old room. No matter how thoroughly she swept the floor before going to bed, there would always be something that would disturb her when she rolled over during the night. Of all her memories over all of her lives, it was a strange one to come to mind now. Still, as with everything where the coding was concerned, there was a reason: it was taking her back to a time when Fen connected strongly with the quarton she kept in her room.

It made her stop suddenly, both hands spread flat on the wall. She was vaguely aware of Pella, next in line, bumping into her and the murmurs of discontent and concern as Shaw and then Don followed suit. 'Why have we stopped?' a voice said, but she was frozen to the spot. 'Fen? Fen?... We have to keep mov...'

Fen watched her younger self wait until Lee had gone and then removed the covering from the skirting board. She watched as she pulled out the quarton block and examined it. She knew every piece of it now – every crevice and crack, every slight bump. It was a thing of beauty for sure, yet so dangerous. Of course, young Fen was not yet aware of that danger. Older Fen wanted to warn her – tell her to be rid of it. Perhaps then, all the bad things that did happen might not.

She watched her younger self, wide-eyed and naive, gradually discover things about her past lives. She was transported to the lake with her, experienced again what she experienced before, shared her wonderment, then her pain and suffering, her sense of loss for wasted lives.

She watched her attempts to protect Klavon, driven by her own noble motives to stop the Garial Bridge being built. Each life was leading to the confrontation on the Friendship Bridge where Klavon would claim victory. She wanted to warn her that it would not be the end; it would go on. She experienced more quarton induced deaths with her, survived the explosion on the Friendship Bridge with her, confronted Arrix and Klavon again and then she journeyed with her back to Garial to learn more about her past.

All of this had been done for a reason. The coding had set out to test her. It had evolved to keep her alive – to find out how far she would go. She had once been prepared to murder her family on Garial to claim the quarton. It would try to break her. Make her do it again. Make her ruthless, more like Arrix, only better.

But, amongst all of it, there were positives. On the Friendship Bridge she had chosen compassion and kindness for Forest over protecting Klavon. She saw flashes of the good life with Sam and Martha, her friendship with Lee in this very place and there had been many good people who had surrounded her when times were hard.

Now as the original scene of her discovering the wonders of the quarton block faded away, she realised that a life of goodness was something the young Fen had wanted, but that the coding had put it beyond her reach.

That made her angry. Very angry. The coding may have thrived on anger. But she would be damned if she was going to let it use hers.

Fen ignored the voices and continued along the wall until she found the air vent. She felt for the cover, wrenched it off with one hard yank and threw it to the ground. Then she climbed up the shaft towards the specks of light shining through from the other end.

Part 6

Lessey

'Feckin' English!' Lessey moaned as she watched the explosion towards the back of the store. 'Call that a missile? I used to let off bigger ones in my back garden on New Year's Eve.'

Understandably, the English PM had been very reluctant to order a missile strike on a building in the capital city of his own country, especially since Lessey had refused to say whether there were any personnel inside, but she had him over a barrel. She had all the countries over the same barrel with the threats of the deton attacks still there, plus she had the MASH's capabilities up her sleeve. She was not that wrong in some ways with her comment about the size of the missile. Mounted on a truck it was one of only five the English maintained – a tiny fraction of the country's capability pre-war. Still, it was there and a shot towards the back of the building had signalled a threat to the people standing outside the loading bay ramp at the front.

'You've got a mighty guilty look on your face, young lady,' she said to Odette who was waiting patiently. 'You wouldn't be getting any ideas about playing dirty tricks on me, would you?'

'Dirty tricks?'

'Suddenly your English isn't so good. Dirty tricks – you know, going against me.'

'Non.'

'Good. If you play your cards right and cooperate, you could end up with a permanent job helping me out. I don't know what the weird girl offered you, but she's out the picture now. I have influence and much better organisation than anything she had. We could go a long way, you and me, and I wouldn't need to keep threatening you with this gun.'

'Okay. I will do what you say.'

Lessey waved the gun in her direction. 'This'll make sure you do, for now, but there will come a time when my people have taken a good look at how this thing works and you won't be needed quite as much. Just remember that.'

Odette nodded and Lessey turned her attention to her flyers which were just coming in to land. By now, they had been joined by the English truck that had fired the missile and another smaller vehicle with several English soldiers. They were all set out in a rough ring a few hundred metres from the store. As her men got out of the flyers, she beckoned over one of them.

'Name?' she barked.

'Captain Thomas, Ma'am.'

'Wait there a second. Update on our missiles, Barrow.'

'All set up. Just need exact coordinates.'

'Give him the necessary, Captain. I want the whole of whatever is left of that building smashed to smithereens, just in case anyone else is skulking around inside. Make sure your men are locked on to the individuals too in case they make a run for it. They've only got basic weapons so you can outgun them.'

'My men are already onto that, Ma'am. We had each target picked out from the air as a precaution before we landed.'

289

'Very efficient, Captain Thomas.' It felt good to be ordering people about and them responding so well.

'Ma'am. Visuals and coordinates sent. With your permission, I'd like to be with my men. Do you need someone else with you?'

Lessey glanced across at Odette. 'No, I think we've come to an understanding. Just make sure every single body outside that building is picked off if they try to make a run for it.'

'Yes, Ma'am.' Rather clumsily, because of the gun in her hand, she returned his salute before he set off. 'Barrow, we may not need you so fire only on my command.'

'Yes, President.'

'Now, young lady... Let's have a look at that group at the front.'

'It looks like Mackenzie and Jerome.'

'They were shot! How the feck did they survive?' Lessey stared out the windscreen in amazement before saying, 'Right, before we blow the whole building sky-high, I want you to show me what this thing can do. You can hit small targets as well as big?'

'Yes.'

'Good. Those two big fellas... Get ready to pick off the one without the beard. I'll teach him to disrespect me.'

'Yes, President Lessey. I can do that. No problem.'

Klavon

Unlike the guards around them, neither Klavon nor Arrix had so much as flinched when the English missile hit the ground towards the rear of the store. Klavon, for one, was too preoccupied with thinking about the coding.

He recognised that Arrix had always been the one in control when they had fought to find the quartons. Always ahead of the game, Arrix was often aware of where each one was even before the rest of them knew they were reincarnations. Yet it had turned out to be an even contest, falling to the last quarton block in London to decide on the fate of the Garial Bridge. Klavon had won that and had done it with no help from Rana. Not being tuned into or understanding enough about the coding could have put him at a significant disadvantage. It was a sign of his strength that, despite that, he was still there and fighting hard. He was convinced that made him special. Special and dangerous, particularly since he was now inside a body that could run through brick walls.

Against the odds and without the benefit of substantial knowledge, he would be the one who would claim the coding.

Fen

Fen reached the top of the shaft. She pushed gently at the grill and immediately found herself showered in rust. A little harder and, with barely a sound, it broke away on one side. There was no one close by so she crawled out through the gap towards a small mound of rubble. From that place of cover, she saw a group of people standing at the top of the ramp that led down to the loading bay.

There were six, possibly seven people. Klavon in Mackenzie's body and the other big man – Jerome, now Arrix – stood out. Not far to her right, she could see several military vehicles and flyers, and in the centre, the MASH with its familiar turret and gun on top. She felt a tingle in her back – there was that connection between

291

the two quartons again. It was possible the other piece was in the MASH. How fitting, in some ways, if it was – typical of Chuck, always the scientist, to keep a piece back.

The coding within her became more active, telling her to push on, urging her towards a resolution. Her rivals were right there, ready to be challenged. Yet she resisted; she would do this on her terms in her own time.

The final piece to the coding may well be in place, but her understanding as to how it all fitted together was not. Actually, she now realised, the key to that understanding could be right here on Earth, sitting inside the body of someone it had no right to be in.

She needed a not-so quiet word with Klavon.

Keeping low to the ground, she skirted back and round to her left to take a position directly behind the group from where she could act. The weapon she picked up along the way would certainly help. It occurred to her that it could easily be the exact shorn piece of railing that Klavon had used to skewer Marston, Arrix's reincarnation, at the Friendship Bridge.

Arrix

It was looking like the coming together that Arrix had hoped for. There was about to be quite the show and the whole world was watching.

Not all the moves would be choreographed exactly, but the performers were all in place and they knew their roles. It was the ending that was important and Arrix was confident of that. The coding would be his – his alone. There was an inevitability to it which was very satisfying.

Arrix took up a position next to the flyer they had arrived in. He had been a little girl then, now he was a man again, inside a body that was physically capable and, best of all, no longer chained up with Klavon. The idea of standing slightly to one side was purely to get a good view of what his former soul mate was going to do next.

What he did next did not disappoint.

It was preceded by a call to his bracelet from Lessey which he put on loud speaker for them all to hear. 'This is President Lessey. I am obliged by rules under the Geneva Convention to give you a chance to surrender. I will not be following this convention. I will, however, give you one minute to enjoy your last moments on Earth.'

'Kind of you,' said Arrix and cut the connection.

This distraction was the cue for Klavon to spring into action. He spun around to face his two guards who responded by raising their guns rather too casually, Arrix thought. They obviously had no real idea of how dangerous Klavon could be. Arrix had an excellent view of Klavon's remarkable strength from behind as, with a loud roar, he pulled his shoulders up and his arms out in one rapid movement. To the astonishment of the guards, the wrist restraints split and he was free. Mackenzie was on them in a split second, taking out the guard to the left with one swinging punch to the head which knocked him spinning onto the ground. The other guard got a shot away which either missed or had no effect because Klavon, his head lowered, simply bulldozed his way straight towards him. There was a sickening crunch as his head made contact with the jaw, and the man was propelled backwards onto a broken metal barrier to the side of the ramp. Klavon remained on his feet, his momentum taking him slightly to his right and towards the pilot who was standing nervously in front of the open entrance to the loading bay. She stood her ground, her firearm pointed directly at him. It was not needed as the two remaining guards came in either side of Klavon in a pincer movement. One hollered at him to stop which, after a few paces further on, he did.

'Arms above your head! Do it... Now!'

Klavon slowly raised his hands before turning ninety degrees to stare directly at Arrix. 'Is that what you expected, Arrix? Have I done what you wanted?'

'Very efficient and very entertaining. Thank you. Now for the finale.' Arrix took a few steps forward to the top of the slope, ready to signal to Odette. As arranged, she would have Klavon in her sights now.

It was then that Arrix wished he had choreographed the show after all.

Lessey

Lessey had been about to give the order to Odette to kill Jerome when Mackenzie had burst into action. Not only was Mackenzie still alive, apparently he was well enough to beat the crap out of two of the guards. And the Frenchman, who had no right to be there either, was just standing watching and smiling. What was going on? It was getting harder and harder to fathom. Then, just as she thought Mackenzie had been contained, the violence started up again, this time from another source.

'What the...?' was all she could manage as Fen, wielding the railing she had found, leapt from nowhere and sprinted directly towards Jerome. Coming from the rear to his right, he had no opportunity to react as she swung her arms back and struck him hard on the side of the head. There was a very short pause before Jerome's knees buckled and the rest of him crumpled to the ground. Barely breaking stride, Fen swung round and came to a halt facing Mackenzie.

'Is that alien-woman?' A horrible knot had suddenly formed in Lessey's stomach.

'Alien-woman?' said Odette.

'Zoom in... quickly!' she snapped, and leant towards Odette's screen to study the close-up of Fen's battered and dirt strewn face. 'Well, for feck's sake, it is her. I thought she'd had it.'

Feeling increasingly flustered, she reached over Odette and pinched the screen to zoom in even further. It was the eyes that had drawn her in, glowing green, with just a dot of black in each. She had seen eyes like that before. She still had nightmares about green-eyed aliens, dressed in black, descending from the skies.

She pulled back, suddenly unsure of herself. There were things happening here which she was finding increasingly hard to understand and she could feel the recently regained confidence rapidly evaporating. 'Right... hang on...,' she said. 'Where's Barrow? Barrow... Barr... no, the captain I spoke to... Is he here?'

Her hands had started to tremble and the array of controls in front of Odette had become a blur. She knew she needed to make a decision, yet that seemed a mammoth task. She blurted out the only option she could think of: 'Direct that thing at the whole building. Just press go and blow up the lot.'

'Non,' said Odette.

'What?'

'Non, absolument, non.'

Totally wracked with self-doubt now, Lessey managed to stammer, 'Go on... fire!'

The girl shrugged – that Gallic shrug that Lessey detested. Geron used to do it sometimes. He was probably doing it right now, shrugging away on a beach somewhere, cocktail in hand, being waited upon. She wished she could be on a beach, away from this, away from so-called aliens, quartons, people. Why was she doing this? At her age, especially.

She was aware she was in danger of completely losing all control. When Odette held up the gun Lessey had been using, she knew she had.

'You should be more careful, President,' she said.

Lessey felt she ought to say something to reassert her authority, when her mouth opened, no words came out. She stared blankly at Odette for a moment before, exhausted, she slumped back into her seat. She had an overwhelming urge to close her eyes in the desperate hope that, when she opened them again, everything would be exactly the way she wanted it. Maybe she might even be on that beach with Geron?

Fen

Fen had taken out Arrix. It had been a huge risk, but it had paid off... so far. Klavon was her target now. Crouched in front of him, the railing in both hands to the side with the sharp point above her head, she was ready to do what she had to do – after he had talked.

She was aware of the pilot and Arrix's guards nearby. Without taking her eyes off Klavon, she growled, 'You're out of your depth. I suggest you go.' There was a pause and then the shuffle of footsteps as they fled the scene.

She wavered for a second. To see Klavon up-close in Mackenzie's body – the body of a gentle man, kind, brave, loyal, a friend to her and Sam – was so tough. Don had said Klavon had occupied it; actually feeling him in it was pushing her beyond the limits of what she thought she could bear. She desperately wanted this part to be over as quickly as possible.

This is Klavon, she told herself. Remember that.

The smashed nose and contemptuous grin on his face helped, as did the way he spoke. The voice was Mackenzie's but the sarcastic tone could only belong to one person. 'You never cease to amaze me, Fen. Here we are again: old friends, colleagues, family, lovers maybe?'

'Never that.'

'You might be right.' He took a step towards her.

'Stay!' she shouted. 'You move one more inch and your head is coming straight off.'

'Fen! No need to be so aggressive.'

His huge hands came up, palms facing her, the tips of his fingers barely a metre away. She fought the temptation to take a pace back; she knew to do so would give him the advantage with his height and reach. Where she was, she could use her greater dexterity to get inside and strike, so she held firm. She could feel metal spurs from the railing digging into her fingers. She did not mind; the pain was helping to keep her alive to how precarious her position was.

'Now, I like that!' Klavon said looking at the railing. 'Just like the one I used to impale Marston with on the Friendship Bridge. When I've finished beating you over the head with it, I might just go and make sure Arrix is finished off in the same way. Was it the left side or the right side I impaled? Ah, you might not know. I think you were busy crying in the corner somewhere. What was it? "Pella, Pella. No, no!" Ah, poor Pella. Perhaps if he had been able to touch that last quarton, things might have turned out differently.'

'Have you finished?' she said.

'Where is Pella? He must be around somewhere.'

She ignored the question. There were things she had to say, gaps in knowledge she wanted filling in. Then she would do what she had to do.

'You know, you weren't the first, Klavon?' she said.

'Weren't the first what?'

'Klavon was not the first incarnation.' There was a flicker to the smile he had painted on. 'I've been back to Garial,' she continued. 'This all started a long while before the Garial Bridge was even thought about. We've been reincarnating for a very long time.'

A slight raise of the eyebrows. 'That makes no difference as to what's going to happen next. You've walked straight into this. You clubbing Arrix has just made it easier.' His face suddenly contorted. 'I'm going to break every bone in your body, find Pella and do the same to him and then...'

She interrupted him. 'Your father knew about reincarnation, didn't he?'

'You know nothing about my father,' he spat. It was true to some extent but, as Rana, she had done some checks before she recruited Klavon to help destroy the Garial Bridge.

'I know he worked with Arrix and that Arrix slaughtered your family. Why? What did your father find out? You never told me.'

His face visibly reddened and the huge knuckles on his hands, by his sides, whitened. It was a dangerous tightrope she was walking.

'Think back. Your father discovered something. What was it?' She was making a bagful of assumptions, trying to join dots that she could not be sure existed.

'My father knew what a heartless bastard Arrix was.' Despite the strong words, Fen detected a seed of uncertainty.

'Go on. What else?'

'There was nothing else!'

She was in danger of pushing too hard. She softened her voice. 'You know more. Tell me, Klavon. It might help us both understand.'

'Understand what?'

'Why we do what we do.'

His eyes dropped and there was a short pause before he said, 'Why we do what we do?'

She said nothing, waited, hoping that her instinct was right and that Klavon had something, anything, that might help her – them, even – beat the coding.

There was a pause as he searched his brain, and then he said quietly, 'I found a data droplet of his. There was something on it about a rogue gene.'

'What sort of gene?'

'He was unsure. It was in Arrix's DNA. Arrix had asked him to study it. The way it was made up – the codes were different.'

'Code, coding... so your father knew about the coding?'

'Yes, he found out that...' Klavon raised his eyes again and his expression had changed. The confidence and arrogance had gone and he looked puzzled, worried, almost lost, vulnerable. It surprised her and she felt her resolve begin to fade. She gripped the railing more tightly. Things could change for the worse very quickly where Klavon was concerned. She risked a quick check past him. Arrix was still flat on the floor and the guards had gone. It seemed quiet for the moment.

'What did he find out? Try and remember.'

'It was so long ago... But, I think... Arrix wanted him to isolate the code. It was mutating and he wanted my father to help him to control it.' He held her gaze. 'My father wouldn't. Said what he was trying to do with the bridge, his grand plan, was wrong. They fell out and Arrix, well...'

'Anything else about the coding?'

'That it's like a virus. He said it could not be controlled.'

'A virus?'

He shook his head. 'That's all I can remember.'

He placed his hands on his chest and stomach, ran them over and across his arms. 'I can feel the coding at this moment. Can you?'

'Always, it seems,' she said thoughtfully. 'Especially now.'

'I thought I could own it,' he went on. She nodded sympathetically. 'Perhaps I can't. It's wild, beyond my control, beyond any of us. We're just its hosts, doing what it wants us to do so it can survive.'

Klavon's insightfulness, so simply put, summarised perfectly the concerns she had had all along. She lowered her arms and the metal railing clanged onto the floor as she let it slip.

To the coding, they were tools, hardwired into a biological programme they could not change. Throughout, they had been so easily manipulated. The way the coding had moved them across the galaxy, backwards and forwards, using the expertise and knowledge of individuals like Pella, Larm, even Taron with the halos. It had played on their motivations, their wants and aims. Her love for Sam and Martha, her need for justice, her desire to save the planet when she was Rana, her guilt at killing her family in that first incarnation, even the anger that had been driving her on now. It had used Arrix's greed and ambition, his determination, his ruthlessness and selfishness, his strengths as an organiser and a leader, his relentless patience. With Pella, it had exploited his intelligence to be able to develop the quartons, used his loyalty to Arrix, at first, and then to Fen, his kindness, his love for Ruby, his humour and positivity to help keep Fen going on Garial. And with the giant of a man standing in front of her now, his physical strength in many incarnations, his callousness, viciousness, hatred towards others, his thirst for revenge at all costs and, conversely, the love he had for his Garalian family.

Even the feeling that she could control the coding, any of them could control it, was part of its ability to manipulate them. They had been conned: she was wrong when she thought she had started it all with her choice at the Brack; she was wrong to think that any of them had ever had a choice with anything they had done. They were being controlled – of that she had no doubt whatsoever.

Even now, with the railing still at her feet and Klavon off guard, potentially at her mercy, the next decision she took was unlikely to be truly hers. Yet, maybe there was something it could not control.

'Klavon, I... I...' she began, but she did not finish the sentence.

There was the crack of gunfire and, involuntarily, she ducked. Cursing herself for her complacency, she turned to see Arrix staggering towards them, gun raised and with blood pouring down the front and side of his face. He fired off several more shots in quick succession, two of which hit Klavon and another scorched through her tattered top below the collar bone. She screamed as Klavon crashed to the floor beside her. Desperately, she tried to stay on her feet and reach for the railing, but another shot ripped through her shin. She twisted as she fell and ended up sprawled on her back across Klavon's legs.

In agony, she looked up to see Arrix standing over her. She had done a thorough job – the upper side of his head was partly caved in, his left eye swollen like a mauve balloon and his cheeks and temples were a mush of blood-soaked hair, skin and shards of bone.

'Good effort, Fen,' he said. Blood sprayed out of his mouth as he spoke. 'You nearly had me.'

'I might yet,' she said through gritted teeth.

'Interesting to hear you two talk. Klavon's father became a pain in the backside. Poor old Arna. Much nicer than his son, though.' Fen's head shook as Arrix kicked Klavon's thigh. 'He was way ahead of his time, was Arna. Genetics. I learnt a lot from him. Anyway, here we are again. Another ending, another miraculous recovery from you? I think not.'

She suspected he might well be right. Still, she owed it to Martha to try. She owed it to all the people who had believed in her to try.

'You can't control it,' she said. It was hard to speak. She suspected another bullet might have hit her because an excruciating pain had now started in her stomach.

'I can.'

She coughed. A salty, metallic taste ran over her tongue before she swallowed the liquid back down. She knew what that was: blood from her lungs. Not a good sign.

'Arna said at the time that I was a genetic freak of nature. He was wrong. As I came to realise, four of us had this gene, the coding, with its wonderful ability to transcend space and stay with us in our minds, our hearts, our souls, wherever we go. Arna was right in the end, though. There is only one. That's me.'

Fen wanted to sleep, get out of the pain she was feeling, yet if she could somehow keep going... She forced her eyes to stay open and shook her head. 'No...'

'You're weak, too nice. It doesn't want nice. It wants nastiness, a will to win at all costs. It's a basic law of nature to allow organisms to adapt, evolve, and get stronger. This is about survival of the fittest and I'm the fittest.'

She heard a macabre laugh and he might have said more, but, if he did, she did not hear. Her time was nearly up.

Lessey

Lessey's only became fully aware that she was still sitting in the passenger seat of the MASH when she felt a hand being slapped across her cheeks. Startled, she looked up to see Don looming over her.

'Good,' he said, 'you're back with us. Right, Lessey, say the following into this bracelet: "Stand the missiles down, Barrow." Got it?'

'What?'

He repeated the phrase twice until she found herself, still shaken, saying those exact words. When Barrow confirmed the action, Don broke the link.

There was someone else beyond Don in the cramped space at the front, looking into a visual projected up onto the front windscreen.

'Major Shaw?' she said.

She was taken aback by his response. 'President, we've got a situation here so, with all due respect, shut the feck up.'

Before she could even think about how to respond to that, there was an urgent shout behind her. 'Fen's in trouble!' Lessey turned to be met by more flashing lights and visuals. Crouched over Odette was a man she had briefly spoken to during the crazy bridge incident last year – he had said he was Ruby's father.

'We might not be able to help her now, Pella,' said Don.

Pella! she thought. What kind of a name was that?

'We're nearly ready to go,' said Odette.

'What's nearly ready?' she asked, but she was ignored.

'Shots fired, Colonel,' said Shaw.

'Fen's down. I've got to get to her!' Pella lunged forward and clambered over Lessey on his way to the door.

'Should I direct our team to extract the girl from the loading bay, Colonel?' said Shaw. 'I assume she's still in there.'

With one hand on the door and his elbow wedged on Lessey's shoulder, Pella stopped. 'What girl?'

'Klavon and Arrix were in a girl's body before they transferred,' said Don. 'Very unfortunate to say the least.'

'What's her name?'

Lessey felt an urge to contribute. 'Ruby. I have to say, that's some weird daughter you had there.'

'Had?'

'Collapsed. Probably dead.'

The man stared at Lessey in horror before pushing her to one side and scrambling out the door. She watched him sprint towards the store.

'Ruby's his daughter?' said Don under his breath. 'I had no idea.'

'What do you want me to do?' asked Odette.

'Just so I'm clear,' said Lessey, 'Odette's not on my side and she's not on the side of the scary girl who was that man's daughter... so who... ' Her ramblings petered out as Don spoke over the top of her.

'Odette, can you operate this on your own?'

'Yes.'

'Okay. This is what I want you to do...'

Lessey tried to interrupt again. 'Can I just...'

'For the last time, stay out of this,' Don snapped.

Lessey nodded weakly. After years of meddling, she was ready to do exactly that.

Klavon

Klavon was hurt, very badly hurt, but he was conscious, just. He had been in similar situations many times before – they all had – and he knew how things usually panned out from here. This time, maybe, it would be different. Klavon knew now he was a victim, part of a programme gone awry. It might not help get him out of this hole, but it gave some comfort as he felt his life begin to slip away.

It did nothing to diminish the loathing he felt for the man standing above him.

He had fallen on his side, his face against the concrete lip of the ramp. It had gone quiet, just the sound of his and Fen's laboured breathing. And then he heard footsteps moving a few paces away, a scraping sound of metal against concrete and footsteps back again. He guessed what was coming next. He felt Fen being dragged off

306

his legs followed by the sole of a huge boot on his shoulder which pushed him hard and forced him onto his back, leaving him helpless with his arms spread either side.

Arrix moved round to stand at the top of his head. Klavon watched as the jagged point of the railing rose slowly.

'Nothing to say, Arrix?' he said quietly.

There was a slow shake of a head and an upside down smile before the lights went out.

Fen

As Klavon was rolled over, so Fen's head went with it, jolting her back into awareness as it hit the ground. It took her a moment to realise where she was and another one to establish that Arrix, having just done the deed on Klavon, was about to do the same to her. She watched the railing's sharp point twitch as Arrix began the downward movement.

'A different path,' she said. From somewhere, she had found her voice.

He paused. 'What?'

'Humans don't... have... the virus.'

'What virus?'

'The coding.'

'So?'

'They can... can choose a different path.' Her eyes, barely open, flicked to his left. She smiled.

'Enough!'

'The human in us is stronger than you think.'

307

The railing moved again. With his badly battered face and only one functioning eye, Arrix looked truly demonic. Only one functioning eye also meant he had a non-functioning eye. It was this blind side which Pella exploited to the full as he thundered in low to the ground, his shoulders smashing into the side of Arrix's knees, and driving him several paces off the ramp onto his back.

'You're a dead man, Arrix.' Pella shouted as he scrambled to his feet and grabbed the discarded railing.

With Arrix on the ground floundering for the gun in his front pocket, Pella swung the railing low and hard, crashing into the fleshy part of his upper arm and sending the weapon flying. Within a second, the railing was up and back down, this time catching Arrix across the knee as he frantically shuffled backwards, the soles of his feet scrabbling for purchase in the dirt. There was a sickening clonk of metal on bone followed by a high-pitched scream, loud enough to reverberate across the whole city. Arrix managed to roll onto his front and was halfway to getting up before he was flattened by another resounding thump across the middle of his back. The wind taken out of him, he collapsed onto his stomach.

Pella struck over and over, punctuating each punishing hit with deep throated grunts until, eventually, Arrix lay motionless. One last grisly crack on the back of his head and it was over.

Pella dropped the railing and, panting heavily, put his hands on his knees. He turned his head towards Fen and nodded. Mouthing a single word, he pointed towards the entrance to the loading bay of the store and staggered off to find his daughter.

It took a few seconds but, just before the beam from the MASH hit and her world changed forever, Fen worked out what her brother had said.

Quite simply: 'Payback.'

Fen

The next few weeks were spent recovering from her injuries in the medical centre in London. Initially, Fen was in a coma. When she awoke after a few days, she was mute, unable to react to anyone or anything. Don waited until she was physically well enough to travel, and then he returned her to Australia in the hope that she would respond to being reunited with Martha. It was a canny decision. The moment Fen saw Martha running across the landing strip towards her flyer, she immediately began to open up. From then on it was about her and Martha. Her, Martha and Sam – she would make sure Martha never forgot her father.

They spent a week with Sam's family and then they returned to New South Wales. With Sam's memories all around them, it immediately felt comfortable there at 'Our Middle of Nowhere House' as Martha called it.

Snippets of past lives returned occasionally, but Fen was learning to live with them. 'Never forget,' she could remember telling herself when Sam was alive. Well, she could now do that, if she so chose, in the certain knowledge that she and Martha were finally safe. Arrix was not coming back, and the links to Garial had been severed forever. Rana, and all the lives either side of Rana's life, would die when Fen died. She was sure of that, because there was nothing inside of her to tell her otherwise.

Fen had refused a debrief, but she got one anyway. Don turned up unannounced one day in a flyer, landing on the other side of the conifers that bordered one length of their garden, scattering the cockatoos in a melee of angry squawks.

'That's not the way in,' Fen said, folding her arms as he stepped through a gap in the trees. 'We've got a gate at the end of the garden.'

'I'm sorry,' he said. 'I wanted it to be a surprise.'

Fen looked up at the white birds, the yellow under their wings glinting in the sunlight as they flapped around indignantly before reclaiming their perches. 'Well, it certainly was that. What do you want, Don?'

'To talk. Get a few answers. Give you a few answers.'

'I'm not ready.'

'Maybe not, but the rest of the world is. It's still on a knife-edge, Fen, after what happened with Arrix. Lessey's antics didn't help much. We think we can sort it by diplomatic means... if I can get the whole picture.'

Fen sighed. 'Martha's having a nap. We can sit on the veranda.'

Don refused the offer of a beer with a smile and a, 'No thanks... I'm driving,' but said yes to ice-cold lemonade.

'A toast to absent friends?' said Fen raising her own glass.

'Absent friends,' said Don.

Alone in their own thoughts, they sat on the swing chair Fen and Sam used to share, sipping their drinks and staring out at thick clouds gathering over the hills in the distance.

'Storm brewing?' said Don after a while.

'Not anymore,' said Fen giving him a pointed look and raising her eyebrows.

Don smiled. 'I hope you're right, Fen.'

'I am. Arrix, quartons, the coding, Klavon, nothing's left... except me and Pella. How is he, by the way?'

'Still in a coma. Doctors think he'll pull through, eventually. On that subject...'

'What caused the coma?'

'Well...'

'Never mind,' she said matter-of-factly. 'I don't need to know. I want to be there when he wakes up. He'll need support when he finds out Ruby is definitely dead. They told me he never reached her, never got to see her.'

An unexpected lump appeared in the back of her throat. Pella had risked everything at the end – for her, for everyone – knowing that Arrix had to be stopped. She had been lucky because she had got her daughter back. Pella had not. It hurt to think about the sorrow he would feel.

Don waited a moment, and then started, 'Fen, I need to...' but she moved the conversation on before he could finish.

'Lessey's locked away, isn't she?'

'Awaiting trial through the international courts. She caused a hell of a stink. They'll put her away for a long time, I hope. We've

311

still got to round up all the members of the organisation Arrix and Klavon set up. There could still be detons out there.'

'I have no doubt that you'll get them, Don.'

'I know we will. Look, Fen. There's a major issue here. Something I – not just me, the whole political world – needs to be clear on. It's why I've come today.'

'That sounds worrying. Go on.'

'Okay... a question: why are you and Pella still alive?'

'I'm not sure I understand what you mean.'

'Alright, let me go back a bit. After we split up from you in London, we headed straight for the MASH. Mac always maintained that we could destroy Arrix with it, and I hoped Pella would know how to use it. As it turned out, Odette...'

'Who?'

'Odette, one of Arrix's followers. Mac had got to her – persuaded her of the error of her ways.'

'That sounds like Mackenzie.'

'Mac all over. Anyway, Odette knew how to operate the MASH...'

'...and she set it off when Pella came to rescue me.'

'Correct. I didn't plan it that way, but it was kind of... how can I say this?... convenient.'

'Pella saving me was convenient?'

'In one way; I needed Pella out of the MASH.'

'I'm not with you.'

'It made my... er... operational decision easier to implement.' Don shuffled uncomfortably in his seat before taking a great interest in the bottom of his glass.

Fen stared at him. 'Operational decision?' she said. 'What operational decision? What are you talking about, Don?'

He was avoiding eye contact. 'You know that the world is still recovering after the Power Wars. The environment's a mess, but there's a real will, internationally, to do the right thing, to rebuild properly.'

'And?'

'Well...let me put it this way...'

He paused again.

'Don! For goodness sake – put it one way, at least!'

'Well, okay.' At last, he looked at her again. 'In a nutshell – we can't have aliens running around threatening the planet.'

She stared blankly at him.

'Look, we're satisfied that the MASH did what Mackenzie said it would do. It extracted every last piece of dark energy from anything connected to the quartons. Klavon and Arrix, in the form of Jerome's and Mac's bodies...' he paused and swallowed before continuing, '...Jerome's and Mackenzie's bodies, they're gone. Quarton fragments, yours and the fragment Odette held, gone. There's nothing left... Nothing left, except you and Pella. Both of you had the coding in you. Putting it bluntly, Fen: You're all connected; how come you're not gone?'

It was a good point. So far, it had been enough to know that Arrix and the coding were no longer a threat.

'Well, I don't know. Maybe when Odette hit Arrix and Klavon with the MASH...'

Don held up his hand to stop her. 'No, Fen, listen. It wasn't just Arrix and Klavon we hit. We went for all four of you... separately. You and Pella too.'

Fen turned her head away and tried to process what Don was saying. Then it clicked, and she looked back at him.

'Because you can't have aliens running around threatening the planet.'

He did not need to say anything more. He was a military man – part of the Southern Alliance. It was what Sam had devoted his life to – 'Out and about... busy saving the world.' Don was doing the same.

He was sitting patiently, waiting for her to speak. She knew he deserved a fuller explanation; she was just not sure she could give it.

'It's definitely over, Don,' she said.' No green eyes... look.'

'Fen... I need more than that.'

'Yes, I guess you do.'

What she had was the certainty that the coding and the quartons were no longer part of her. She was not gone; they were, and that was all that was important. But how to convince Don? She thought carefully before, eventually, she spoke.

'Don, I've done all of this so that Martha doesn't have to experience what I've been through, what we've all been through. Sam, Mackenzie, Chuck – they can't have died for nothing.'

'No....' Don pursed his lips and lowered his head. He had lost people close to him too. 'No, Fen. I suppose not.'

'I can't explain why we're not gone, but I can say that if the threat from Arrix wasn't over, I couldn't live with myself. More importantly, I couldn't live with Martha. She's the ultimate test. I'm accountable to her.' She placed her hand on top of his. 'It's all about Martha. It always was.'

Don held her gaze for a moment before nodding. 'I get that. Sam got that too, didn't he?'

She moved her hand away to tackle a tear forming in the corner of her eye. 'Yes, yes he did. And Mackenzie and Chuck.'

'All good people.'

'The best.'

'The best.'

Don emptied his glass then stood up. Business-like, he straightened the belt on his uniform trousers and adjusted his tie,

'Well,' he said, 'now I guess it's my job to convince the rest of the world that it definitely is all over.'

She gestured for him to give her his glass and then put it down on the table next to her own. 'You're very convincing. You'll manage,' she said preparing to ease herself out of the seat.

'I guess I will. I have no choice.'

She stopped midway, momentarily surprised by his words, and then stood up to face him.

'That's not quite true, Don,' she said seriously. 'We all have choices. We wouldn't be having this conversation now if we didn't.'

Epilogue

Fen watched Don's flyer take off. Just as it began to disappear into the distance, Martha came running out and crashed playfully into her legs. Giggling, she grabbed round Fen's waist with both arms and put her bare feet on top of Fen's.

'Walk, Mummy, walk!' she cried.

Stiff legged, Fen set off back towards the house complaining what a lump Martha had become and how her own legs were going to fall off after all this effort. When they reached the veranda, she extracted her daughter's hands, bent down and gave her a kiss on the cheek.

'Go and find your shoes, young lady. Otherwise the spiders are going to eat your toes, one by one.'

She playfully patted her bottom as she ran up the steps and into the house towards her bedroom at the back.

Fen followed her in and headed straight into the kitchen. She took a blue wooden box off the old-fashioned Welsh dresser that Sam had insisted they buy to provide more cupboard space, and put it on the kitchen table. The box was not locked, but the hinges were loose and the lid flopped back lazily when she opened it. Carefully, she took out the contents and placed it on the table next to the box.

Martha joined her, her hands and chin resting on the edge of the table. 'What's that?' she said.

Fen held it up for her to see. 'What do you think it is?'She turned it round slowly.

'It looks like one of those things angels wear on their heads.'

'A halo?'

'Yes, a halo. What's it do?'

'Protects Mummy, I think. It may have saved Mummy's life. And Uncle Pella's. He's got one just like this, I reckon.'

'Who's Uncle Pella?'

'Ah, you've not met him yet, but I promise you will.'

'Can I hold it?'

'Best not.'

'Why?'

'Because it could be dangerous.'

'You should throw it away then.'

'I might.'

The girl lost interest and skipped off happily to look for something more interesting to play with, leaving Fen to put the halo back into its box, wondering if she was right about it giving them protection. If she was, where was Pella's halo now? Don had not said anything unusual had been found on him.

Of course, Fen had had the option to ask if anything unusual had been found, but she had not. She had not mentioned the halos.

That was her choice.

Checking the lid was on properly, she placed it back where she had got it. Perhaps she ought to find somewhere more secure for it, although, like the ones on Arrix's statue in Garial, she could argue it was kind of hidden in plain sight.

Whatever happened, she was determined that no one else would get their hands on it. The world was not ready to deal with another powerful object like the quarton.

Not yet anyway.

Acknowledgements

Publishing your own books is quite a task. I could not have done it without the love, support and encouragement of family and friends around me. Self-published authors are not blessed with a team of professionals and most, like me, rely on the skills, kindness and time of people we know to help out.

I want to, in particular, thank my daughter, Abbey, who, without her specific feedback and amazing encouragement on the whole series, there would not have been a Quarton trilogy. I used to open up her texts and emails with slight dread, on occasions, because the comments were invariably blunt, but they were always spot on! Exactly what an author developing his trade needed. Thanks also to my wife, Angela, for a similar role and to my author friend, another Angela (Cairns), who has shared her self-publishing experiences with me and been a great support. Proofreading can be seen as a chore and my gratitude goes to my mum, Glad, who ploughed her way through this and the last book.

Finally, thank you to you, the reader. If you've got this far and bothered to read the acknowledgements too, then you are a real star! I just hope you don't think they are the most exciting thing about the book...

I value feedback of all types and read all my reviews. If you feel able to spare some time to write a review on Amazon, Goodreads or anywhere else, I would really appreciate it. They really do help to get authors' work out there.

Thank you.

Appendix

Below is a list of names and references connected to the main four characters – **Rana, Pella, Arrix and Klavon** – who were killed on the Garial Bridge in the first book and feature throughout the trilogy.

After that are some of the other significant characters from all 3 Quarton books.

<u>Rana</u>

Rana is the leader of the rebels on Garial who helped destroy the Garial Bridge which Arrix had built. She is the sister of Pella in this incarnation. Rana and Klavon, for different reasons, want the bridge to be destroyed so, when it is, they end up on the same side against Arrix and Pella, trying to prevent the bridge from being rebuilt. Rana becomes Klavon's protector in future incarnations.

She is also...

Fen – a scavenger in a war torn London in 2067, she is the main protagonist and Rana's most important reincarnation. Fen becomes aware of her previous reincarnations as the story unfolds in book 1.

Jeanie – the first book starts with a scene on a lake in Montana, USA in 1998. Jeanie is the first incarnation that Fen becomes aware of.

Anne-Marie – a young French girl in Brittany, France in 1851, who is caring for her sick father.

The mother – near Gaza city in 1348.

The old man – in New Zealand, 1752 who grabs the spear to stop the Chief (Arrix) killing the warrior (Klavon).

The hunter's sister – African Savannah, 500BC. The first reincarnation on Earth.

Sunan – a miner in the diamond mine, South Africa, 1896. In book 2, Sunan finds a quarton in the mine and tries to take it out to one of the gang leaders (Klavon), but he is caught by his uncle (Pella) and the owner (Arrix).

Paul – Chuck's adopted brother. In book 2, Paul tries to explain to Chuck about Arrix and the quartons but Chuck does not believe him at the time. He was killed by Marston in Prague trying to get to a quarton block.

Pella

Pella is Rana's brother on Garial. He is an engineer and is recruited by Arrix to help design and build the bridge. After their deaths on the bridge, every time Pella is first to a quarton and touches it, that quarton disappears and is held as one which could be used to help join the Garial Bridge to Earth. Arrix is his protector in all subsequent incarnations.

He is also...

Forrest – the young girl who Fen helps when she joins the Westsider Scavengers. In this incarnation, Forrest is also the sister of Sal and Bill.

Jeanie's mother – she steers the car into the lake in the opening scene because she has felt the presence of the quarton.

Papa – Pella is the dying father of Anne-Marie in Brittany, 1851.

The girl who touches the quarton in the desert – near Gaza city in 1348.

The slave boy – New Zealand, 1752

The hunter's father – African Savannah, 5001BC. The first reincarnation.

Sunan's uncle – diamond mine, South Africa, 1896. See Rana and Sunan.

Lenny – Lenny was one of Sal's henchmen who was knocked over by Fen near the Friendship Bridge. When the keystone quarton was destroyed, Pella transferred into the body of Lenny. Lenny later became a pilot.

Mark – Mark is the father of Ruby (see Klavon and Arrix). Mark was killed in an aircraft accident when Lenny was the pilot. Pella transferred into Mark's body when Lenny died. Mark is with Fen at the end of book 2.

Arrix

Arrix is the master schemer. He has been reincarnating for some time before he becomes Arrix and is aware of the power of the coding. To hold onto the coding he needs to have a ready supply of quartons and Garial is running out of quartzite, its main constituent. That is why he builds the bridge to Earth. He is Pella's protector in all their incarnations.

He is also...

Alistair Marston – He has an influential role throughout book 1 having found the last quarton and then lost it when the missiles struck London. He also appears in book 2 in flashbacks.

The baby sister of Jeanie in the opening scene at the lake.

Doctor Martinez – the doctor brings a quarton to the house of Anne-Marie and Papa in Brittany. He mocks Anne-Marie (Rana) because Klavon's incarnation is not even around at the right time to challenge.

The brother – near Gaza city in 1348.

The Chief – New Zealand, 1752

The hunter's mother – African Savannah, 5001BC. The first reincarnation.

The mine owner – diamond mine, South Africa, 1896. See *Sunan* and Rana

A beggar boy – in Prague. He used to watch Chuck and his brother, Paul's, movements before he beat them to the quarton at the top of the clock tower. He killed Paul.

Ruby – Ruby is the daughter of the original Mark (see Mark and Pella). Ruby is killed just before Arrix's warriors land. When Lee (Klavon) and Arrix are killed at the end of book 2, they transfer into Ruby's body together.

Klavon

Klavon wants revenge on Arrix because he killed all his family and so joins Rana on her quest to destroy the Garial Bridge. His father, *Arna*, used to work with Arrix. Every time Klavon touches a quarton in each incarnation, it is destroyed. Rana is his protector in all reincarnations.

He is also...

Bill, the leader of the Eastsider scavengers. She only realises she is Klavon in the last scenes. She is also the sister of Sal and Forrest in this incarnation. They were all separated when the missiles struck.

The stranger – in the opening scene at the lake

The father – near Gaza city in 1348

The warrior – New Zealand, 1752

The young hunter – African Savannah, 5001BC. The first reincarnation.

The supervisor at the mine - diamond mine, South Africa, 1896. See *Sunan* and Rana

Other significant characters

Sal – Sal features in book 1 and is the leader of the scavenging group called the Westsiders, of which Fen is a member. He has many of the traits you might expect in Klavon – a tendency towards violence and domination. In fact, he is the Earth brother of Bill (Klavon) and Forrest (Pella), but has no direct connection with Garial.

Dougie – is also in book 1. He is Marston's sidekick and challenges Marston for control of his operation towards the end of the book.

Liz – is Fen's subgroup leader and Sal's partner. She crops up briefly in book 2 when she nurses Lee (now Klavon) back to health.

Larm – Larm is Arrix's assistant in book 1. She appears again in book 2 having been put into stasis until Arrix's life-force returns to Garial into Arrix's body double.

Lee – in book 1, Lee, Fen's roommate when she was scavenging, is killed by Marston. In book 2, we discover that Klavon transfers into her body after the keystone quarton is destroyed. Klavon's story on book 2 is largely told through his new body, Lee.

Ruby – Ruby is the daughter of the original Mark (see Pella and Mark). Ruby is killed just before Arrix's warriors land. When Klavon and Arrix are killed, they transfer into Ruby's body together.

President Lessey – first appears on book 2. She is the leader of the Western-French-Irish (W.F.I.) Alliance. An ambitious lady, she refuses to admit to the existence of aliens.

Chuck Lawrence – Doctor Charles Lawrence, a good friend of Mackenzie and brother to Paul (see Rana). Chuck is a prominent character in book 2 and is responsible for building the MASH which tackles Arrix and his warriors towards the end.

Mackenzie Ingles – a member of the Southern Alliance (a peace keeping organisation), loyal friend and associate to Chuck.

Don Berretti – a major in the Southern Alliance who helps Chuck and Mackenzie at the site where the Garial Bridge landed.

Sam – Fen's husband. Also a member of the Southern Alliance, Sam rescued Fen at the Friendship Bridge.

Martha – Fen's daughter with Sam. She is left back in Australia with her grandparents when Fen and Sam go to England to tackle Arrix and the black hole that appeared.

Major Shaw – President Lessey's major who is monitoring things in England when the black hole appears.

Vice President Geron – Lessey's second in command

Barrow – heads up Lessey's military wing.

Taron – one of Arrix's warriors.

Jerome – loyal follower of Ruby in book 3. Next in command who provides added muscle.

Odette – another follower of Ruby. She is an I.T. expert.

Arna – Klavon's father on Garial

Author note (2) – no plot spoilers! I have not included details of incarnations that might be relevant to this book, The Payback.

The books in 'The Quarton Trilogy'

Quarton: The Bridge

Quarton: The Coding

Quarton: The Payback

Available on Amazon in paperback and as an e-book

About the Author

In the last book, I said that nothing much had changed about the author since the previous book. That is still generally true, though the world seems to have changed quite drastically around me. Lockdown has given authors like me even more opportunities to create new worlds for you, the reader, to immerse yourself in. I hope you are finding lots of good books to enjoy.

Having finished with Garial and the world(s) of Fen, I am already moving onto pastures new. I have two sci-fi books for younger readers just about finished and I am dying to introduce the world to Maggie Matheson, an eighty-year old grandmother and spy who I hope will bring some light and mirth into the homes of older readers.

Please tell me what you think of this book. I would love to hear from you on any of the social media links below.

Or why not leave a review on Amazon or Goodreads? Thank you!

Follow Ian on:

Website	www.ianhornett.com
Facebook	@ianmichaelhornett
Twitter	@Iancolufan
Instagram	@ianhornett

Printed in Great Britain
by Amazon